IN THE ATTIC

Cobwebs came spinning toward him from all sides—growing, multiplying at a fantastic rate. Stringy cobwebby fingers reaching for him, encircling him, crawling across his skin and around his body. He couldn't move—and now the horrible sticky tendrils were creeping across his face, his eyes! *He couldn't see!*

Peter opened his mouth to scream and cobwebs flowed in, blotting his strangled cry like a thick wad of cotton. And now there were tendrils slithering into his ears and crawling into his nose. He couldn't breathe. *He couldn't breathe!*

Even as the cobwebs drew him up toward the rafters, even as the last breath was squeezed from his body, Peter Beaufort kept telling himself that this all had to be some kind of macabre joke, because things like this didn't happen . . .

And never in the daytime.

LISA W. CANTRELL

THE MANSE

TOR HORROR

A TOM DOHERTY ASSOCIATES BOOK

THE MANSE

Copyright © 1987 by Lisa W. Cantrell

First printing: November 1987

A TOR Book

Published by Tom Doherty Associates, Inc.
49 West 24 Street
New York, N.Y. 10010

ISBN: 0-812-51673-7
CAN. ED.: 0-812-51674-5

Printed in the United States of America

0 9 8 7 6 5 4 3 2 1

for my husband

ACKNOWLEDGMENTS AND THANKS

To Jim Allen for starting this;

To Melissa Ann Singer for her excellent editorial input;

To M. A. Foster for remembering what a beginner needs to know;

To Pam Emick for being a special friend;

To M. Scott Gilliam and Theresa Phillips Gladden for advice and support above and beyond;

To Ruth Brinker and Teresa Reeder for help and encouragement;

To Bud Harmon, Robert Shively, Steve Chase, and John Hance for technical assistance;

To Barry Cantrell for allowing me to adapt his lyrics for ''Tin Cup Man'';

To Jimmy, Gramp, Steve, Suzie, Kelly, and the Bear for patience, support, and understanding;

And to Jim Allen—again, because he deserves my deep thanks first, last, and always . . .

Excerpt from *The Merrillville Weekly,*
October 2, 1985, Samantha Evers, Feature Writer:

. . . and in October 1975, the Merrillville Junior Chamber of Commerce staged its first annual Halloween House of Horrors. The fund-raiser, held at the old Beaufort family estate at the north end of town, proved a huge success for the civic group.

During the next few years, the Jaycees expanded their program, gradually extending the number of nights as attendance increased dramatically. This year a full three weeks of nightly presentations are scheduled to begin at the Manse on October 11.

Over the past ten years, the Jaycee fund-raiser has become one of this area's largest attractions, drawing record crowds from neighboring towns and counties, taking in record proceeds, and scaring the skin off hundreds of people nightly for the weeks preceding Halloween.

PROLOGUE

The Manse: October 31, 1985,
Halloween Night, 11:53 P.M.

Approaching midnight.

The witching hour, say some. Time to be about night-time business—sleeping, watching the late show, making love to your wife or husband (or someone else's):

If you're Joe Dawson, you're slapping your six-year-old son, Davy, in the mouth for crying about not being allowed to go to the Halloween House with your older son, Randy;

If you're Pearl Rollins, you're lying awake in a darkened bedroom, feeling the ache of old bones and the deeper ache of old fears that sometimes, like tonight, just won't let you sleep;

If you're old Doc Wilson, you're on your way to Country Manor Retirement Home, where one of the Beaufort Twins, Miss Flossie or Miss Bessie (the message service didn't say), is having a bad night;

If you're the drunk called PoJo, you're sleeping off a gutful of eighty-six-proof supper in an alley across the street from the old Beaufort house;

And if you're one of the Merrillville, North Carolina, Jaycees, you're just coming off the eleventh successful staging of the Annual Jaycee Halloween House of Horrors at The Manse itself . . .

Sherman "Tank" Worley lounged against the waist-high wooden swing gate that stretched across The Manse's driveway and waited for the final tour group to straggle from the old house. Almost midnight. They tried to have all the spectators through the house and out by midnight. Generally this wasn't a problem; most people came early, lines beginning to form even before it got dark. But a few holdouts always thought the later the better for a House of Horrors, though by eleven o'clock the Jaycees working the inside setups were usually so tired and hot they'd begun cutting bits and pieces off the scenarios and rushing them through.

Tank was glad to be pulling outside duty this year. It was damn hot inside the house. He tugged at the elaborately tied neck cloth enveloping his tree-trunk neck and unbuttoned his confining coat. The turn-of-the-century costume felt sticky and uncomfortable tonight, making him feel less like the ghost of the ill-fated swain he was meant to portray and more like the drowned, dead-weight body that, according to legend, had been dragged from a well here on the grounds. Tank shifted position and gave in to a large, audible yawn.

Even in repose, an almost visible boisterousness embraced Tank Worley. Sound clung to him, thrumming from the pores of his massive body, stirring the air like vibrations from a tuning fork. It was as though feedback from something that had boomed forth earlier still resonated around Tank.

He stripped flimsy plastic from a bourbon-flavored toothpick, pocketed the wrapping (since the Jaycees were responsible for keeping the house and grounds in order, and Tank was on the cleanup crew, it made one less piece of litter to pick up later), and placed the wooden sliver in a corner of his mouth. Pungent whiskey smell immediately assailed his nostrils; a slight burning sensation branded the side of his tongue and lips, not unpleasant. A bit like cinnamon.

A grayish-yellow late-autumn moon hung full but listless in the sky, giving a washed-out look to the grounds surrounding The Manse. If anything, it enhanced the eerie effect they'd worked so hard to achieve this year, lending a haunted quality almost impossible to duplicate mechanically, at least for a group of budget-strung amateurs like the Merrillville Jaycees. Perhaps that *Star Wars* bunch · . . .

Tank glanced at the house. The Manse looked pretty eerie on its own, even in broad daylight and minus Halloween embellishments. Anyone with a mental template of what a haunted house looked like would no doubt find the Manse fit from cupola to cellar. Night suited the huge old house, making it look like an illustration Tank had once seen on the cover of a horror comic, all shades of crypt gray and ghost white and flat black—a perfectly normal setting for a perfectly normal House of Horrors . . . except for maybe a few bats swooping around the rafters and

eaves. Something to think about for next year? Bats, yeah.
At least one the size of Mothra.

Tank stifled another yawn, tugged again at his neck
cloth, and shifted against the gate, getting restless now.
The gate groaned in protest and he eased his weight off,
just to be on the safe side. Tank had no desire to spend a
few extra hours tomorrow repairing a broken gate. Especially in this heat.

It was too hot; unseasonably hot. Even this late, the
night heaved with it, the kind of heat that felt like it was
building toward a humdinger of a storm. Now, that would
have added a dramatic element to the setting: boiling
thunderclouds belching jagged spokes of lightning over
The Manse. From where Tank stood he couldn't see the
front of the house and the great effect they'd rigged in the
third-story attic window—a flashing blue strobe light behind a swinging noose. It welcomed the crowds as they
walked up the stone stairs from the street and loomed over
them while they stood in line along the walkway. What a
backdrop a raging windstorm would have made. As long
as it didn't rain. Rain was a sure crowd deterrent.

A finger of sweat traced a line down Tank's back. He
shrugged his shoulders against the tickle, then squirmed an
arm around to scratch. Damn, it was hot! Taking a breath
felt like gulping a lungful of tepid water.

Apparently other night creatures were feeling the same
sort of ennui. Hardly a sound broke the stillness . . . an
occasional cricket noise . . . the trill of a distant night bird,
a lonely sound in the darkness . . .

In the distance, the old town clock began to strike the

midnight hour . . . slow, heavy, echoing bongs that hung
on the night air like hollow warnings—

Now, why did I think that? Tank listened intently to the
stately sound as it ebbed and flowed across the half mile
between Merrillville proper and The Manse. It was a
superstitious thought, a precognitive thought, not at all the
type of thought that usually graced Tank's well-grounded
mind—and almost immediately another thought supplanted
it:

Someone's out there . . .

For a moment Tank went utterly still, mind edging
toward uncertainty, thoughts bending slightly off rational
center. Then he grinned, and his body relaxed. Using only
his tongue, he skillfully maneuvered the toothpick to the
opposite corner of his mouth.

"Okay, guys. Zack? J.T.? Remember, this is the Tank
you're running the ball on. I know all the plays, and I can
get mean. Come on out . . ."

Nothing.

"Come on out now, assholes . . ."

Nothing.

An involuntary shiver feathered up Tank's spine. Something not quite right hovered about the stillness, something
not precisely wholesome.

A sigh of wind trailed past Tank's face with hot fingers
and a sour smell. Dead leaves rustled, dry crackles of
sound. A rag of dark cloud drifted across the sallow moon.

Tank produced a small, withered chuckle, a facsimile of
his normal booming laugh. It almost sounded like the
crackle of the dead leaves.

"Damn," he murmured under his breath. "This place is getting to me."

Yet there was just something . . . something not quite right—

The crunch of footsteps on dry leaves.

Tank froze—six feet four inches and 228 pounds of visible sound put on hold. The footsteps were coming toward him with a stealth that reminded Tank of that time he'd been last in the locker room after a night game when someone turned off all the lights and he cut off the shower and stood there dripping water and soapsuds and heard heavy breathing and slow, crawling footsteps come down the hall and into the shower.

Moonlight filtered from behind the ragged cloud and Tank saw the last group of spectators walking toward him. He released the breath he'd been unaware of holding and grinned sheepishly under the camouflage of remaining shadows. The shower room monsters had been Zack and J.T.; the ones coming toward him now were Buddy Grey, Vince Colletti, and the older Dawson boy.

Tank slowly straightened as the boys loped across the yard, banishing his momentary lapse to spineless jellyfish— something he'd never in a million admit to Zack and the others—as though it had never been. He eyed the approaching trio: Vince Colletti, looking like a junior version of Al Pacino, in the lead; Buddy Grey, wearing his tall, gawky adolescence like a bandage on a sore thumb; and— what was the Dawson boy's name? oh, yeah, Randy— Randy Dawson, bringing up the rear, your average afterthought. Three representatives of the up-and-coming generation, fourteen, maybe fifteen, going on eight; rebellious going on hardcase; prospects unlikely going on nil. In a rare moment of honest introspection, Tank wondered if he and some of his high school chums had been this close to the edge of nowhere when they were fourteen, maybe fifteen.

Taking a step forward, toothpick working up and down in his mouth, thoughts turning toward home, Tank waited impatiently for the three to amble on down the path. Thank God this was the final group and he could lock the gate after them, help close the house, and then go home to Rosa and a cold beer, not necessarily in that order.

Tank shoved the bourbon-flavored toothpick to the side of his mouth. The flavoring was almost gone, like his patience and good nature.

"Let's go, guys. Haven't got all night." He laid a suggestive hand on the top bar of the swing gate, dispensing with his ghost-of-the-well routine.

One of the boys mumbled a reply which Tank didn't catch. No doubt he'd made a mistake trying to hurry them. Now they'd do their best to make a twenty-second walk last four minutes, a typical teenage rebel's answer to any voice smacking of authority. He should have told them to take their time.

Finally the trio reached the gate. It surprised Tank to see that they looked just a bit shaken. And they were acting rather subdued, too. Unusual for this group of JDs on the rise. Could it possibly be that the House had done a real job on this hard-core element of Merrillville society?

Tank performed a neat, no-hands maneuver with the toothpick, turning it end to end, as first Vince, then Buddy moved through the open gate. Randy continued to take up the slack, a good little camp follower.

Damned if they didn't look shaken. Though everyone tended to pale in the moon-bleached yard, theirs was a pasty look. Tank chuckled softly, proud of this year's scenarios and special effects that he'd been involved with, delighted that they'd grossed out even the older kids. They were definitely getting better at this haunted house thing.

What he really should do, Tank thought with typical compassion, was wait until they filed through the gate, then jump out behind them and let out a bloodcurdling scream. They wouldn't be expecting anything else after leaving the House, wouldn't be prepared for a little encore. Like that movie: "Just when you think it's safe . . ."

As though reading Tank's mind, Vince Colletti squared his shoulders. Seeing this, Buddy and Randy flashed Tank a couple of "Made in Taiwan" grins, meant to convey bravado. The effort sat sticky on them, like a blob of peanut butter catapulted from a spoon: *Here, have a spoonful of backbone, ka-thwunk.*

Tank grinned back, the all-American variety. "Scared, girls?"

"Up yours," Vince Colletti threw over his shoulder, not willing to challenge, or acknowledge, Tank's gibe with eye-to-eye contact, while Buddy Grey made up for this lapse of etiquette by turning toward Tank before shooting him the bird.

Another chuckle rolled out of Tank and plodded off into the night. He almost missed Randy Dawson's final comment, "That was a pretty bad trick they staged in the back garden, man. How they rigged a statue to do that number . . ." He moved on down the driveway, taking his words with him.

Tank continued to vibrate with residual chuckles as he watched them round the first turn in the driveway, catching a few more words—something from Randy about being glad he hadn't had to bring his brat kid brother, that the little creep would be having shit-fits by now from that last thing in the back garden—then he folded the chuckle and put it away, leaving only a crease of sound to circle lazily on the hot night air. Yes, it had been a good House this year, particularly the alien-encounter routine which he'd done most of the work on. No one expected the blob to explode.

Closing the gate, Tank secured the latch, his big body moving as sluggishly in the heat as his thoughts. He stared into the darkness, the residue of a grin lingering on his cheerful features. Working the toothpick around his mouth to leach out its last faint sting of flavoring, Tank was about to turn toward the house when a sudden thought struck him:

"Wait a minute," he murmured, puzzlement etched into the usual booming solidity of his tone. "We didn't stage anything in the back garden . . ."

Excerpt from *The Merrillville Weekly,*
October 8, 1986, Samantha Evers, Feature Writer:

. . . an old house where "bad things" are reputed to
have happened is a familiar setting in most small
towns. The house is usually large, a showplace in its
day, now a bit run-down and deserted. It fits everyone's stereotyped idea of sinister, and most visitors
greet it with an involuntary shiver. The Manse is such
a house.

PART ONE

The Manse: October 31, 1986,
Halloween Night, 9:45 P.M.

Chapter 1

The town of Merrillville (population 2,042) is located in the eastern Piedmont section of North Carolina, about midway between the Atlantic seacoast and the Blue Ridge Mountains. Founded by Jason Merrill in the late 1800s as a base of operations for his textile mill, Merrillville quickly expanded to tidy size. The new residents were mostly postwar indigents and dissatisfied sons of area farmers who flocked to the new mill to work fourteen-hour shifts, six days a week, for seventy-five cents a day and board. After a time the town stopped growing and began to bask in changeless mediocrity.

There is not a lot of affluence in Merrillville, but there is no great amount of poverty either.

The crime rate falls on the impressive side of the state average and tends to be of the misdemeanor type or petty variety.

Other than the 1975 state championship football team, the town has produced no Olympic-quality athletes.

Other than one state senator back in 1912, the town has produced no favorite sons.

There has been no great fame, fortune, or glory accredited to anyone from Merrillville; but neither is it overly rife with infamous past inhabitants.

Strong passions certainly exist in Merrillville, as in all places, but their exposure is kept to a minimum.

For almost a century, Merrillville has maintained an unexceptional existence.

The only abiding extreme in town is The Manse. Strangely enough, the house was not built by Jason Merrill, but by John Beaufort, a gentleman of independent means who married Merrill's only daughter. A Victorian-style mansion constructed on a heavily wooded rise at the northern end of town, it faced Merrillville's one long Main Street business district, and added a touch of gilt-class lacquer to an otherwise lackluster town.

Now untenanted, its former elegance grown slightly tarnished, the estate has remained intact for nearly a hundred years, having passed to its current owners, Miss Florence Mae and Miss Fanny Elizabeth Beaufort (fondly known as Miss Flossie and Miss Bessie, or simply the Beaufort Twins), some forty years ago. Spinsters in their eighties, neither had ever married, though Miss Bessie is quick to tell anyone she was once affianced to a "young man who died."

With the determination born of a fierce devotion to their ancestral home, the elderly Beaufort sisters, who were forced by circumstance of age and economics to move into a nearby retirement home, have always done their best to keep The Manse as it was during their youth. Unfortunately the ladies were unable to secure adequate funding from various historical preservation societies. The Beaufort Twins then entered into an ''arrangement'' with the Merrillville Jaycees. The Manse is used each year for the Jaycees' major fund-raising project, the Halloween House of Horrors; in return, the Jaycees pay the sisters a modest stipend—enough to supplement their necessities—and maintain the house and grounds on a year-round basis. A renewable lease was signed by both parties, the local bank and realtor were empowered as overseers, and The Manse remains the focal point of Merrillville—except, of course, in October, when it becomes quite something else indeed . . .

Chapter 2

The 12th Annual Jaycee Halloween House of Horrors was in full swing.

About two blocks up from where Route 225 circled The Manse and formed a T with Merrillville's Main Street, PoJo shuffled along the sidewalk, hands jammed into the pockets of his ragged coat. He muttered to himself as he walked, every now and then scowling at the house that stood sentinel above him, the house he'd been kept out of for the past three weeks. Usually a dark and silent standing invitation to an old drunk on a cold night, a place he could squirm into through a loose basement window, The Manse was currently alive with the rituals of the season.

"Halloween," PoJo muttered, glaring at the house. "What a pisser."

PoJo was something of a fixture in Merrillville, living

off the town, taking odd jobs and handouts with equal disdain. Nobody knew where he'd come from or remembered when he'd arrived. He'd simply showed up one day and stayed. Said his name was Joe. Poor Joe, they called him at first; now just PoJo.

There was a shabby dignity about him, like he'd looked into the eyes of life a long time ago and refused to be intimidated. Perhaps it was this that made the townsfolk upgrade his standing to ''town character''—a more acceptable term than ''town drunk'' or ''town bum'' or plain ''wino,'' according to general Merrillville opinion. Perhaps it was something less noble that motivated them—humanity is rarely averse to having a ''There but for the grace of God go I'' example to feel superior to.

The cops shook him down a few times, looking for drugs. They didn't find any. PoJo didn't do drugs. ''No drugs,'' he'd tell them. ''Wouldn't touch 'em. Bad stuff, that. Eats the sane outta your brain.'' After a while they let him alone.

He could be spotted shuffling around town at odd hours, looking for a bite to eat, the price of a bottle, a place to hole up and grab a few hours' sleep. Just a harmless old vagrant with shuttered eyes, part of the local scene, like the boarded-up theater on Main Street.

Town was buggy with kids tonight. Older ones bunched the three-block Main strip or cruised by in look-alike cars, all decked out for the occasion, PoJo supposed, though to him they looked like they always did. They shouted kid stuff back and forth. It sounded like gibberish.

The younger ones, mostly wrapped in nonflammable ''night-brights,'' grasping little orange plastic jack-o'-lantern buckets in one hand and parents' hands in the other, were gathered down at Tully Ryerson's photo shop where Mr. Picture Man was giving two-cent trick-or-treats and snapping little Frankie Stein's or Cindy Rella's picture for "Just five bucks a shot, ma'am."

From time to time, people went running past PoJo, heading up to The Manse, where the heavy stuff was going down. Big people and little people in their Halloween trappings, smiling and laughing and playing their games. Mostly they'd rush by him as if he weren't there, but occasionally someone would toss a comment his way, or he'd catch his name being thrown into the conversations that passed him by.

PoJo ignored them all. He was thinking about Florida.

Flarida, yessir. That's where I'm goin', PoJo would tell anyone who would listen. *This here's just a rest drop, just a gappin' point 'tween high north and low south, a place to set a spell and ponder things before travelin' on.*

He'd been telling the townsfolk this for years.

Rounding the corner where Main Street dead-ended into the loop of highway that circled the old Beaufort estate, PoJo favored the house on the hill with another baleful glance. A blue-white light flickered crazily in the highest attic window, making the heavy noose suspended there look like it was swaying and jerking with the death dance of some invisible horse thief. Looming over the darkened window of the opposite spire, a huge black bat gleamed red-eyed and malevolent, wings a-flapping in the wind, bleeding crazy shadows from the yellow spotlight attacking it.

"Bats," muttered PoJo. "Bats."

The night air was cold, unseasonably cold. For weeks it had been getting colder and colder and tonight was coldest of all. PoJo hunkered down in the old navy pea coat that had come to him through another branch of the service—the Salvation Army—and continued shuffling down the broken sidewalk that sketched along for a couple of blocks this side of the highway before turning into dirt and rattrap buildings. He walked with his head down, shoulders hunched, hands stuffing coat pockets. *Allays watch where yer steppin'*. A good rule. Kept him out of puddles and holes and that.

There was a hole in his left pocket. PoJo balled his hand into a fist and ignored it.

Coming to the alley between the back of Lawson's real estate office and the west side of Gibson's warehouse, PoJo slipped into the narrow slot that separated the two buildings. He eased his body down just inside the opening and leaned against the cold cinder-block wall. The ground sat hard and uncomfortable here, but the walls provided some windbreak and it was a good vantage point to maintain watch on The Manse.

Tonight would be the last night of these foolish goings-on. When midnight came they'd tuck away their ghosties and goblins for another year and give the house back to the empty darkness. If he took care, PoJo thought he might slip in later, get out of the cold.

Reaching into an inside pocket, he pulled out a pint bottle of rye whiskey and carefully unscrewed the cap with fingers that felt like they were brittling up. Pausing a

moment, he put his fingers to his mouth, breathing heavy
on them. Breath misted around his hand like fog on a cold
mountaintop, but it helped a little. He finished unscrewing
the bottletop, took a nip. A dram of warmth drifted
through him . . . comforting, familiar.

PoJo held the bottle in one hand, its cap in the other,
and regarded The Manse sullenly. It looked pale tonight, a
white tombstone rising wraithlike from the ground, surrounded by gnarled old trees with spindly, leafless branches,
a place where elves and demons and spirits were cavorting
and prancing and casting their evil spells . . .

*Only that was just tales and this was kids with stupid
people tryin' to scare 'em.*

Stupid people was pretty good at tales, he reckoned.
Been lotsa tales about him. Some parents scairt their kids
away from him, said he was crazy, said he'd mess with
'em. Now, that hurt. He wouldn't mess with no kid,
wouldn't hurt no kid. Had a kid once. Little girl name of
Jenny. But then his old lady died and he couldn't keep no
kid on the road. So they took her, homed her out to some
button-down folk. He visited for a while, even after the
man gave him all that talk about bad images and stayin'
away. Then one day he went to visit and found them up
and gone. No one knew where, or leastways no one would
say. So he just started bummin' south. Got this far. Liked
it enough to stay a spell. But allays meanin' to bum on
south—

*Down to Flarida, yessir. Where the weather don't
come in through the holes in your shirt and grab you to
the bone . . .*

PoJo took another swig from his bottle and eyed The

Manse. For a moment it seemed to be looking back at him, sizing him up. Shrieks roamed the night and giggles skittered back and forth on the wind.

"Halloween," muttered PoJo. "What a pisser." He settled down to suck his bottle and think about Florida.

Chapter 3

A shiver crawled up Davy Dawson's seven-year-old spine. *Haunted house*. Just thinking the words gave him goose bumps, conjuring up shadowy visions of things better left unseen, things with cold hands and sunken eyes, things that walked through graveyards at midnight and skulked about old houses . . . Davy looked up at The Manse . . . like this one. He craned his neck toward the big black bat that was hovering over the top of the house. The bat glared back at him, directly at him, its glittering red eyes picking him out of the crowd below. Any minute now it was going to swoop down and grab him up in its long, curling claws and carry him away to its deep dark cave and . . . *and probably eat me*.

The line moved up, and Davy was close enough then to hear the huge bat wings flapping in the wind. They sounded spooky. If he shut his eyes, he could pretend it was the big flag down at the post office on a real windy day, except there you could also hear the chain hitting against the metal flagpole. Besides, he didn't need to pretend the bat was a flag. He wasn't a baby anymore. He didn't have to pretend away scary stuff. Scary stuff was fun. Big black bats were fun. *This* was fun.

Davy looked around for his older brother, Randy. There he was, back down the line with Buddy Grey and that turd Vince Colletti. Well, that was okay. Davy didn't need to have his hand held anymore, and if they went through the House together, Vince the turd would probably just hassle him, the way he always did. Davy smiled to himself. This way he'd get to see stuff first, be leader for a change instead of having to hear Randy complain about dragging him along. Let the three of *them* hold hands with each other. Davy stifled a giggle at the thought.

This was an adventure, thrilling and scary at the same time. Like the time his dad had dropped him off for the Saturday kids' matinee at the new mall theater, some stupid movie about a silly princess who couldn't do anything right. He'd sat through about ten minutes of it, then sneaked out, gone into the bathroom for a while, then sneaked into the part of the four-theater building where *Zombies From Outer Space* was about to start. That had been really fun, not that scary at all. Of course, he'd had to leave before it was over and go back to the stupid princess. Then he'd be sure to come out with the proper group at the proper time so his dad wouldn't know what he'd done. But he'd seen almost to where the zombies landed on earth.

Another shiver passed through Davy's small body, making his scalp prickle and his skin contract. Would there be zombies in the haunted—

A hand gripped his shoulder. Davy jumped and swung around, staring into the angry, red-rimmed eyes and hairy face of the Wolfman. A small whimper escaped Davy's throat.

"All alone, little boy?" the Wolfman hissed through gleaming yellowed fangs and thick pale lips all smeared with red. The hairy paw-hand crept along Davy's shoulder, inching toward his neck.

Davy managed a little shake of his head while his body stayed as still and cold as chilled glass. "My . . . my brother . . ." He didn't want to look away from the Wolfman, but he glanced toward Randy and Buddy and Vince the turd, quickly, without moving his head.

The Wolfman lightly traced a path around Davy's throat with a hairy claw-tipped finger. "Pity," he growled softly, for Davy's ears alone. "But he won't be watching all the time, will he?" The Wolfman moved away.

Breath returned to Davy's body, little icy darts of air that stung his insides. He quivered where he stood. A man next to him chuckled.

The man said: "Don't be afraid, kid. It was just someone dressed up in a werewolf costume." The man was looking at him strangely now, his eyes studying Davy, slightly narrowed in the dim light. "You know that, don't you, boy?"

Davy managed to nod and flash the man a grin. "Course I do," he said, and his voice sounded pretty normal. "Everybody knows there's no such thing as a wolfman."

The man reached down and ruffled Davy's hair, making Davy think of his dad's friend Lewis, who always did that whenever he brought Davy's dad home from drinking too much. Davy didn't like it.

"That's the spirit, kiddo," the man was saying. "It's just a game, just like a game. Don't let it scare you."

Davy nodded politely and turned to look back down the line at Randy. Maybe he'd better stay with—

Randy and Buddy and Vince were gone. Davy searched the crowd, but there was no sign of them.

Behind Davy, the Wolfman was fingering another little kid, and a Vampire Lady glided toward them. Everyone around the kid was squealing or laughing. The kid wasn't. As Davy watched, the kid began to cry.

Crybaby, thought Davy in disgust. *You won't catch me being an old crybaby. Even if the* real *Wolfman tried to get me.*

He turned back toward the house, moving a few paces forward as the line crept ever closer to The Manse. It seemed colder than before. Davy could see his breath in the night air. He moved up another couple of paces. It would feel good to get in out of the cold—

Screams suddenly burst from just inside the front door. Davy shivered, counting the heads in front of him. Seven. He'd probably get in with the next group.

He pulled out his ticket so he could hand it to the Old Witch at the door. The Old Witch cackled each time she took a ticket; her fingernails glinted long and red in the porch light. Davy tried to smooth his slightly crumpled ticket. He didn't want to make the Old Witch mad.

Once more, Davy glanced back, looking for Randy.

Randy wasn't there. He faced the house again, moving up
the steps with the next group—*his* group. The Old Witch
took a ticket, cackled, and took another ticket. Davy realized he was squeezing his, bending it in the middle. He
eased his grip.

It was okay. Okay. He didn't need to be with anyone,
even if the Wolfman did come back around. That old
Wolfman had just been someone dressed up in a costume.
He knew that . . .

But for a few moments, when the paw-hand had gripped
his shoulder and he'd looked into those red-rimmed eyes
and felt that hot breath hiss between those gleaming yellow
fangs, it had been *the* Wolfman menacing young Davy
Dawson.

Frank Morrison was ready for a cup of coffee. Six hours
on the road and five more to go till he reached the end of
his haul and could drop this trailer at the terminal and grab
a few hours' sleep before heading out with another load.
He hoped he could start getting some loads going south
pretty soon. Atlanta or even Birmingham, and then west,
maybe. And without the rinky-dink back-road side trips
like this route.

It was moving toward the time of year when Frank
didn't like to work the small-town northern routes. Particularly the Virginia and West Virginia mountains, or into
Tennessee, where an icy splotch on a hairpin turn could
throw you down the side of a cliff and add an ironic twist
to the term "truck stop."

Black ice, that was the worst. A thin sheet of clear glass
coating the road, it let the asphalt show through and

looked like it wasn't there at all. Until you hit it. Then it became all too evident, and things like brakes and steering wheels and prayers went skidding into oblivion with your rig.

The dark miles clicked by: a mile a minute, eighty-eight feet per second. Frank felt reasonably safe running sixty in North Carolina, even on the two-lanes like this. They tended to allow you a few extra miles over speed limit, particularly at night. In Virginia, now—which might be for lovers like the tourist ads claimed but sure wasn't for truckers—you'd better keep it parked on those old double-nickels. He'd heard horror stories from some drivers about being pulled for doing fifty-eight in a fifty-five zone and getting their trucks impounded and being carted off to spend the night in some podunk jail. Frank had no firsthand experience of how Virginia dealt with lead-foots, and he had a strong suspicion that the drivers who had were embellishing a mite, but he had no wish to put it to the test.

Coffee . . . where to get a cup of coffee?

This was a lonely stretch of road once you passed the big Union 76 Truck Plaza (*why hadn't he stopped there?*). Not much stayed open on the back roads after dark. And he wouldn't make the interstate for another ninety miles. But, he remembered, there was a dinky little all-night truck stop just the other side of Merrillville. Yeah, the C&P Truck Stop, that was it, about forty, fifty miles on down the road, roughly another hour's drive at most— allowing for the slow-down where Route 225 looped through the little shade-tree town of Merrillville.

The C&P, he could wait till then, and he'd probably be ready for a fried ham sandwich to go with that coffee . . .

Darkness.

Total, absolute darkness. The kind of darkness you could reach out and touch. The kind of darkness that could reach out and touch you.

Not even a crack of light showed around the edge of the door that had just closed. Davy knew he was surrounded by ten or twenty people, could feel the brush of someone's arm, smell the musky scent of someone else's perfume, or after-shave, he couldn't tell which. It made his nose scrivel.

The door to outside lay only a few steps from where he was standing . . . but which way? He was completely disoriented, without any reference point to back or front, right or left; he was beginning to feel a little dizzy, like maybe up and down were trying to change places. He remembered the man. He put out a hand and his fingers immediately made contact with another person in the group. The person gave a little start of surprise at his touch; he heard a nervous giggle. Not the man. Davy moved closer to the

Sound.

A low keening wail had begun to twist its way through the darkness, a needle threading the air with shrill tunelessness. It grated against nerve endings, set teeth on edge, hit eardrums like bone on bone.

A gasp. Someone whispered, "Look. There."

Davy slowly turned his head around to the

Light.

A blue-white sliver of light marked the end of a dark

tunnel. The fan of light started at a point about five feet off
the floor and spread out like a V. It seemed to be floating
toward them, gliding silently down the corridor of darkness. Inside the light gleamed

A face.

Starkly white, bleached and burning white like the picture of an animal's skull Davy had seen once in a book
about the desert. A face carved in frost; a face of milky
white like the marble angels on his grandfather's tombstone. And Davy knew, *knew* that if he reached out and
touched the face, it would be as hard and cold as the
marble angels' cheeks, as hard and cold as his grandfather's hand had been when he reached over the side of the
coffin and pressed his finger to it. Cold and hard and dead.

Davy closed his eyes as a shudder racked his body.

Someone jostled up against him. His eyes blinked open,
moving with the crowd. By instinct, they all backed away
from the cold white deadface. The face was almost to them
now. Davy could see eyes in it. They looked vacant and
glassy, fixed on a point somewhere above.

Suddenly the people closest to the deadface gave a
collective gasp and took several steps backward. As they
shifted, Davy saw

A hand

floating up to join the face. A hand that was not a
hand but skeleton bones, long, spidery skeleton bones
glowing blue-white in the dark. The skeleton hand rose
smoothly, stretching beyond the face toward the crowd.
Slowly the hand formed a fist, first finger extended, a
spine of glowing bone pointing toward the ceiling. As
one, the group looked up.

At first nothing but darkness hung overhead, then pale, flickering lights began to appear, quivering lights, candles maybe . . . No, not candles, Davy saw as the lights grew stronger; little pointed light bulbs in a hanging chandelier that gave off fluttering light, sullied, yellow light . . .

"The ceiling's moving," someone behind Davy said; then, "Oh, ugh! Yuk!"

And as other people began joining in with groans and gagging noises and sounds of disgust, Davy saw the

Spiders.

The ceiling was crawling with spiders; big ones, little ones, black ones and brown ones, sending long-legged shadows prowling from the flickering light.

"Oh, gross, they're *moving*—they're alive!" someone said loudly.

And it was true. Spiders squirmed and quivered all over the ceiling. And then one of them dropped!

Someone screamed. Davy flinched with the impact of sound, his eyes still glued on the ceiling that was crawling with spiders, and as he watched, another one dropped, and another . . .

And then more people were screaming as the spiders fell all around, bouncing up and down, and in the flickering light it looked like the inside of a cave made of spiders, and they were attacking the people, attacking him—

Davy scrunched down, throwing his hands and arms up to cover his head, hardly aware that he was screaming too because his screams were lost in the other screams as something hairy brushed against his arm.

And then the light began to die and the screams began to melt away.

Davy cautiously uncovered his head and looked up. The spiders had retreated. He watched them blend into the darkness as the flickering lights faded to black. The attack was over.

Around him, people were straightening, uncovering their heads, sharing little nervous titters of relief, whispering, "They're gone" and "Thank goodness they took them away" and "They damn sure looked real to me!"

Why didn't the people understand? Didn't they see? The spiders weren't gone. They were still up there, still crawling across the ceiling just like when the lights had been on to see them by. Darkness didn't take things away, it only gave them hiding places.

The face was back.

Everyone turned and a hush fell over the group. What would the face do now?

Vacant eyes stared at them, moved over them slowly, unseeingly. The face was dazzling white against the blackness. The skeleton hand began its rise, a ghost hand exhumed from beyond the grave, pointing down the long, narrow tunnel from where it had come, pointing the way they were to go . . .

And as the floating deadface moved back into the shadows and the glowing hand stretched to show the way, a hollow, unearthly voice echoed from the darkness:

"Welcome to the House of Horrors . . ."

MERRILLVILLE 42 MILES.

The sign whisked past as Frank wheeled the huge semi down the road, eating up miles at a steady pace that would have him to the outskirts of the little shit of a town in less than an hour.

Traffic had been fairly heavy tonight, but most of it was going in the opposite direction. Later it would dwindle to night-shift workers coming off second or going on third, a few late-night daters and travelers, and truckers like himself. Frank didn't like to travel this highway during the high-traffic daylight hours if he could help it. Despite being only a two-lane road, this was a major artery between Virginia and North Carolina and the traffic at peak times was a pain in the butt. He knew there'd been a number of bad wrecks on this stretch of road, several fatalities, in fact, but still it remained two lanes only.

"Wonder how many people they have budgeted to die before it makes four-laning cost-efficient?" Frank murmured to himself, and shook his head ironically. "Dangerous, that's what it is," he added, "plus a pain in the butt having to go through Shitville."

The four-lane bypass picked up on the other side of town, which was completely incomprehensible to Frank. Why hadn't they just extended it another couple of miles instead of making highway traffic poke through town?

"Shitville."

The visitors moved single file down the dark corridor, clinging to a handrail on the left wall, inching forward by touch rather than sight. Davy thought he was about midway in line. He gripped the railing firmly every few steps, then quickly slid his hand along it to a new squeeze point. It made him feel safer having the firm round bar to hang on to, made his breath stop coming in ragged little gasps.

He breathed deeply. The air had a stale, musty taste. Davy put the jumping spiders out of his mind. They'd been left back at the entry hall (Davy glanced up toward the ceiling into thick darkness)—at least he guessed they had. The air felt heavy in his chest. He slowly released his breath.

The line was slowing down. Someone ahead of Davy whispered, "Which way?" Davy had supposed someone up front was leading the way, since they'd left the floating deadface back with the spiders.

The line stopped. In the distance ahead, a sudden burst of screams disturbed the silence; then faint laughter could be heard. As though this was a cue to resume normal behavior, around Davy the crowd came alive.

"Are they just going to leave us here?"

"Who's supposed to be in charge?"

"What the hell kind of shit is this?"

Davy didn't care what kind of shit this was. He'd just be glad when—

Light came on in the corridor. Not regular light but black light; Davy knew it from the arcade. It made things look—

With a little gasp, Davy cringed against the railing, eyes fastened on the opposite wall. All around him people were reacting the same, squeezing away from the sight, making sounds like when you lose your supper.

The opposite wall oozed monster heads, grinning, gaping, drooling monster heads, with monster teeth and monster hair and monster eyes *all looking at him!* Davy felt the monster eyes hammering into him, pinning him to the wall like a bug to a board.

There was blood. Lots and lots of blood, dribbling from glistening fangs, seeping from gaping wounds.

A sudden gust of wind moaned down the corridor . . .
or maybe it was the crowd that moaned, because the heads
were beginning to move toward them, a wave flowing
sideways, undulating toward the crowd. Glassy eyes flashed
and glittered; shiny scales and fangs glowed unearthly
colors; blood shone dark red and dripping.

Davy's legs felt weak and his stomach began to churn.
Again, the darkness had hidden something horrible.

Tearing his eyes away from the staring monster heads,
Davy turned toward his right, searching for another person—

He recoiled. The people around him had turned into
monsters too. A white face with glassy eyes and a grinning
mouth looked down at him. It was laughing; Davy could
hear its unearthly laughter. He swung around, searching
for someone who looked right, but everyone had changed.
Then Davy saw his own hand. It was blue-white and alien,
a hand that belonged to something dead. Davy stared at it in
horror. The hand disappeared!

Davy thought at first that he'd shut his eyes, shut out the
sight of his own monster hand. He blinked twice to make
sure.

The wind had also stopped. Once again they stood in
total darkness.

Davy felt his heart pounding against his chest, heard a
roaring in his ears; but even as he listened, the sound
began to fade into whispered conversations and laughter.
Slowly Davy began to understand. It was just people
around him, not monsters. The heads had been just cheap
dime-store masks pinned to a sheet. His hand was still his
hand . . .

Davy suddenly realized he was still gripping the railing

with his left hand. His claw-hold had all but paralyzed that side of his body. He tried to let go of the railing, and felt his heart start thudding again when he thought he couldn't, thought his fingers had become frozen forever to the cold metal rail. Taking a deep breath against rising panic, Davy put his right hand atop his left and gently pried his fingers loose.

Someone bumped him from behind, murmured, "Oops, excuse me." The line had begun to move again, and Davy moved with it, by rote. *Just a game,* he thought, remembering what the man had said. *Just like a game. Follow the leader, one, two . . .*

Up ahead another floating deadface appeared, just like the one they'd left back with the spiders. *One face two face . . .*

He could see it bobbing in and out of sight as the people in front of him filed past it. *One pace two pace . . .*

Then it was his turn to pass the face. He saw the pointing skeleton hand and quickly hurried on by, turning left down another corridor, going the way the hand indicated. For a moment he thought about turning around, going back the way they'd come, all the way back, all the way to the front door and back outside and across the street and down to the car. But the hand had pointed this way and Davy was afraid of what would happen to him if he turned back. The house might not like that.

He stumbled along with the crowd, not knowing what else to do.

Dim light seeped from the end of the tunnel. Davy could make out the people moving in front of him. Some sort of doorway lay up ahead, a double door made of small glass panes. The door opened onto a glassed-in porch. Davy followed the crowd through the doorway and out onto the dimly lit porch, moving along the inside wall as others filed out behind him.

The porch stretched to Davy's left. Along the front and sides, windows reached from the ceiling to about his waist. Beneath the windows it became solid wall. The floor was tiled and empty. It was cold out here. Davy could see his breath, little puffs of mist.

Outside, across the yard, trees formed a dark boundary. As Davy watched, a single spot came on. The spot began moving back and forth among the trees, looking like the headlight of a train coming from around a bend.

All at once the spotlight picked out something in the trees and stopped. Frankenstein! It was Frankenstein! Arms held high, ten feet tall, coming toward them.

Unbelievably the spotlight moved away and found another monster—a zombie! No! *Two* zombies, moving with the shuffling, stiff-legged gait of the Undead.

Again the light moved on . . . to Dracula! Davy watched the vampire begin stalking toward them, his cape billowing out on either side, its crimson lining two gashes in the darkness, black wings dripping blood.

The light became frenzied now, flashing back and forth, picking up other monsters emerging from the trees, coming toward the house.

Davy shrank against the wall, away from the windows and the approaching monsters. Some of the crowd was doing the same—but some of the people were actually going up to the glass, pressing themselves closer to the oncoming monsters, talking and laughing and pointing first at one, then another.

The monsters reached the windows, scraping against them, beating on them, wanting in, inside with the people so they could kill them, eat them, suck their blood!

Horrible moans and snarls assaulted the glass as the monsters found the barrier. Davy held himself tightly, grasping his arms with his hands, hugging himself, straining against the back wall. *Please, God, don't let the glass break—if the glass wasn't there—*

A sound exploded on Davy's right—the sound of a door being thrown open! Someone screamed.

A bullet of dread shot to the bottom of Davy's stomach. There had been another door, hiding in the darkness, a door to the outside.

A little whimper escaped Davy as he watched Frankenstein stalk up the outside steps and through the door.

As one, the crowd moved back, away from the oncoming monster.

In a spasmodic burst of flight, Davy darted from the wall, weaving between people who weren't moving fast enough. He had to get away before the monsters—he glanced back over his shoulder and saw the two zombies follow Frankenstein onto the porch—got close enough to touch him. Davy felt his stomach heave at the thought of being touched by one of them. He closed his eyes, and then he was at the far doorway, and through it, and off the porch that the monsters had taken for their own.

Davy looked almost gratefully at the floating deadface waiting in the darkened inside room. This monster was becoming familiar. It was a monster you could count on.

A glowing skeleton hand pointed the way.

Davy fell in among the moving people, scuffling along with blank devotion, feeling some comfort from those who were coming behind, filling in the cracks between him and the monsters, but he was beginning to feel *very* small, *very* alone, and *very* sure that this wasn't so much fun, after all.

Chapter 4

Leroy James Hopkins, "Dood" to his friends—
and enemies, if he had any—pushed the heavy black cowl
from his wiry, short-cropped black hair and favored the
ghoul in front of him with a flourishing bow.

"The scepter of office, Your Ghoulishness," Dood pro-
nounced in stately, sepulchral tones, holding out a black
Eveready flashlight topped by a blue-tinted lens.

In a reverse gesture the ghoul, also known as Phillip
Handy, pulled his own black cowl carefully into place and
took the flashlight with his left hand, which was encased
in a plain black glove. Tucking the body of the flashlight
under the front of his robe, he flicked it on. Blue-white
light shone upward from just beneath his chin, highlighting
a face heavily coated with luminescent white pancake
makeup and dramatically shadowing the eye areas which

45

were shaded black from brows to cheekbones. It created an eerie imbalance that was a combination of stark white and strangely mobile shadows. The eye sockets looked sunken, round hollow pits in the deathly pale face. Shadows swelled and contracted with each slight movement of the flashlight. It was a good effect, and one repeated throughout the house: the Jaycees were using ghouls this year for tour guides. *Step right this way, folks, and let me turn you over to your friendly neighborhood tour ghoul.*

"How do I look?" Phil slapped on a deadpan expression and struck a pose.

Dood brought up his right hand, still covered by the glowing fluorescent skeleton glove, its elongated first digit held rigidly out by the pencil taped to his finger inside. With great deliberation he slowly fingered his chin, eyeing his fellow ghoul critically.

"Well . . . if you were a bit taller and a few pounds lighter—there's so little demand for short fat ghouls this season. Yes, that's it, of course." Dood snapped the skeleton finger away from his chin and, waggling it at his companion, did his best impression of Miss Beulah Dowling, his fifth-grade teacher. "Please grow five inches and lose twenty pounds at once!"

Phil muttered an oath under his breath. "Gimme a break, Dood, I've got to go take your place in the front hall before the next group comes in."

"Oh, well," Dood said in mock exasperation. "In that case you look *mahvelous*, dahling, simply *mahvelous*."

Phil reached out with his own skeleton-gloved hand and patted Dood's white cheek. "I'll bet you say that to all the ghouls."

Dood cackled with delight. "I love it, Phil, I love it!" he exclaimed in his normal voice. "Except I should have said it."

"You will." Phil's tone was dry. He turned and went through the door leading to the front hall of The Manse.

Dood watched him leave, still chuckling with amusement, then sauntered off in the other direction, shaking his head slowly. "You're right, Phillip my boy," he murmured, grinning widely. "You're so right."

Circling through the unused east wing of the old house, Dood headed for the enclosed breezeway that connected the body of The Manse with the kitchen annex, originally constructed as an outbuilding to lessen the possibility of a kitchen fire spreading to the main house. The breezeway had been added at a later date, probably by the Beaufort Twins, who would no doubt have found it a bit of a task to make the trip back and forth in all sorts of weather whenever they wanted a cup of tea or finger of milk toast. The kitchen building now served as lounge, makeup facility, dressing area, and private entrance for the Jaycees, who also made use of its small bathroom.

The kitchen was far enough from the main house and insulated sufficiently by a door at each end of the breezeway that the Jaycees didn't have to worry about being seen or heard by spectators going through the tours. They'd even draped black cloth over the windows so no light would show through.

Dood opened the door to the breezeway entrance, and found himself face-to-face with Frankenstein's monster.

"Hi, Tank," Dood said as the seven-foot monster clomped toward him, surrounded by an aura of noise-on-the-move and the light aroma of bourbon. "Been at the juicesticks again? You really should consider joining Tooth-picks Anonymous."

Tank Worley answered him with a large groan. "My feet are killing me!"

"Concrete overshoes ain't for everyone," Dood said in sympathy, stood out of the way, careful to keep his toes well off the beaten path as the Frankenstein monster clomped by.

"Look out for Zack and Samantha," Tank threw over his shoulder. "They're having at it in there."

"Thanks for the warning."

As Tank clomped off, Dood became aware of a rather heated discussion emanating from the kitchen. Coming through the closed door on the other end of the breezeway, the voices were muffled, but they were clearly male and female and hot enough to cook a turkey.

Not wanting to be that turkey, Dood exited the breeze-way through a small side door to the yard. He needed a smoke anyway, and you couldn't smoke inside the house—strict fire laws plus the Beaufort Twins' insistence on a no-smoking clause in their contract—but the grounds were exempt, although they were cautioned to be careful if it was dry.

There'd be no problem tonight, Dood saw as he strolled down the couple of steps and walked out onto the grassy side lawn; there was a heavy dew already forming from the sudden drop in temperature after a sunny afternoon. Re-moving his gloves, he pulled a Tareyton out of a flat leather cigarette case and lit up, cupping his small, elegant butane lighter to protect its flame from the wind. He replaced lighter and case in an inside pocket, unconsciously rubbing a thumb over the smooth leather. The Dood liked nice things.

Dood stretched his shoulders up and down a few times. It was colder than the ace of spaces out here. And dark. Clouds kept drifting across the moon. Yet despite the biting cold, the air had a heavy feel to it, lacking the usual late-autumn crispness. It held a stale smell, too; definitely not the fresh breath of night air he'd expected to enjoy— rather like being inside a huge walk-in freezer, or a mauso- leum. The heavy, stale coldness seemed to lean against a body, weight it down.

Dood brought his left hand up and briskly rubbed his right arm from shoulder to elbow to stimulate circulation.

In the distance a night bird hung a plaintive cry on the wind. Dood shivered at the sound.

Suddenly he didn't want to be out here by himself anymore.

Taking a final long drag from the cigarette, he dropped it in the grass and crushed it carefully beneath his shoe, despite the sizzle he'd heard as glowing tip met damp lawn. He scuffed at the pieces until satisfied that no spark remained, then walked back up the stairs and reentered the breezeway. Now he could use a cup of coffee, strong and hot.

The moment he closed the outside door the voices hit him again. "Still at it," he murmured, and headed toward the sound, ready to intrude. After three hours of taking little-bitty sliding steps on a strip of carpet to make it appear that he was a disembodied face floating down a corridor, and re-coiling the tacky plastic spiders that were attached by rubber bands and paper clips to guide wires strung across the ceiling, he was ready to prop his feet up in the kitchen and relax a spell. Phil would be working hall duty for a couple of hours, and while a short fat ghoul couldn't hold a flashlight to the Dood—

Angry words reached into his head and interrupted the modest self-evaluation he'd been about to make; temperatures in the kitchen were apparently reaching new highs. "Not seeing eye to eye again," Dood murmured as he hesitated on the threshold, aware, as were all the Jaycees, of the internal problem that existed within their official ranks.

For the past several years, Jaycee membership had been open to women. Although some chapters throughout the state still maintained the bipartite structure of "Jaycees" and "Jaycettes," the Merrillville chapter had consolidated, mainly due to the efforts of Samantha Evers, former Jaycette president, now honorary co-president of the Jaycees—at least until the next election, when she planned to run against the current president, Zack Dalton. The new arrangement had produced mixed emotions among the male Jaycee membership. Further complicating matters, Samantha and Zack had been high school sweethearts and, for a time, live-in lovers. It promised to be an interesting campaign.

"That little girl was scared to death, Zack," Samantha Evers's voice blazed from the kitchen. "A little girl, for Chrissake! Can't you prey on the ones you know can take it?"

A harsh laugh indicated Zack Dalton's opinion. "What's this, Miss Liberated Womankind? Werewolves should be reserved for boys only? Leave the little girls to their sweet little fairy tale princes?''

''Dammit, Zack, don't try to twist this into some sort of pseudo-sexist game. You terrorized that child. Her family had to take her home and God knows what the repercussions will be.''

''You think they'll try to sue?'' Zack's voice suddenly became cautious.

Samantha made an obvious sound of disgust. ''I'm talking about the effect this might have on the child. Haven't you ever heard of nightmares? Traumas?''

There was movement in the room, the sound of a chair being dragged across the floor. ''All kids have nightmares.'' Zack's tone was matter-of-fact.

''You're a pig, Zack, you know that? You sprawl out in that chair and prop your feet up on the table and you don't give a damn about a little girl you just frightened half out of her wits. I saw her fear. I tried to calm her down, but she was hysterical by then, scared to death of me even when I took off my wig and tried to show her we were just dressed up in costumes. What's the matter with you? I've never seen you treat a child that way.''

''Get off it, Sam. The kid shouldn't have been here if she couldn't take being scared. That's what a goddamn House of Horrors is all about.''

''You sadistic bastard!'' The words trembled out of Samantha. ''If you do that to another child tonight, I'll—''

''You'll *what*?''

The sound of a chair falling to the floor. Footsteps crossing the room.

"You'll what, Sam?" Zack's words were soft this time, but as though shoved through clenched teeth.

Dood took a step forward.

"Let go of me, Zack." Samantha's tone was packed in ice, but she sounded in control.

A moment of silence followed. Dood hesitated.

"You know, Sam"—Zack's voice had changed again, become husky—"if I were to judge this little disagreement by several of our past encounters, I might think it was leading up to something."

"Stop it, Zack. That's all over."

"Is it? Is it really, Samantha? You remember the arguments so well, but what about the way we used to end them? Don't you remember making up? God, it was so good . . ."

"Zack, let go of me." There was a sudden touch of alarm in Samantha's voice.

Dood reached for the doorknob.

"Come back to me, Samantha. It can be the way it used to be for us. Remember how it was between us? Remember this . . ."

Again, Dood hesitated. He didn't believe there was a chance in hell that Samantha Evers would go back to Zack Dalton this time, but he'd thought that before, and their on-again, off-again relationship persisted.

The sound of a scuffle. A slap.

"Damn you!" Zack growled, and there was an ugly edge to his voice. Real ugly.

Dood decided it was definitely time to intrude. He thrust open the door and stepped in, displaying his broadest smile. "Interrupting something, I hope?"

The scene reached out and grabbed him with a wrench that brought a distasteful dryness to his mouth, then took on the classic motions of a one-act farce.

A tall, slender redhead draped in flowing white nylon, a crimson-lined black cape clasped at her throat and slung back over her shoulders, stood rigid in the arms of a big man dressed in a werewolf costume, minus the headpiece. The expression on Samantha Evers's face was a mixture of loathing and fear, and it shot through Dood like a needle of ice. Intimidation, in any form, was disgusting—and this form particularly so. He felt the beaming smile freeze on his face and maintained it with difficulty.

Samantha had turned to see who had entered. Now a look of relief passed across her features and the spark of anxiety shimmering in her green eyes faded.

Zack Dalton had not moved. Dood wondered if he was even aware that someone else was in the room. Zack's large hands, bereft of the hairy, claw-tipped gloves of his costume, were clamped around Samantha's forearms as though he had been shaking her, or more likely, pulling her toward him. Samantha's hands, balled into fists, were crushed against Zack's chest. Both were breathing heavily.

"Having a small difference of opinion, children?" Dood inquired in the blandest of tones.

For a moment Dood thought Zack was simply not going to respond to his presence. Dood took another step forward, not sure precisely where this thing might go. Then Zack turned toward him.

Dood somehow kept his smile in place, but his eyes narrowed sharply. Zack's face was suffused with color, one cheek mottled, apparently from the slap Dood had heard. Ice-blue eyes stared at Dood like he was a stranger, glittering with a cold, dark fury, and at the same time clouded and heavy with a kind of passion. It was a look more suited to the wolf's head lying on the kitchen table.

"Hey, my man." Dood somehow kept his tone light and bantering. "Chill—"

Abruptly, Zack released Samantha, strode over to the table, snatched up his wolf's head and the claw-tipped gloves, and stalked past Dood out of the room.

"—out," Dood finished, staring after him. He knew Zack Dalton was something of a hothead; he'd been that way since high school and probably before, but this was a bit much.

Shaking his head once, Dood closed the door, then turned back to Samantha. The smile had left his face. "That was a rather nasty little scene."

She began to massage her arms where Zack had gripped them, giving Dood a quick glance and a small, humorless laugh. "You don't know the half of it." Her voice was husky with a combination of emotions that Dood recognized as anger, disgust, and a residue of fear.

"For a moment there I was really afraid of him," she continued. "Afraid of *Zack.* Jesus, I lived with the guy for over a year and we never had a scene like that, even the night I told him I was leaving. It's not like Zack to be that vicious." Samantha's voice was soft, almost like she was talking to herself, and her eyes stared blankly at something only she was seeing.

Dood took a couple of steps her way. "Hey, Freckles, you okay?"

Samantha met his look of concern, then beamed him a

smile. There was genuine amusement in it this time. "Why
do you call me that? I don't have freckles."

Dood shrugged, relaxing. "You should have. A redhead
without freckles, unreal. Want me to stop?"

She shook her head. "Nope. I don't mind." She sank
down in the big easy chair someone had dragged in from
another part of the house and stuffed in a corner. "It's
better than *Sam*." A frown clouded the smile. "I hate
being called Sam."

Dood strolled over to the big makeup mirror propped
against the left side of the kitchen sink and nonchalantly
began touching up his white theatrical pancake makeup. It
had rubbed thin enough in spots to let the dark skin
beneath show through. Daubing a smear of white onto his
left cheek, Dood watched Samantha's reflection out of the
corner of his eye.

"You know," he said, pitching his voice loudly enough
to make sure it penetrated her blue funk, "I think the
Dood is becoming rather fond of this white face." He
patched a place at the edge of his hairline. "Yeah. Everybody going around saying, 'That's really white of you,
Dood.' " He eyed himself critically. "With this face, the
Dood could even try for Mr. Interlocutor, if they still had
minstrel shows."

In the mirror, he saw Samantha glance up at him. He
flashed her his best homeboy grin. She didn't return it.

"Do you really think that kind of joke is funny, L.J.,
even if you're the one who makes it?"

Dood let the tinsel smile melt away. He regarded her
carefully for a moment, their eyes locked in the mirror.

"No," he finally said. "No, I really don't."

"Well, neither do I." She got to her feet, breaking their eye contact, and went to pick up her wig off the table.

Dood returned to his makeup repairs, feeling at ease. He'd known Samantha Evers a long time. They'd gone through school together, spent a good part of their small-town growing-up together. Somehow, along the way, they'd become friends.

Samantha's face reappeared in the mirror, just behind Dood and to his left. She began putting on the long black wig streaked in white at the temples that was the crowning touch to her Lady Dracula outfit. The silence between them lengthened, but it was the comfortable variety, the kind of silence between friends who feel safe lowering barriers in front of each other.

Bloodred nails flashed in the mirror as Samantha adjusted the wig, then reached to apply fresh lipstick the same color. She picked up the soft, plastic Drac fangs lying on the edge of the sink and turned to go.

In the mirror, Dood watched her walk away. "Hey, Freckles . . ."

She turned.

"I'll be around if you need me."

An easy smile covered her face. "You're a nice person, L. J. Hopkins, you know that?"

Spreading his hands wide in a gesture of exaggerated humility, Dood pasted on his best homeboy grin and turned toward her:

"I'll bet you say that to all the ghouls."

MERRILLVILLE 31 MILES.

The big dual headlamps stabbed the sign, flashed back a

glare, then swept on down the tarmac, bringing the somber
black asphalt to sudden light before racing past, dragging
the darkness along behind. Slender strips of yellow rushed
by Frank's left, a line of solid white ran beside him on the
right, sandwiching the rig into the middle of a race that
Frank sometimes felt would go on forever, toward a finish
line that wasn't there.

"I'm getting tired," Frank murmured to the night, aware,
with the subconscious knowledge of the professional trucker,
that such fanciful thoughts were often a prelude to dozing
at the wheel. He'd done that once, not in a truck, thank
God, which would have put a blot on his safety record, but
in his ex-wife's old Nash Rambler. Of course, she hadn't
been his *ex*-wife then . . .

He'd just come off better than forty-eight hours on the
road, pushing the limit of his endurance, adjusting his
logbook to reflect the mandatory requirements of maxi-
mum fifteen out of twenty-four, wanting to make it home
before their anniversary moved another year away. He'd
made it to the terminal, then gotten almost halfway home . . .

That night had been like this one, cold and overcast, the
full moon blotted by banks of clouds, lines zipping by on
his right and left. He remembered thinking he could hear
them sing, singing just to him, a chorus humming in the
background of his consciousness. He'd woken in the
hospital.

Many times since, Frank had wondered what might have
waited for him at home that night, wondered if he might
have walked in on the same scene that had greeted him
half a year later. As he had those other times, Frank ended
the reminiscence with the thought that even though the

ensuing six months had been merely a pretense he hadn't
recognized, he was glad his marriage hadn't ended on their
anniversary.

The room was full of light. A large central fixture
dominated the ceiling. Around the walls, sconces added
their warm glow to the overhead lighting.

Davy filed past the pointing deadface that stood just
beyond the light spilling from the room, blocking the
group from continuing down the darkened hallway. He
was becoming more used to the floating faces with their
skeleton fingers pointing the way to go—signposts detour-
ing you this way and that, making no threatening moves,
as long as you followed their directions, Davy thought,
resolving to continue doing just that. He didn't think he'd
be able to stand it if that long, glowing finger were to
touch him. It might make him shrivel up, turn black and
wrinkled. Davy shivered, a little rigor of reflexive movement, and hurried with the crowd into the room.

The room spread large and empty and comfortingly
bright after the thing-filled darkness of before. Davy glanced
around, looked up at the ceiling and down at the floor. No,
nothing scary here. The back- and far-side walls had thick
draperies drawn across their windows, barring the night
outside. To Davy's right and about midway down the
inside wall, a door loomed ominously. But the door had a
bar and heavy padlock on it, the kind of big lock that not
even a monster hand could break.

Davy relaxed and allowed himself to be herded into the
middle of the room as those behind him filed in. The
crowd milled about, reacting to the light and warmth with

normal-tone conversations, jokes, some light horseplay between a small group of teenagers. The knot in Davy's stomach began to loosen. Maybe from here on it would be okay.

A policeman strode into the room. He held a clipboard and was marking on it with a pencil. He strode up in front of the padlocked door, turned to the crowd, and lowered the clipboard.

"Security check, folks," the policeman said. "Nothing to be alarmed about," he said, smiling to emphasize the truth of this statement, "but there's been a report from headquarters that a deranged killer has been seen in the area and we're just making sure everything's locked down tight before continuing tours through the house."

He raised the clipboard, poised the pencil over it. "Has anyone seen anything out of the ordinary around here?"

Giggles from the crowd.

"Nothing strange going on? No one lurking about?"

Laughter.

Davy saw nothing all that funny in the policeman's words. A killer on the loose was nothing to laugh about. He searched his memory for any clue that might help the officer.

"Okay, then, folks." The policeman looked up and flashed them another smile. "Tours will resume shortly." He jotted something on the clipboard and turned to leave, then turned back. "Oh, by the way, the killer keeps his pet with him all the time. It's a big, black panther."

Titters from the group.

"I'll just check this lock before I go, make sure it's on

good and tight.'' The officer reached out and gave the padlock a firm jerk.

The padlock came off in his hand!

At the same time, the overhead light went off, leaving only the wall sconces illuminated, but they now seemed to be giving off shadows instead of light and lacked the warmth of earlier.

The crowd reacted with a soft murmuring sound and moved away from the door. Davy felt the air around him begin to breathe, like a draft from an open window. He looked toward the heavy drapes on the side wall. They were undulating sluggishly.

The crowd moved back another pace. Davy's eyes darted to the front again, seeking out the big smiling policeman, the uniform that meant help and safety and protection, the person to run to if you're lost or hurt, the one to call if something bad happens.

The policeman was backing slowly away from the barred door. The broken padlock dangled from his fingers. ''I think I hear something,'' the policeman said, and his voice sounded scared. ''I think I hear something behind that door.''

Why didn't he pull his gun? Davy moved with the crowd as they eased away from the wall where the door was—

With a sudden crash the bar fell from across the door.

Davy jumped at the sound, then shivered as a breeze blew across the room. It seemed to be trying to blow out the lights. They had dimmed almost to nothing.

A sudden gust, and the door in the wall began to open. The creak of rusty hinges rasped in the silence. The crowd swayed back, away from the opening door, away from what might be hiding in the darkness on the other side.

Davy squeezed himself into the middle of the group, trying to surround himself with people, block off what was happening, what was going to happen. The knot had come back, but to his chest this time, not his stomach. It was bigger than before. It lay there like a wad of half-chewed bread, and he couldn't swallow around it.

Slowly the door creaked open, holding every eye riveted, including his own, Davy realized with abstract interest even as he felt his body freezing around him. His mind was a mass of contradictions, operating on two levels. He wanted to look away—but he couldn't look away. His eyes were fixed on the widening black space behind the opening door. Fascination held sway over fright. He felt as he had that time he'd stayed up late with Randy to watch *Shock Theater*, covering his face with his hands at the scary parts, but somehow always giving in to some weird urge to inch his fingers apart ever so slightly and peer past the darkness at what was happening on the flickering screen.

The door had stopped moving. It was open all the way back to the wall now. The crowd had gotten quiet and still. Davy waited for what would come, waited for whatever thing lay hidden in this darkness. He felt his skin begin to crawl. Someone was watching him, something was watching him from the darkness, from the darkness beyond the door.

Some of the people in front moved backward again, making the rest of the crowd back up, bunching them closer together, pressing them toward the back wall. Davy nestled into their closeness, wrapped it around him like the eye of a storm. Then he heard it.

The scratch of claws on floor, stalking, coming nearer. A soft rumble of breathing, rhythmic breaths, ebbed and flowed in the otherwise silent room, not human . . . *Not human!*

"Eyes . . ." someone whispered.

And Davy saw them. Yellow-green eyes, slanted eyes, with centers of glittering, diamond-shaped red. Davy felt impaled on those eyes, held spellbound by the eerie beauty and cold threat within them. The eyes were moving toward him.

The crowd backed up.

The animal breathing was louder now, growing as the eyes came forward from the darkness. A low, throaty roughness moved into the room like a separate thing, alive.

Then the smell hit Davy's nostrils. A smell sour and pungent, an unwashed, zoo smell; the smell grew worse, vying with the swelling sound and stalking eyes.

Davy backed away with the crowd, back and back until they were surely almost as far back as they could go—and still the sound and smell and eyes came nearer, looking at Davy now, picking him out of the crowd. The panther was coming after him!

A scream ripped from somewhere in the group. Davy whirled toward the scream, eyes darting wildly from person to person. The scream came again and again and again . . .

Huge monster hands and arms had sprung from behind the heavy drapes and twined themselves around one of the teenagers. The boy was struggling, grappling with the arms and hands, trying to get away. Beside him a girl was screaming and screaming.

Frantically, Davy pushed between people, shoved his way toward the side wall, away from the screams, putting the crowd between him and the screams. He flung himself up against the wall, then turned to make sure the thing behind the curtain hadn't followed.

The screams turned to laughter; the long monster arms began to flop around like rubber snakes, grabbing blindly at the spectators. Davy shook his head, little jerks of nonacceptance. Everyone was laughing, jumping away from the flopping monster arms, moving to the hallway door where the floating deadface had suddenly reappeared, skeleton hand pointing outside and down the hall.

One by one the crowd obediently filed out. The policeman left with them, pushing closed the door where the panther was as he passed. The policeman was laughing too.

Davy continued to watch, pressing himself against the wall, a small boy trying his best to look smaller. In a moment, the heavy drapes were pushed aside. A guy in a T-shirt and jeans walked out, pulling off the monster arms, chuckling to himself as he left the room.

Nobody noticed Davy. Nobody turned around to see him standing there. They just walked away, taking their laughter with them.

The lights had come back on.

Davy edged over to the far corner, the corner farthest from the door with the eyes. He squatted there and continued his vigil, watching the door where the panther was. A tear leaked from his left eye and slowly trickled down his face. Davy hardly felt it, didn't make a move to wipe it aside.

Drawing his knees up to his chest, Davy grasped them with his hands, grasped them with white-knuckled intensity—something to hold on to. He didn't understand the laughter, didn't know why there had been so much laughter.

"It isn't funny," he whispered defiantly to the empty room, then bit his lip as he heard the sound of his own voice, a sound that might call attention to his corner of this awful place. *It isn't funny*, he thought grimly.

Faint laughter and distant screams stirred the silence of the dimly lit hallway that led from the kitchen annex through the unused east wing of The Manse and into the central structure that formed the nucleus of this year's House. Although the Jaycees were using the glassed-in side porch off the west wing for their "Walk Through Terror," most of the main scenarios were set up in the core structure, utilizing parts of all three floors and the cellar.

Dood strolled along the deserted hallway, his thoughts matching his easy pace. He was not all that anxious to go back and relieve Phil in the front hall, but it was no big deal either. Couple more hours and this ghoul would bite the dust for another year. Next House, the Dood was going to opt for one of the outside jobs—maybe the ghost from the well or the ax-happy gardener. Of course, if it turned out to be as cold next year as it was this year, he would rue that decision.

Rounding a turn in the hallway, Dood started up the

corridor that would take him to the room just off the entry hall where Phil would be waiting for him, or would meet him when he got through with his current group of spectators. Dood began humming a chorus from one of his favorite Dead Red Sampson blues songs, then moved on into the lyrics:

> "Tin cup man comin' down the road
>   He's shufflin' along an' draggin' a dog,
>   Wearin' a sign 'round his neck, it said:
>   'I am blind an' my dog is dead' . . ."

Light poured across the hallway and splashed the wall opposite the open door to the panther room. Now there was an innocuous, enjoyable little scenario: focus crowd attention on something coming at them from the front, then zap 'em from behind. Worked every time. Dood was beginning to lean a bit toward the conservative element in Jayceedom who were questioning the increasingly graphic scenarios and violence in their Annual House as becoming too intense for younger children, and even the older ones. After what Wolfman Zack had done to that little girl tonight, this opinion might be echoed by certain members of the Merrillville community, particularly the—

Dood frowned, stopped walking, turned around, and went back to the open doorway he'd just strolled past. Had he seen a kid in there . . . ?

Yep. Dood stood at the doorway a moment, eyeing the small boy bundled into a back corner of the room. The little guy seemed wedged as tightly as he could get into the V where side and back walls came together—knees pulled

up against chest, hands grasping knees. The only things
exempt from the classic fetal position were his head and
shoulders, which were rigidly upright as though bolted
against the wall. The kid had on jeans, a white hooded
sweatshirt, and tennis shoes, one of which had come untied. The laces lay on either side of his shoe like twin
strands of long, limp hair. The small pinched face looked
troubled, forehead slightly drawn as though thoughts were
churning double-time behind it. A pair of strangely neutral
eyes were fixed on the wall to Dood's right, studying
something intently. Dood glanced at the wall, saw nothing but the closed door that connected this room with the
one next to it where the panther mock-up was.

Dood sighed, beginning to understand. The kid was
either waiting for the next group to do the panther scene
again or—Dood's frown returned—he was too scared to go
past the door, even to get out. Where were the kid's
parents? Surely this little guy hadn't been going through
the House alone.

Dood stepped into the room. The Dood didn't like no
little guy to be scared.

The kid's head snapped around to face Dood. His eyes
went from oval to round, dilating into big dark holes of
suspicion. Dood stopped where he was.

"Hey, little guy," he tossed out in a light, cheerful
voice. "What's hap'nin'?"

The kid remained utterly still, a little stone kid.

Dood reached up, slowing his movements when he saw
the kid wince, and pulled back the cowl he'd just spent
five minutes positioning properly in front of the makeup
mirror in the kitchen.

"Hey, my man, don't be afraid of the Dood, now. The Dood is in disguise, here. Normally I do Gumby but this year they're into black and white." Dood slowly began walking toward the kid, hoping his banter would soothe away the fear. "It's all the rage."

The kid shifted his gaze to Dood's hand—the one with the skeleton glove. Without looking down, Dood began to remove the glove, maintaining his measured, easy approach to the boy, doing his best Eddie Murphy jive routine. The kid continued to stare at the glove as Dood pulled it off, focusing his gaze on it, looking at it with a sort of horrid fascination—then, as Dood pocketed the glove, he realized it was his hand the kid's gaze was now locked onto.

Reaching the kid, Dood stopped walking and knelt down to put himself on the same level. The boy's eyes remained fixed on Dood's hand. Dood sighed. His hand was still black, even after he'd removed the glove. For some reason the little guy couldn't quite make the transition.

Dood thought of a scene they'd done last year where a horrible monster had been unmasked for the crowd, only to reveal a gruesomely mutilated and scarred human face.

"Hey, little guy, that's just my skin you're putting your eyeballs on, nothin' more to take off." Dood flipped his hand over and wiggled his fingers back and forth. "It's just a hand, see?"

At first the kid had flinched away from the movement of Dood's hand, then he blinked his eyes a couple of times, seeming to come out of his trance, and looked up at Dood. His expression returned to its former speculative study.

"The name's Dood," Dood said amiably. "What's yours?"

It almost surprised him when the kid replied:

"Davy. Davy Dawson."

The kid's voice sounded steady and strong. Maybe he'd been wrong about the fear he thought he'd seen.

"Well, Davy Dawson, is there some way I might be of service to you? Are you lost?"

Davy shook his head. "I want to go home."

"Okay. Let's go find your parents."

"My dad's at home."

The way he said it made Dood suspect there wasn't a mother. "Then who did you come with, Davy?"

"My brother. I came with my brother, Randy, but he got in line with Buddy and the turd and I was going to go through the House first and tell them they were the scaredy cats." The words tumbled out. "But then there was so much dark and things inside the dark and now I want to go home," he finished with a rush.

Dood sighed. The kid had no doubt wanted to impress his brother with his fearlessness and instead had bitten into a can of worms.

"Where are you supposed to meet your brother, little guy?"

"At the car," Davy answered, sounding forlorn and a bit embarrassed.

"And where's the car?" Dood prompted.

"Across the street, about a block up."

"Is the car locked?"

Davy shook his head vigorously. "No, sir. They left it open so I could get in if I got there first."

"Fine." Dood carefully reached over—seeing only a small flinch this time—and tied Davy's shoe. He stood up.

"Tell you what I'm gonna do, Davy my lad. I'm gonna show you the special way out of here, the one that we Jaycees use. You won't have to go through any more of the House and you won't even have to tell your brother about this. You can go outside and around back and come out by the exit path where all the other people are coming out. It'll look like you went the whole way through, just in case your brother or his friends see you coming out. How's that sound?"

Davy's eyes had been glued to Dood's as he listened to the lifeline he was being offered. He indicated his approval by vigorously nodding his head once more.

Dood gave him a grin. "Let's go, then, big guy." He started to put out his hand for the kid's, then thought better of it.

Davy scrambled to his feet and together they left the panther room.

Retracing his steps of moments before, Dood kept up a steady monologue of light chatter, easing them down the dimly lit corridor and through the darkened east wing with a winning combination that was part Eddie Murphy and part blue-lensed flashlight.

They came to the breezeway.

Dood opened the first entry door and held it for Davy to precede him. Warm sounds of muffled conversation and laughter filtered from beyond the closed kitchen door, a rather striking contrast to Dood's previous visit.

"Right here, my man." Dood flicked open the door to the yard and led the way out, saying, "Three steps down,"

as a warning to the small boy who gratefully followed him
out of the house.

Holding the door open with his left hand, Dood pointed
with his right. "Just head around back and go through the
rear garden. On the other side of the house, there's a flight
of cement steps leading up from the cellar—that's where
the tour groups are exiting. Just blend in with the first
crowd that comes out and you're home free."

Dood glanced up at the moon that had moved from
behind a bank of clouds. It was full, and although rather
cold and constipated-looking as opposed to the jolly yellow giant that typified midautumn nights of countless tales
and songs, at least it shed sufficient light to see by—Dood
snapped off the flash to be sure—yes, even when some
clouds got in the way. The kid would be all right.

Davy took a few steps forward and turned around.
"Thanks, mister." He shot Dood a grin that was at least a
seventy-five percenter.

"Gotcha covered, my man." Dood gave a little salute,
adding, "Nothing between here and the exit path, Davy.
Nothing at all. Just you and the man in the moon."

Davy nodded, and with a little gesture that was part
wave and part a copy of the salute Dood had given, turned
and walked away.

Dood watched him go, suddenly feeling the cold settle
around him like it had earlier, though the biting wind of
before had died away. Moonlight emphasized Davy's white
sweatshirt, making it clearly visible even after the blue-
jeaned bottom half of his small body blended into the
night.

"Nothing between here and there," Dood murmured to

himself abstractedly, as the small white sweatshirt receded like a beacon down a tunnel. "Nothing at all. Just you and"—the moon went behind a cloud—"the dark."

A frown touched Dood's forehead. There was something not right out here, something . . . Why had he thought it was light enough for the kid to see?

The white shirt was barely visible now, a rip in the black curtain draping the yard. Dood released his clutch on the door, noting as he did so that he'd been grasping it with a vengeance. His fingers felt cramped from the grip. Flexing them, he took a step forward.

The moon filtered out from behind the cloud, spilling cold, silvery light across the yard once more. Davy's white sweatshirt was clearly visible again. The boy stopped and turned around; his face was blanched colorless by the moonlight. Dood watched Davy's hand move upward in a repeat of the little salute—a small pale dot on the end of a snow-white arm.

For a moment something reached out to Dood, something in the boy's stance that made him think: *Don't abandon this kid*. He started to step forward again, call out to Davy: "Wait, wait for me. I'll take you from here to there and it'll be you *and me* and the darkness, which makes for better odds . . ." Then the moment was gone.

Dood felt fear prickle up his spine and crawl onto his neck. The hairs at the base of his scalp sprang erect. "Jesus, what the fuck?" Dood whispered to himself.

He breathed deeply, cold air rushing into his lungs with a thousand tiny pinpricks, clearing away his sudden sense of dread. He looked up. The small splotch of white was gone.

Dood shook himself slightly, reached for the door, gave a little laugh. The kid was probably halfway to the exit path by now. He'd no doubt made a beeline around the house and through the back garden as soon as the moon came out. Dood glanced up. The moon was still shining coldly, no clouds nearby.

Dood walked up the steps and reentered the breezeway, feeling an unnatural relief. The kid would be all right.

MERRILLVILLE 17 MILES.

Thinking about his marriage always made Frank melancholy. One of the most melancholy thoughts of all connected to that brief span in his life was that he and Doris never had a kid. A little girl with Doris's dancing brown eyes and long hair; or a little boy to take to the stock car races over at the local dirt track. But Doris had kept putting it off, saying "Not yet" whenever he'd talk about having one.

Frank could understand. Although he'd been born into a family of nine—five girls and four boys—he was the baby of the lot and was exempted from most of the constant, backbreaking chores of a working farm. They had been a close-knit family, the hard times liberally sprinkled with laughter and love.

Doris had been the oldest of four. Her three brothers were born within two and a half years of each other, but not until nine years after Doris's birth. When her mother died eighteen months after her last delivery, Doris had shouldered the burden of raising her brothers. She got little help from their drunken father.

Frank thought it had soured her on kids, giving her all

of the problems and none of the joys. He'd tried to tell her it would be different with her own; with her own there'd be joy. She'd never disagreed with him, just smiled and nodded and said, "Not just yet," then taken him off to bed to do what she did best.

With a muttered curse, Frank reached over and turned on his radio, switching the dial around until he found what sounded like a country station—at least Willie Nelson was singing at the moment. Getting where it was hard to tell, there was so much of what they called "crossover" nowadays.

Frank turned up the volume and settled back to the wheel, enjoying the raspy voice and twangy guitar. Old Willie could sure talk to you, tell you about life—his life, your life. Frank let the music wrap around his thoughts and bundle them away.

On his right a sign flipped past: "Prepare to meet thy God."

Frank grinned, then laughed out loud. *In Shitville?*

Chapter 5

The cold felt like he was wearing it. It hung on Davy the way his old terry bathrobe would feel if he dipped it in ice water before he put it on. Beneath the sweatshirt his skin felt clammy from the thin film of perspiration that had layered his body inside the house.

His sneakers scuffed through the damp grass, soaking in moisture as he walked, beginning to make little squishy sounds. The left one hurt; the man had tied the lace too tight.

As he neared the end of the house, Davy caught faint sounds of laughter coming from a window just above his head. He looked up toward the sound, feeling its comfort steal some of the tenseness from his limbs and move a smile closer to his face. This could take the place of the man he'd left behind, give him someone nearby.

(If I can hear them, then they can hear me.)

But the window was covered with black, shutting him beyond its comfort and warmth.

(I wish that man was here.)

Davy realized he'd balled his hands into fists. He stuffed them into his pockets and walked on.

Tall, unfriendly tree giants stood along the edge of the yard to Davy's right. They hovered over him, leaning slightly inward, poised the way a huge wave looms just before it crashes down. Davy glanced up. The branches overhead seemed locked in some endless wrestling match, grappling hands and arms. He lowered his gaze to the bushes squatting in between the trees—sumo wrestlers, arms akimbo, ready to jump forward into the arena and do battle.

Davy quickened his pace as he rounded the end of the house, moving away from the line of trees that marched silently around the perimeter of the back garden, stumbling once when his foot scuffed a rough spot in the grass.

The garden stretched before him, a huge square of yard with some sort of stone thing in the middle, bounded on three sides by the trees and on one by the house itself.

Davy stopped, regarding it solemnly: an island of blue and black and stone gray surrounded by a green-deep ocean.

Moonlight filtered from behind a cloud, casting a silver coverlet on the landscaped square, an intricate pattern of light and shadows—like his grandmother's crocheted quilt, Davy thought, the one that always lay atop the blue spread on the big old high-poster bed at her house. He'd always liked the way the blue peeked through the holes and squiggles, liked to crawl up on it and sit right in the middle, pretend he was on an island surrounded by water full of things that wanted to get him but couldn't because he was safe above and beyond their reach. He had often filled that ocean with things he wanted to drown: bad things, fear things, hurt things.

Davy glanced down. He was standing in the ocean. Quickly he stepped across the boundary into the patchwork yard, immediately feeling safer.

His eyes moved toward the edging of trees that lay greenish black around the island-garden. It reminded him of the icky, slimy stuff that grew on stagnant water. He'd touched that stuff once, where a backwater pool gathered from the creek that ran beside the old Mackaby place. The icky stuff had stuck to his finger, clung to it like a thick piece of dark green skin, all slimy and cold. He'd only gotten rid of it when he raked his finger across the dirt.

Davy eyed the woods on the far side of the island-garden and became very still. He was supposed to go over that way, over there where the monsters were hiding. The man had said there was nothing bad between him and the path to home.

(Nothing between here and there but you and the man in the moon.)

And there wasn't. They would be waiting for him when he got over there—Frankenstein and Dracula and the zombies. Just like the ocean around his grandmother's bed, the ocean around the island-garden was filled with nightmare things.

Davy moved on toward the center of the island-garden, away from the edge of the green-deep sea. His eyes darted back and forth along the line of trees surrounding his safe spot. Tree trunks became dark wooden piers trying to hold back a night-green ocean lapping at the edges of his island, seeping through the cracks, a silent incoming tide, restless and churning and full of hiding things. Davy imagined himself trapped in that tide, covered with dark slimy green stuff.

Above his head the branches began to whisper in the wind, the trees passing secrets to one another. Davy plunged his hands farther down in his pockets and pretended not to hear.

His gaze roamed the monster side of the yard, watching it from the safety of his island. Nothing moved. Maybe the monsters were gone now. Several dark openings split the trees. They could be pathways. The man had said follow the pathway.

Davy studied the openings skeptically. None looked inviting, none looked worth trading his safety for, even though they might lead home. One of them. But which? Davy couldn't be sure which one would be right.

Moonlight shifted, and the line of woods now became a huge grinning mouth, moonlight on the tree trunks making them slivered monster teeth, the pathways gaps between where more teeth should have been. Davy didn't want to go over there alone.

A vision of the wall of eyes and mouths and teeth flashed through his mind.

Davy gave a little shudder and pushed the memory out of sight. There would be people coming from the house, the man had said. Groups of people exiting the house and taking the path toward home. They would know which path to take. All he had to do was wait.

Davy glanced behind him at the back of the house. It rose to meet the night sky, getting skinnier toward the top as if it had been partially pulled out of the ground by a giant hand. The top looked squeezed together, with little jagged pieces jutting upward, escapees that had oozed between the fingers as the pressure of the hand increased. Dark windows were punched here and there, holes gouged out where the giant hand's thumb and fingertips had gripped.

(Surely someone would come out soon—the man had said so.)

A light ground mist was beginning to creep across the yard, lumping in spots, adding to the quilted look that already lay there. Davy took a couple of steps toward the center of the garden, watching the mist swirl lazily around his feet. It bothered him; he looked away.

In the middle of the garden, a statue stood solemn and watchful; stone benches squatted around it, one at each corner of the central court. The benches were all slightly curved. Davy imagined them all scuttling forward on their squat stone legs to join up and form a perfect circle, dancing around and around the statue.

It was a fountain, Davy saw as he stepped nearer; a round, stone-rimmed pool with the statue jutting up in the middle. The statue looked vaguely like a fishwoman, he thought, though in the dark and rising mist it was hard to tell.

Momentarily distracted from the things that lurked outside the boundaries of his island, Davy wandered toward the fountain, becoming aware of a soft gurgling and spattering from several spouts and jets. A walkway circled the fountain, creating a little island within the garden, inviting a tour of inspection.

Davy moved closer. The statue was larger than it had looked at first. It *was* a fishwoman, he saw, a fishwoman made of stone. The fishwoman's face was turned away from him, but he liked the way her long hair hung in waves down her back and curled along the curve of her hip. Water cascaded from the locks of her hair. She held her hands outstretched to either side, palms raised as though offering gifts. Small streams tumbled from her hands and fell from slender fingers with little tinkling splashes; small, merry waterfalls given to the pool by the friendly fishwoman.

Mist gathered on the pool, thicker at the base of the statue. It rolled sluggishly across the water, curling over and around itself in slow motion. Every now and then some would spill over the stone-rimmed sides of the pool, small avalanches of mist here and there. Cloudy tendrils had begun to roam around the fishwoman's lower body, coiling slowly upward like cold white snakes. Davy could almost feel the slithering tentacles, touching, reaching, crawling up the moist gray stone. He shivered, wishing the mist would go away and leave the fishwoman alone.

The moon sank into a cloud. Darkness immediately swallowed the stone rim around the pool, and the concrete walkway lying cold and gray in the filtered light faded to black. Only the statue retained a nimbus of light, a moonbeam caught and held fast by the fishwoman—only now it wasn't the fishwoman at all, but a milky pillar of mist that rose at the center of the pool.

The pillar seemed to move.

Davy caught his breath, held it, eyes glued to the statue.

The mist undulated in silent, mocking innocence. Davy shook his head slightly, letting the breath escape. Of course the statue hadn't moved. Statues couldn't move. It was only the swirling mist.

Davy regarded the mist-covered fishwoman carefully, aware of the way her hands jutted out sharply from the cloud that covered her body. A picture flashed to Davy's mind of something he'd seen on television or in a movie, where two men were carrying a box with smoke boiling out of it, manipulating it with long pipelike devices connected to the box's handles. There had been some reason why they couldn't touch it and Davy vaguely remembered big thick gloves and strange bulky suits.

The statue moved again.

This time Davy was sure. He took a single step back, pulling his hands from his pockets.

The mist had thickened around the statue, molding itself to the fishwoman's body like liquid skin, matching the fishwoman's shape.

Suddenly it was alive!

Davy's small body iced over with gelid sweat. Fear bubbled up inside him, a gush of rancid fear that splashed through his pores. Wet tennis-shoed feet froze in place as a rigor of numbing terror stiffened muscles and sinews.

Davy watched the cloudy form slowly begin to pivot on its pedestal base and turn toward him. Horrid fascination filled him, joining the fear that had welded his frozen body to the ground. He wanted to run. He wanted to get away before the mist-form finished turning around. He wouldn't like its face, *knew* he wouldn't like its face, but he couldn't seem to move his legs. They didn't want to work because something else was contradicting the orders from his brain, something else was waiting to see the face, even though he knew it would be bad.

A safety valve popped open in the back of Davy's brain. Words of reassurance rushed into his consciousness. Davy, it's okay, it's only a game like all the other games tonight and soon there'll be lights and laughter and a friendly floating deadface to take you away to the next game. Please, God, let there be a floating deadface when I turn around and look.

(The man had said there was nothing between here and there. The man had lied, lied, *lied*.)

Davy's spine arched in a spasm of uncontrolled reaction. A thin scream formed at the pit of his stomach and sped upward; cold, needle-sharp sound ripping from his guts and through his heart and past his throat and shooting out of his mouth and off into the night as the mist-thing's face turned all the way around.

(Bad, oh, God, the face is bad, it's all covered with eyes. The mist-thing's face is covered with—)

Gaping, staring, horrible yellow *eyes* stared at Davy; piercing, stabbing, blazing yellow eyes; a face made of eyes, hundreds of eyes, all looking at him.

And Davy knew this wasn't a game. He'd known it all along, somewhere behind the lies, but now he had to peel the lies away. This wasn't part of the House—this was a thing all by itself, a thing that had nothing to do with games or pretend or floating deadfaces.

This was real.

In the span of a moment, Davy graduated from abstract fear to specific, mind-shattering terror. In the span of a

moment, he left childhood's cushioned haystacks behind
and entered a world built of pitchforks.

Hardly realizing his body had begun to move, Davy
took a step backward, then another, prompted by some
instinct spliced into his genes from a distant past when
survival came programmed into existence like eating or
breathing, self-preservation designed to take over when the
conscious mind failed. Davy moved back another step.

The mist-wreathed head had begun to swell, the eyes to
merge, blending into each other, colors running together
into darkness. Pain shot across Davy's face; he realized
that he was gouging at his cheeks with his own hands. He
heard a noise that sounded like the scream of a baby animal
his dog had caught and killed, and realized it was coming
from him. A flood of warmth soaked his groin and coursed
down his legs, and Davy knew he'd wet his pants and
somehow this was the worst thing of all.

Slowly the head swelled into a grotesque, grinning parody of a human face, a human face made of eyes, neither
manface nor womanface but something in between. Little
hands of water began sprouting from the swollen cheeks,
spanning the distance to Davy with slow-motion grace as
he stood, program stalled, mesmerized, unbelieving, watching them come, seeing them grow larger as they reached out
for him, the waterfingers turning into gleaming, glittering
claws.

(But they're only made of water and water can't hurt
you unless you drown in it.)

A claw-hand ripped the air. Davy felt it coming and
then it was slicing across his cheek. A slash of pain

stabbed into Davy's shell-shocked mind and brought him screaming into motion.

Stumbling backward, scrambling to get out of the way, Davy threw himself to the ground, screaming, crying, rolling sideways as once again the claw-hand descended. He felt another lightning jolt of pain as the claw-hand caught an edge of his shoulder and tore through shirt and skin and muscle. A flow of warmth poured down his arm and soaked his sleeve. An ice-pick stab of pain followed; Davy reeled, catching his breath in a ragged gasp, changing his scream to the moan of a wounded animal. Still moving, still trying to get away, Davy swung a look back toward the statue, his vision a dancing blur of light and color on darkness.

Oh, God, the statue was starting to change again, becoming distorted, distended, bulging toward him like an overblown balloon. More hands of water were sprouting from the mist, tiny little hands becoming bigger as they formed, scrabbling hands, reaching, groping, arching toward him. The statue's entire body was growing hands—long hair becoming hands, hands expanding outward, hands with fingers forming into long talons, hands coming for him.

A part of Davy's brain closed down; the part that had to do with reason and rationale and saneness. This was all the monster stories he had ever heard come to life; it was all the fears he'd ever had; it was his worst nightmares, his most horrible imaginings.

It was coming after him!

Scrambling to his feet, Davy began to run. As fast as his small legs could be thrust forward, he ran, heading for the trees that had turned from a monster hiding place to a refuge. He felt his right shoe come off, the one with the laces that weren't too tight. It didn't matter. Nothing mattered except his ability to run.

Run, Davy, run.

Nothing would ever matter so much again.

Run, run, RUN!

Davy felt the cold slam against him with a stunning blow. He tried to hunch away from what he knew was coming, tried to shrink his small body from the claw-hands that were after him, bearing down on him.

Pain exploded across his back and sent him tumbling forward. He turned his mind off, jumped to his feet, and began to run again.

Run, Davy, run
Run from the horror behind you
Run from the darkness closing in, the cold closing down
Run toward the light . . .

————————— Chapter 6 —————

Sᴘᴇᴇᴅ Zᴏɴᴇ Aʜᴇᴀᴅ.

The sign tumbled past Frank as he backed off the accelerator pedal and prepared to gear down the sixty-thousand-pound rig for the necessary crawl through town. If he paced it right, kept his RPMs up, he might not have to gear down at all. Forty-five was the cutoff point; forty-five miles per hour minimum, if you wanted to avoid gear-down. Barring hills or red lights—and Frank remembered neither—he could probably maintain it. So long as he didn't have to stop completely, Frank thought. Once stopped, he'd have to grind his way back up through all ten gears.

Bᴇɢɪɴ 45.

Frank checked his speedometer. It read about fifty. A couple of cars coming from town sped past him on the left,

85

gathering speed as they reached the flip side of the sign: RESUME 55. Frank rumpled his nose and sniffed. That was okay. He'd have a sign like that waiting for him on the other side of town.

MERILLVILLE CITY LIMITS.

SPEED LIMIT 35 UNLESS OTHERWISE POSTED.

SPEEDS STRICTLY ENFORCED.

The trio of signs hailed Frank's entry into town. Frank shrugged, looked at his speedometer. Forty-seven. That was probably pushing it. He eased up on the accelerator, reluctantly geared down once, and watched the needle drop back to around forty-three. They could take your license for doing fifteen over limit.

One of those round Chamber of Commerce signs popped up on his right. You could never really read them, even at a crawl, but you knew what they were the way you knew golden arches and HoJo motels.

Up ahead the road began a long left curve where the highway, as Frank remembered, cut between town and a big old abandoned house standing on a hill. You couldn't help but notice the house . . . an impressive old soldier standing watch over the little town of Shitville. Frank supposed that one day someone would come along and tear it down to build Shitville Shopping Center or something. No profit in old soldiers these days, folks.

BEGIN 30 AHEAD.

Frank's foot felt heavy as he lifted it up a tad more to comply with the sign just passed, then sank back down again as he saw his RPMs drop almost to the next gear-down point. He'd be damn glad to get through this small burg and out to the bypass and coffee at the C&P. That fried ham sandwich was becoming more and more attractive to his taste buds, too. With mustard and a thick slice of onion . . .

Frank's foot began to tremble from the effort of holding it half off the pedal. He relaxed it a bit more. It lay gently against the narrow strip of rubber-coated metal beneath, pressing only a tad heavier than before, within the designated parameters—Frank's designated parameters—anticipating the end of the slow zone.

Something darted out into the road. A small animal? A deer or something? Out in front of him . . . Frank's headlamps speared it, caught it on their powerful halogen beams, stopped it in its tracks for a split second, momentarily holding it frozen . . .

A kid! A goddamned kid! Running toward him now, reaching out toward the truck lights, grabbing at the beams, snatching at them, flailing at the light as though trying to catch hold of it, climb up it into the cab with him.

Frank slammed on brakes, jerking the air horn, swerving to the right—

But it takes time to stop a semi . . .

========================= Chapter 7 ======

PoJo's right hand rhythmically worked the dirt on the ground beside him, fingers stretching, contracting, moving with unconscious regularity across the loose topsoil. Fingernails scratched light paths along the packed-down ground, adding fresh soil to the dusty mound already accumulated.

Somewhere in PoJo's mind the movement of his hand was being traced, cataloged, and recorded, but it was sand, not dirt, PoJo was feeling, white powdery sand, the fine white sand of a Florida beach, hot and dry. Back and forth his hand moved, in time with the waves rolling up against a long white shore, breaking with the sound of muffled thunder in the background of his dream-clear vision.

Warm sun beamed down on PoJo, a friendly, smiling, lemon-yellow sun filling a corner of his dream . . .

*Like the pitchurs his little Jenny used to draw . . .
allays the sun stuck up there in the right-hand corner,
beamin' down on Jenny's pitchurs, bright yeller suns allays shining, shootin' little streamers down . . . Be like
that in Flarida, allays the sun shootin' little streamers
down . . .*

A sea gull glided by, cutting across PoJo's warm blue
sky, winging and soaring . . .

The sea gull let out a screech that became the scream of
locked-down brakes, tires shedding rubber, and an air
horn.

PoJo's sunny dream shattered into the dark, cold reality
of a Merrillville alley. The hand in the dirt grew still; the
opposite one tightly gripped the neck of the bottle it was
holding, a purely reflexive movement, protecting the thing
most dear, keeping it safe from possible harm.

A thump split the momentary silence, the solid, dull
thump of a bat hitting a softball.

PoJo looked up the street toward the sound.

A small body catapulted across his vision, rag-doll arms
and legs flopping almost comically in the cold night air,
splayed open in total abandon. PoJo gave a small wince as
the body completed its flight and landed with a sound like
the last hundred-pound bag of fertilizer landing in the back
of a farm truck.

Another sound grabbed his attention; he turned his head
and saw a big truck skidding to a stop, sprawling across the
road just up from his alley, about half a block beyond
where Main Street met the highway in front of The Manse.
One huge tire came to rest on the right-hand curb, the cab

jackknifed at a ninety-degree angle to the trailer hitched behind.

As PoJo watched, the driver forced open the door on his side and climbed down to the street, almost falling in his haste. The man began running toward the bundle of flesh and clothes and bone lying in the weeds at the side of the road, twenty or thirty feet beyond him. The big truck lamps gashed a path to the scene, like a spotlight lighting up a play. PoJo heard the man crooning, "Oh, my God, oh, my God, I hit a kid, I hit a fucking kid," as he rushed down the middle of the street, waving his hands frantically at a car just approaching from the opposite direction. The car squealed to a stop.

A shout came from across the street, from the front yard of The Manse; another. PoJo glanced up at the house and saw several forms already making their way to the scene, one man scrambling down the incline that sloped to where the crumpled body lay, others moving to the stone stairway set into the hill.

Holding his bottle tightly in his left hand, PoJo cautiously backed into the alley, moving away slowly, feeling his way with his right hand trailing along the cold stone wall of Gibson's warehouse. Once, he had to leave the wall and move around a gathering of garbage cans, then he was right back against the wall, gliding back like a wraith on the wind until he was deeply embedded in the shadows.

PoJo listened a moment to the sounds seeping down the tunnel of his hidey-hole, muffled, faraway sounds that had nothing to do with him, couldn't get in enough to touch him here. Sinking to the ground, PoJo set about squirming himself another place in the dirt, a comfortable place. That done, he leaned back against the cold wall, carefully unscrewed the cap of his bottle, and took a neat swig. Wiping his mouth on the back of his right hand, he turned his thoughts away from what was happening outside, satisfied with his response to it, and once again began the trip south.

If there was one thing you learned on the road it was keep your nose to yourself and your hands outta someone else's trouble pot. Yessir. Allays best to keep your hands outta someone else's trouble pot . . .

Excerpt from *The Merrillville Weekly,*
October 2, 1985 (continued), Samantha Evers,
Feature Writer:

Built by John Beaufort in 1873, The Manse has its
tales to tell . . .

PART TWO

Merrillville, North Carolina: November 1, 1986, through October 30, 1987 . . .

_____ Chapter 8 _____

The Manse is, at the best of times, a rather eerie place. Thick brush and old trees have been allowed for decades to grow untended on its five acres of land. In John Beaufort's later years little attention was paid to the outer grounds, care going first to the house, and then to the immediate surrounding gardens. Straitened circumstances encroached on the Beaufort family even then.

The term "grounds," as in "house and grounds," applies to the manicured back garden with its elaborate fountain sculpture, the small stretches of smoothly cut grass running lengthways on either side of the house, and the plainly neat front yard.

Over the years the trees have grown taller in their straight lines along each side of the house and across the edge of the back garden, gradually curving slightly inward toward The Manse, as if their upper branches were trying to gently cup the structure's roof and hold the very air inside. Even when autumn strips the leaves from the gnarled old branches, the trees grow close enough, with modest evergreens among them, to cast a pall of gloom across the estate, filling open spaces with permanent shadows and encouraging premature night.

The temperature in the front yard is lower than in town by at least ten degrees, even in the sweltering dead zone of summer. Most times there is a dankness, a mustiness, as if the air around the house had stagnated over the years, as if it were the very same air that lay there when John Beaufort walked the grounds.

Some folks think that a place bears the taint of its past, particularly that intense or violent emotions concentrated in a certain spot over a period of time can leave a residue that settles down into that space like a negative charge— bad vibrations, some say. If that is true, then surely fear is the chief emotion at The Manse, for when you walk alone through its grounds, or go into the house itself, a brush of something whispers:

I'm afraid . . .

===================== Chapter 9 =====================

I'*m afraid* . . .

The thought popped out of nowhere into Samantha Evers's mind. She immediately dismissed it. Ridiculous. The basement of The Manse was dank and musty and full of shadowy silence, but it was the middle of the day and there were Jaycees by the dozen all through the house. They were dismantling this year's House of Horrors, packing it up for storage until next October. All she had to do was call out and someone nearby would answer. *Wouldn't they?*

It was just so quiet down here, quiet and cold and overlaid with cellar darkness, the kind that crouches around a lighted area and nibbles at the edges. And the air smelled faintly sour, as though sometime in the not-too-distant past a small animal had perhaps crawled into a forgotten corner and died.

That had almost happened here once, long ago, Samantha shivered, *to a child.* Occasionally they used the old tale, threaded the plaintive whisper-cry of a little girl lost through the darkened basement. It gave a chilling, eerie effect that made scalps tingle and skin roughen. Samantha had never particularly liked the scenario, never liked playing on the legend child's misfortune. It always made her wonder how she'd feel to be locked by mistake in one of these dank cellar rooms, unable to draw attention, trapped for days.

The sour smell again intruded, calling Samantha back from the reverie that had almost, but not quite, hung an echo of a child's cry on the shadows. She wrinkled her nose in distaste, banishing an accompanying tremor. The odor clung to the air the way cigarette smoke lingers for days after a party, despite open windows and cans of room freshener. But that was no reason to be afraid.

Yet something had caused Samantha to hesitate in the middle of her cleanup chore. A sound? No. The absence of sound. It was *too* quiet down here. Solid quiet. Stealthy quiet. There should have been sound: the creak of a loose floorboard as someone walked overhead; the thumps and clatter of boxes and crates being carted off to upstairs storage rooms; the burst of laughter or muffled conversations from those working in groups . . . None of that penetrated here. It was as though the house was in stasis . . . or holding its breath.

Suddenly she felt weighted down with the silence, vaguely threatened. A rash of chill bumps slid up her arms. She rubbed her skin and felt the bumps subside. She was just cold, and like all of them, feeling a bit down after the dreadful accident last night.

The house was freezing, even though Samantha knew the old oil furnace was working and the thermostat set at sixty-eight, which was plenty. She tugged down the sweater sleeves she'd pushed up when starting this job, welcoming their soft warmth on her lower arms. She wished she could as easily pull sweater sleeves over the niggling unease that still lay at the back of her mind, then returned to the job of packing Mrs. Bates.

Queasiness nudged her as she picked up Mrs. Bates's disembodied head. The face was grotesque, its decayed, skeletal features a morbid contrast to the old-lady wig innocuously framing it; the high school art department had done wonders with the molding. Dingy, gray-streaked hair was parted in the middle and drawn back to a neat bun at the nape of Mrs. Bates's neck. When attached to the padded, round shoulders of the full body and seen from behind, the head looked real enough to turn around and say "Boo"—which, in effect, it did. They'd spent a good deal of time working out this *Psycho* scene, from the part in Mrs. Bates's dingy hair to the tips of Mrs. Bates's old-lady-comfort shoes.

It was a popular scenario, and an easy setup, one they'd staged down here before and would use again. Strictly visual scenes worked best in the basement because of the narrow stairs and choppy room arrangement. With Mrs. Bates, tour groups could be led slowly down the cellar stairs, their attention drawn to her form sitting beneath a gently swinging light bulb. An unseen Jaycee rotated the swivel chair to cause the effect. Then the group exited via a maze to the stairs leading up to the backyard.

Samantha had always liked this scene, finding it a good

scare no matter how often they played it. But today she was getting slightly nauseous handling the head.

She began carefully stuffing eye cavities with tissue paper. Though the head wasn't all that delicate, it somehow seemed important that the empty eye sockets be filled— maybe to keep out vermin.

"Yuk," Samantha murmured to the empty basement as a picture of squirming things crawling from eyeholes infested her mind. "Hate to be the one unpacking you next year if that happened . . ." She finished her stuffing and gently placed the head in its storage box, glad to be almost done with this chore.

"Talking to yourself again?" Dood's question floated down the stairs.

An almost overwhelming relief flooded Samantha, spreading the soft warmth she'd wished for earlier over the unease that had tunneled in at the base of her thoughts. *Not alone anymore.*

Samantha turned to see Dood's slight, well-dressed form descending the basement stairs. As usual, the Dood looked like he'd just come from a photo session for *GQ* magazine, though he'd been up on the roof taking down the bats. He wore his fashionable attire with the same casual nonchalance as he wore his smile.

"I was talking to Mrs. Bates, here," Samantha corrected, quickly adding, "and if you say 'Why, Mrs. Bates, do pull yourself together,' I'll behead you!"

Dood pulled on a pained expression as he glided down the last few steps and strolled over to peer at the decapitation Samantha had deposited into its packing box and was now surrounding with tissue paper.

"Credit me with a bit more creativity, my dear Freck-les," Dood said, studying the head. "At my worst I could come up with a better head line than that—and you the Lois Lane of Merrillville, *tsk-tsk*." He waggled an admonishing finger.

Samantha shook her own head slowly and put the lid on Mrs. Bates. "Unfortunately the only response I can think of at the moment is sever it, L.J., which is only a cut above stuff it."

"But a slice below my Bate-à-tête," inserted the Dood.

"And which would groan me out to say, so I won't," finished Samantha.

"I'm still ahead of you, and—"

"I know, I know," Samantha interrupted, "it's—"

"—better to be ahead than a behind!" they choroused.

Dood chuckled softly, pulled up a chair that had all its legs but only a cracked back, grabbed a dust towel from atop a pile, wiped the seat, and sat down astraddle it. Folding the towel neatly, he draped it over the break, then propped his arms across the padding and looked at Samantha, who was eyeing this ritual sardonically. "Need some help?" he asked, flashing her his standard homeboy-helper grin.

Samantha raised one eyebrow. "You certainly look in a position to be of service."

Dood spread his hands in mock helplessness. "Supervising's a dirty job but someone's got to screw it up."

"As I always suspected." Samantha finished taping the box closed and tied a cord firmly around it. "There." She patted its top. "Sleep well 'til next year, Mrs. Bates."

"Where's the rest of her?"

Samantha set the small box atop a large one to her right, feeling suddenly subdued. "Here," she said.

"Head over heels," Dood murmured, staring at the two containers, as though needing to say something to sustain the mood, even something unworthy of his talent.

"Ready for head quarters," Samantha added, trying to do her part, matching her tone to the softness of his, her eyes also drawn by the neatly stacked boxes.

The silent moment seemed to extend tentacles of deeper, unspoken thoughts, peeling away the veneer of forced gaiety.

Uneasiness crept back into Samantha's mind, nudging aside the comfort of Dood's presence. She felt as though they were the only two people on a small, removed world whose boundaries were defined by the ring of light coming from the single naked bulb crouched above them. Beyond that boundary lay an unkind darkness, an underworld where something waited.

Samantha caught herself glancing around at the darkness beyond their little incandescent world. She felt exposed; she felt that if she were to turn all the way around and look behind her, she'd see eyes implanted on the shadows, eyes moving toward them.

With a little dart of movement, she threw a glance over her shoulder, almost laughing at herself. Of course there were no eyes. Of course there was nothing watching them in the basement of The Manse. Of course. But if by some twist of chance that one light bulb went out, Samantha knew she would scream.

"I sent him out there, you know." Dood's voice was almost a whisper.

"What?"

"The little Dawson boy. I found him in one of the rooms—the panther room." Dood gave a little humorless laugh. "He was wedged in a corner like the room was shutting down on him. His shoe was untied."

Dood stared at the boxes, but was looking somewhere else; his eyes were steady, his voice flat and even.

"Tell me," Samantha said softly.

For a moment she thought he hadn't heard, or wasn't going to respond, then Dood snapped back to live action with an offhand gesture and a quick shrug that was almost a spasm. "There's nothing to tell, not really. The kid was alone. His brother sloughed him off." Cold contempt swept through Dood's eyes. "He'd tried to bluff himself through the House, but didn't quite make it. I talked to him awhile, he seemed okay, just wanted to go home. So I showed him out through the breezeway door, pointed him in the right direction, and sent him on his way." Dood winced. "I should have gone with him, walked him across the street."

"Maybe," Samantha stated, "but I know you've got reasonably good judgment, L.J. If you thought the child would be all right, then it was a well-based decision."

"He was only seven, for Chrissake!"

"Seven's old enough to know how to look both ways when you cross the street. Look, Dood, I know that Dawson bunch. The mother's dead and the father might as well be. There's an older sister who sleeps around for the price of dinner at McDonald's, and the brother, Randy, is a high school dropout who's already had a couple of brushes with the local law. Kids like that learn early—they have to if they want to survive."

Dood stabbed her with a sharp look. "This one didn't."

Samantha sighed. "I know. But, dammit, it's not your fault! Don't take a guilt trip on this thing."

Dood nodded slowly. His eyes turned downward, toward his hand. He made a fist, put out a finger, and lightly rubbed it across the dark skin. "Kid was scared of the dark," he said, more to himself than to Samantha. "Scared of the dark."

Samantha glanced around again. "Actually, I'm not too fond of it either. Let's get out of here."

Dood looked up at her, suddenly intent. "You feel it too, then?"

Samantha lifted a hand and slowly began rubbing her arm in an almost unconscious gesture of nervousness. The gooseflesh had popped back out at the tone of his voice. "Feel what." She made it a statement rather than a question, trying to keep it light, as if to convince herself that the thoughts lurking just under that nicely formed lump of common sense weren't really there at all.

Dood held her eyes with his, the look both evaluating and introspective. After a moment he gave a slight shake of his head. "I'm not sure. But I felt it before—last night, in fact." He frowned, started to say something more, then changed his mind.

"Look, L.J., we could sit here in the cellar psyching ourselves out on spook tales—no pun intended, dammit," she interjected when he quirked up an eyebrow and the corner of his mouth, "until we start seeing ghosts come out of the walls! Don't be ridiculous."

Dood grinned slyly, lifting his eyebrows. "Who are you trying to convince, me or yourself?"

Samantha opened her mouth to retort, then closed it and answered Dood's grin with one of her own, a rather sheepish one. "Yeah."

With a chuckle of acknowledgment, Dood removed his arms from the padded chair back, tossed the towel back on top of the pile, and stood. "Let's get out of here."

"Good idea. I even thought so when *I* suggested it."

"Now it's unanimous." Dood moved over to the packing boxes, picked up the small one, and handed it to Samantha. "Here's the pate crate; now head 'em up," he intoned, reaching for the larger box, "and move 'em out."

Samantha started up the stairs, glad she was in front of Dood instead of the other way around. He made an excellent rear guard. With each step, the anchor of rational thinking took firmer hold. It was surprisingly easy to talk or think yourself into a peculiar state of mind, Samantha mused, and less easy to move out of it again. Like once you've opened a door and seen what's on the other side, you can never completely erase the vision.

Suddenly realizing she didn't hear Dood behind her, Samantha hesitated, then glanced back over her shoulder. He was still standing by the carton, head bowed, body tensed. His hands were balled into fists at his sides.

"L.J.?"

Immediately Dood picked up the box, shouldering it.

"The body brigade is coming, Freckles my dear."

His tone held its normal light bantering quality, and Samantha grinned at him as he looked up and headed for the stairs. Yet as her gaze flicked one final time around the

shadowed basement chamber, unbidden the thought popped
into her mind:

I'm afraid . . .

Ted Nathan was coming up the front walk as Samantha
exited The Manse and stopped to hold the door open for a
couple of Jaycees going in. She automatically nodded to
the pair, her eyes on Ted.

A tall, rangy man of medium build and reserved temperament, Ted Nathan was something of an enigma. He'd
moved to Merrillville about a year earlier, joining a local
law office that had for decades been the sole prefecture of
the Hamilton clan. Despite the fact that only one Hamilton, a bachelor in his late sixties, remained, the firm was
still Hamilton, Hamilton & Hamilton and probably always would be. Ted Nathan's insertion into their hallowed
ranks had obviously been a necessity, but Samantha suspected it would be more likely for Ted to change his name
to Hamilton than for Hamilton, Hamilton & Hamilton to
ever become Hamilton & Nathan. As she also suspected
Ted was handling an increasing work load, she wondered
why he seemed so predisposed to the status quo. In his
place, she'd have demanded a full partnership by now, an
opinion impulsively voiced once, which he'd shrugged off
with a lack of concern that made her five parts angry for
him and five parts angry at him. Rumor associated the
surviving Hamilton with Ted's father, so maybe a family
connection existed somewhere. It was really none of her
business, anyway.

Since Ted had been thirty-five when he moved to
Merrillville—the Jaycee age-out point—he never became

a member. He had, however, almost immediately taken over all their legal work from Charles Hamilton, and as their attorney maintained a fairly close tie with the group. He seemed to be the kind of lawyer who took an extra interest in all his clients. He was a rather solitary man, deft at turning a conversation away from himself and onto you, so that only later did you realize you'd spent the majority of your time telling him things you wouldn't tell your priest and knew no more about him than before—except that he was a damn good listener.

He was such a quiet man . . . Yes. That described him perfectly: the Quiet Man. Samantha remembered that old John Wayne movie, one of his classics. Ted had a look of that early Wayne, an element of that style. She wondered if he, like that other Quiet Man, held some cloistered flaw in his past. Yet his quietness did not seem laced with guilt or etched by atonement. Probably just making more of a situation than the evidence warranted, she decided, a dangerous side effect of being a professional snoop.

In spite of the overcast day and brisk, biting wind, Ted's suit jacket hung looped on a finger and slung over his left shoulder with an unconcern that belied the strictness of the pin-striped dress shirt, dark silk tie, and neat silver collar pin. He somehow managed to look conservative and slightly rakish at the same time.

He smiled when he saw her, not increasing his pace, yet conveying a sense of pleasure, Samantha thought. As he neared, she could see his smile crinkling the small creases at the corners of his eyes. He smiled with his whole face, the kind of slow smile that was less a grin and more a merger—mouth sharing it with face, face spreading it around so that the smile came at you from all corners. It was a warm smile, an honest smile, quiet like the rest of him. His eyes were soft gray and held an openness that was an unexpected contrast to his innate reserve. Light brown hair, neatly combed, fell on the short side of prevailing taste, though not unfashionably so.

Samantha decided again that she rather liked this tall, quiet man, liked his lack of pretension, liked his easy manner—which was convenient since she'd been seeing him, casually, for about two months. A couple of dinners out, a few lunches, a party at the club—no unpleasant surprises so far, no uncomfortable demands. Their time together had been light but not shallow, friendly but not seeking—the kind of relationship Samantha thought she'd been needing for a long while, the kind, at their age and stage of life, that was probably difficult to come by. Or was she being cynical? Giving herself an acceptable excuse to settle for something less than exploding stars and clanging bells? Lately Samantha had found herself inching into the no-man's-land between relief and disappointment because of her platonic relationship with Ted, but it was better not to rush things. Liking someone was a good start, but it wasn't always grounds for diving into a deeper commitment—at least, it wasn't for Samantha.

"Hello." Ted's voice was another quiet attribute.

"Hello, yourself," Samantha said as she reached him and stopped walking. For a moment she felt satisfied just to stand there silently trading smiles with him. He was comfortable to be with, restful. The strange uneasiness that had claimed her in the house drifted away.

Ted broke their silence: "How's the cleanup going?"

"Oh, fine." Samantha waved an offhand gesture at the house. "We'll get everything packed up and stored away today. Then we have all weekend to house- and ground-clean. So far the only real damage we're aware of is one broken windowpane—Tank Worley, a.k.a. Frankenstein's monster, got a little overzealous scratching to get in."

Ted laughed softly. "I'm driving out to see the Beaufort sisters on another matter and thought I'd stop by for a status report to take along."

"That's nice of you." Samantha gave a little sigh. "Miss Bessie, poor dear, has never quite reconciled herself to her beloved home being used for a Halloween carnival. She's always so relieved when the season is over and The Manse is back to normal with no harm done. Each year she convinces herself that by next year she'll get the proper funds appropriated from some preservation society and will be able to tell us to find another house to haunt." She shook her head in sympathy. "Just tell her that all's well for another year and that I'll stop by to see her sometime this weekend."

Samantha had appointed herself as liaison between the Jaycees and the Beaufort Twins, and she didn't at all mind visiting them. Though Miss Flossie seemed to be going downhill lately, Miss Bessie was always a trip.

"Why don't you come with me?" Ted suggested, swinging the jacket off his shoulder and tossing it across his arm instead. "We could have lunch along the way."

With a touch of perversity, Samantha wondered if this was a spur-of-the-moment idea or if that thought had also played a part in Ted's stopping by The Manse. She had no intention of probing, which would be rude, she told herself, preferring this excuse over the possibility that his answer might not be the one she wanted; anyway, the matter was academic, because she couldn't go.

"I'd love to, Ted." She paused, watching his gray eyes for a spark of pleasure; they stayed coolly uncommittal, and she experienced a prick of annoyance at herself for playing childish games. "Unfortunately I can't," she hurriedly added. "I've got to drive over to the county courthouse and pick up some copy for next week's paper. If I don't get it in today, our typesetter has threatened to be creative in the 'Court Report' space. Sorry."

"Me, too." Again, his eyes remained steady and bereft of any overt disappointment. Nor did he revise the suggestion into an invitation to dinner, or lunch tomorrow, or a weekend in Tahiti.

A memory clouded Samantha's mind, the memory of a weekend she and Zack had spent at a friend's small cabin in the mountains. They'd had one of their worst fights ever the first day there. And they'd also had one of their most passionate nights together.

But that had been Zack, and that was done with at last, and this was Ted, and was she looking for something in him that wasn't there? Or was she losing her appeal? Samantha was surprised to find herself beginning to fluctuate between "A gentleman, thank God," and "Let's get this show on the road." Of course, *she* could simply say: "How about dinner tonight—or lunch tomorrow—or a weekend in Tahiti." She didn't say any of those things.

"How about . . ." *a rain check*, she was going to compromise with as she glanced back at Ted. The look on his face stopped her.

He was gazing at the old house. His eyes had narrowed slightly and an intensity robbed them of their normal warmth. The look on his face was positively grim.

Samantha frowned, a bit disconcerted, not understanding what had just changed but knowing something had. Uneasiness slithered out from under its rock. She was about to ask him what was wrong when he said:

"I don't like this place."

The words didn't surprise her at all, not even coming from Ted Nathan. They seemed to reach down inside her, all the way down to that place where unadulterated truths lie dormant and waiting, and there met her own worries— her worries and fears.

"Why do you say that?" she asked, not willing to reveal herself yet.

Ted shook his head slowly. "I don't really know. I've never liked the house. It seems to be . . . brooding." Somehow the statement didn't sound as ridiculous as it should have.

Nevertheless, Samantha tried a laugh, to lighten the strange mood beginning to chunk up around them. It fell flat. "Dood said something like that to me earlier, down in the basement," she admitted, not forgetting her own feelings just before he'd joined her, but still reluctant to voice them. For a crazy moment, she felt like they were all rushing headlong toward something she didn't want to reach, and it was up to her to put on the brakes before it was too late.

Ted turned to her. His eyes had a sharp look she'd never seen before. "Really? And what reason did he give?"

Samantha tried to shrug off the conversation's heaviness,

but couldn't. "Nothing specific, just a feeling." She tried another laugh. "I think maybe Dood believes The Manse is haunted."

As she expected, Ted quirked an amused eyebrow at this, but then he turned his gaze back on the house. "I'll admit there is something uncomfortable about being here. It's there when I walk onto the grounds, and sinks in the longer I remain on the premises."

"That's ridiculous!" Samantha exclaimed, almost too readily. The strange flights of fancy she and Dood might fall prey to could be dealt with, laughed at, and tucked away. Ted Nathan was a separate entity. She didn't like hearing him express such fancies, it made them seem too real—and they couldn't *be* real. "Ridiculous," she said again for emphasis.

He looked back at her and the sharpness left his eyes. He smiled. "Yes, isn't it," he said in his normal quiet tone, yet Samantha sensed no amusement, no levity behind the words. None whatsoever.

"I expect the accident is affecting us all today," she offered.

"I expect so," he agreed.

They looked at each other a moment.

"Walk you to your car?" he asked, breaking through the mood a bit.

She nodded.

They strolled in silence to the parking area on the left side of the house. Closer to the trees the shadows thickened, giving the feel of late afternoon rather than midday.

Across the way, Samantha caught a glimpse of Tank Worley, J. T. "Attila the Hun" Hunsinger, and no doubt the rest of Wolfman Zack's subcult of ex–football cronies tossing something back and forth in an exaggerated display of sandlot football. They were supposed to be cleaning the grounds. A group of good old boys still playing high school football. She remembered challenging Zack with that very accusation, not long before she'd broken off their relationship this last time—she accused him of living like he was always on the football field, running full speed for the goal line, running over whoever got in his way, expecting her to always be right there on the sidelines cheerleading him on. She'd done it in high school, caught up in the excitement of their status and popularity; and again later, caught up in their discovery of passion. But she wasn't a cheerleader anymore.

Ted had also noticed the impromptu game. "The Jaycees should have their own football team. They've certainly got the talent. Those guys were on a state championship team, weren't they?"

"I'm surprised you have to ask," she replied, tossing him a glance. "They rarely miss a chance to talk about their good old days of football."

Ted lifted an eyebrow. "You make that sound like an indictment."

"Do I?" Samantha studied his face a moment, a bit stung by the comment, then looked away. "Maybe I do."

They reached her dusty maroon VW Rabbit and stopped walking, "Sherman Tank Worley, Attila the Hunsinger, Micky 'Mick the Kick' Wainwright." Samantha gave a short laugh. "They're okay really, just big kids still on their way to growing up."

"And Zack Dalton?" Ted's face gave no indication of whether the question was pointed or random.

Samantha treated it casually, unsure what Ted might have heard about her relationship with good old Wolfman Zack, captain of the team. "Zack played a year of college ball, then the Marines got him. When he came back, it was too late for the pros." She remembered that time, one of the lows in their relationship. "Zack's holding on to the past with both hands and trying to drag it along with him."

"It's not always easy to let go of the past," Ted murmured, "or for the past to let go of you."

Samantha glanced at him sharply, not at all sure to whom he was referring—Zack Dalton, Samantha Evers, or Ted Nathan. "You make that sound like a judgment, or the passing of sentence."

He smiled and shook his head. "No."

Samantha didn't think she wanted to pursue this line of conversation.

"Don't mind me," she said with a laugh. "I'm just having a temperamental day, it seems. I'm not usually this . . ." She paused, searching for the right word. It didn't want to come.

"Philosophical?" Ted supplied helpfully.

She gave him a smile that held a touch of irony. "That's nice of you, but 'critical' comes closer to the mark," though that wasn't quite a proper fit either.

Ted shrugged, a noncommittal gesture accompanied by a faint smile. He looked at the house again.

Emotional, maybe that was the word. Samantha noted Ted's absorption. Emotional, yes, that came closer to describing the mood at The Manse today and yesterday. She thought about last night's violent scene with Zack, the edgy feel to this morning. Did it go back even further? Were all their emotions emphasized lately? Embellished somehow? Confused, Samantha reached over and opened the car door. "I really must go."

As she swung the car door open, Ted put out his hand and grasped the top, causing her to hesitate and turn back to face him. The shadows seemed heavier than before. They cast his face into seclusion; made his eyes opaque, unreadable. He almost appeared to be looking at her now the way he had looked at the house, as though the—how had he said it?—the *brooding* had insinuated itself between them.

Silence stretched like ripples expanding on a fathomless pool. Samantha had a sudden inexplicable urge to reach across the gap, reach out before it widened beyond her span, and touch the man who held her with his eyes.

And maybe Ted felt something of that same impulse, for slowly, as though the least hint of haste might jar the moment, scatter the ever-so-tenuous strand of web-silk intimacy being woven between them, he leaned toward her and brushed her lips with his. It was an infinitely tender gesture, gentle, with the added charm of being totally unexpected. This was the first time he'd kissed her.

For one more moment, he held her eyes with his, so close she could feel his breath, feather light against her face. Then he straightened, turned, and without a word began walking back the way they'd come.

Samantha watched him walk away, tall, lean, once again

hooking the jacket on his finger and shouldering it. Pleasure and expectancy fluttered to life inside her.

"How *very* touching."

The words struck the fragility of her thoughts with an insolence that made Samantha wince. She momentarily squeezed her eyes shut against the injustice of a fate that would rip this moment from her before she'd even had a chance to examine it, try to understand what it might mean.

Then she whirled on Zack Dalton, feeling her fingers ball into fists, her jaw tighten with anger at the curl of his lip and the look in his eyes.

Beneath the scruffy old baseball cap he always wore, Zack's eyes mocked her, stripped the half-formed images from her mind and shredded them to the cold wind.

"Is that the best he can do?"

Zack's voice was full of contempt, the kind of absurd contempt a man of basic passions will use to attack an emotion that falls short of his ideal measure. Tenderness wasn't in Zack Dalton's book of plays.

Samantha found herself unable to formulate a response, glaring at Zack because he made her feel defensive.

Then he laughed. A slow, deliberate, *knowing* laugh that swept over her body with the same calculated challenge as his eyes. She felt the familiar weakness betray her, flush her cheeks with memories that were still too close to the surface, and much too vivid. She wanted to hit him, to curl her fingers into claws and rake them down his mocking face.

A shout split the air: "Zack! Heads up!"

With the quickness of a cat, Zack swung toward the call, his body poised, immediately alert. Something flicked through the air—a small tennis shoe?—and he arched upward, slightly to his right, made the catch. Tank Worley's booming laugh rang out. Zack responded with a laugh of his own.

Samantha flung herself into the car, slamming the door, firing the engine with a wrench to the starter and a stomp to the accelerator pedal. She was wildly furious—at Zack Dalton for taking something gentle and new and trying to maul it, at herself for being susceptible to his crude baiting tactics, and at some nebulous enemy that seemed to be twisting everything out of shape.

She threw the gears into reverse and without looking at Zack's position, spun the car backward in a forty-five-degree arc. Applying the brakes, she thrust the lever into drive—then glanced left, at Zack.

He was watching her, looking directly at her, his eyes penetrating with an intensity that was almost a violation. Undiminished desire bombarded her. And, God help her, she was responding; like an alcoholic for his gin, her body was saying, "Yes. I still belong to you." Then he smiled, the slow, sensual, caressing smile Samantha knew so well, and gave her a little mocking salute. With a quick lunge into the air, Zack tossed the makeshift football back the way it had come, returning to the game.

Samantha pulled her gaze away from him. She pressed the accelerator and swung the car out of the parking area and down the driveway, fury her chief motivator. But fear was a close second, fear that Zack had become an obsession she'd never be free of.

Barely stopping where driveway met street, Samantha gunned the car to the right, into the road. Luckily nothing was coming. She forced herself to slow down, taking several deep breaths to calm the emotions seething within her, feeling confusion replace fury as the car distanced her from the scene. It wasn't like her to be this tempestuous; nor was it like Zack to be so cold-bloodedly vindictive, so contemptible. Even Ted had behaved uncharacteristically.

Why? What was the matter with them? With her? What the bloody hell was the matter?

Dood picked the last of the packing straw from his Generra bulky weave and sauntered down the front walk-way toward the cement staircase leading to street level. They'd had a time wrapping Tank's Mothra for storage because of its size and welded wire frame—it couldn't be folded, spindled, or mutilated in any way. Finally they'd hung it from an attic rafter and draped packing straw around it, topping that with a cocoon of plastic cleaning bags.

"Bat's in the belfry—all's right with the world," Dood mumbled, taking the stairs two at a time. He purposely averted his gaze from the spot where a small body had lain broken and dying only hours before.

Whistling away a residual chill, Dood flashed a wave at Ted Nathan as he paused at the intersection then turned his car to head out of town. "A bit on the passive side, but the man has style," Dood said softly, his unerring eye auto-matically making the judgment from the glimpse he'd had of Ted's attire—and behavior. "Conservative but classy; keeps the stuffiness at bay."

"Yo, Dood!"

The call accosted him from across the highway and Dood glanced over to see Phillip Handy coming out of his Main Street Swap Shop. The sales, salvage, and second-hand store had bloomed from a blemish of a junk shop to the business that allowed Phil to drive a vintage Jaguar and thumb his nose at the nine-to-five set. Dood wished his own video rental store did half as well.

Phil was also Jaycee Chief Procurer in Charge of Cheapo Paraphernalia and Special Effects Gizmos for their Annual House of Horrors. Between him and the high school art department, the Jaycees were able to net a killing on their Halloween fund-raiser, which meant the bourgeois bake sales, concession stands, and car washes rated 1.0 on the Richter scale—hardly worth a shudder.

Dood stretched up a hand in acknowledgment, then sprinted across the highway to the corner where Phil now waited.

"Phil, my man. Out scavenging today, or merely fleecing customers?" Phil had been noticeably absent at the morning's cleanup session.

"Neither. My accountant's screaming 'bookwork.' End of month, you know."

Dood nodded sagely; his own accounting system at the video store consisted of two composition books, four shoe boxes, and a cash register. And if April didn't come around once a year, he'd use trash bags.

"I'll drop by later with the truck"—Phil indicated The Manse with a nod of his head—"and pick up the stuff they don't want to keep. Right now it's lunchtime. Want to join me? I'll buy."

Dood swung an arm around Phil's plump shoulders and started guiding him up Main Street toward the Merrillville café. "An offer I can't refuse, old buddy, and since I don't have to open up until one—"

"You, boy . . ."

The interruption came from a small break between two buildings, a narrow alleyway. A little old black woman stood just inside the opening, garbed in black from hat to shoes, both hands clutching a pocketbook in front of her like a challenge to a purse snatcher. The entire ensemble was Sears, Roebuck circa 1950; the old woman looked timeless.

Her hail had checked the lunch processional; now Dood turned more fully toward the woman, removing his arm from Phil's shoulders. Lifting a finger to the middle of his chest, Dood mouthed *Me?*

The old woman nodded quickly, little darting birdlike movements that caused her prim black hat to bounce against the pins that held it.

"Be right back," Dood told Phil absently, and walked over to the woman. She looked vaguely familiar; he thought he'd seen her around town. "Can I help you, ma'am?"

"No, boy, you can't help me. But I can help you."

"What?"

"Listen to me, boy! Listen tight. There's trouble up there"—she jerked her head toward The Manse—"all the trouble you could ever nightmare up. You stay away from there, boy. And you make those others stay away too."

Her eyes darted sideways again, and Dood felt himself turn involuntarily, look up toward the house perched on the wooded hill. Echoes of his recent past came tumbling

back to him: Davy Dawson; the strange touches of irrational fear; Samantha's discomfort in the basement—all rolling forward like a snowball filled with rocks, grasping,
growing . . .

Dood pulled his gaze away from the house that suddenly
seemed ominous and turned back toward the alley. "But I
don't—" The small black woman no longer stood in front
of him. He glanced down the narrow slit and saw her
receding form.

Phil had stepped up beside him, eyes following the old
woman's retreat. "Who *was* that masked man?"

For a moment, Dood felt incapable of movement, of
speech . . . then he shrugged. "Beats me. Town's full of
. . ." He couldn't quite bring himself to say weirdos, not
even as a joke. The old lady had been weird, definitely
weird, but she wasn't a weirdo.

"Yeah," Phil finished for him and took his arm. "Can
we go have lunch now?"

Dood smiled a response and resumed his pace at Phil's
side. Somehow he didn't feel quite as hungry as before.

Chapter 10

Randy Dawson sat in the back of Vince Colletti's car, head leaning against the seat, eyes pasted to the inside of the roof, hands wrapped around a can of Pabst Blue Ribbon. Every once in a while he'd sit up, raise the can, and transfer some of its contents to his mouth. He played a game with the routine, trying to time his swigs to the lull between the bumps that jostled his body on the vertical plane and the curves that slung him left and right. There was an art to drinking beer in a speeding vehicle. Lurch to the right, or left or up, shift back into position, can up, drink, can down. Randy smiled. The secret was in the wrist movement.

From the front seat, Buddy Grey turned around and held his can of Budweiser aloft. Buddy always drank Bud. Vince, on the other hand, would drink either Bud or Pabst—whatever one of them bought.

"How you doing back there?" Buddy trilled in his shoe-string voice.

Randy smiled again, closing his eyes as his head rocked back and forth on the seat with the rhythm of the moving car. "Fine. Just fine and dandy. Dandy Randy, that's me."

Buddy laughed, a quick, high-pitched giggle that sounded like something that ought to be coming from inside a padded cell. "Dandy Randy, Dandy Randy," he chanted until Vince growled, "Shut the shit up!" from the driver's seat. Buddy immediately shut the shit up.

"Got any money?" The question came from Vince, and Randy knew it was meant for him. They'd already spent Buddy's on a joint and beer. He also knew better than to lie about it.

"About fifteen dollars," he told Vince, hoping that would satisfy.

"Need some gas." Apparently it did.

Vince wheeled the car into the parking lot of the C&P, slowing only when tires met gravel, still sluicing up enough stone pellets to risk knocking off a tailpipe or putting a hole through the muffler. He swung in beside the self-serve pumps. "Ten dollars' worth."

Randy was mildly surprised. Apparently the other five was intended for something else. Without a word, Randy tossed the empty beer can to the floorboard and climbed out of the car, knowing his place in the scheme of things. He went inside, paid the man, came back out, and began pumping his ten dollars into Vince's gas tank, feeling the biting night chill seep past the alcohol-induced warmth.

Why did he do this stuff for Vince? Randy sometimes wondered, not too often, but sometimes.

The pump clicked off. He replaced it, crawled back into the warm car. With a spray of gravel they were away.

"Where to?" Vince asked.

"Anywhere you say," chimed Buddy.

Another game. Randy didn't even bother to join the chorus. Let good old Buddy have a solo on this one.

The joint was long gone up in smoke, but the beer lingered on. Randy pulled another from its plastic headgear and pushed in the top. It made a whooshing noise and geysered out a fine spray of beer mist.

"Hey! Whatcha doing back there?" Buddy swabbed at his left ear.

Randy felt a pang of relief that it was Buddy, not Vince, he'd sprayed. Vince's reactions to things were never predictable. "Just being thankful," he told Buddy. "It's Thanksgiving, isn't it? Time to be thankful."

Buddy answered with a sharp giggle. "That was last Thursday. This is Monday. Thursday. Monday. There's a difference, you know."

Randy closed his eyes. Not for him.

"What you got to be so thankful for anyway?" Buddy taunted. "Your old man kicked you out of the house. You got fired from your job for coming in drunk—"

"Hey, I've got you guys, don't I?" Randy cut in. "Good friends like you? Shouldn't I be thankful for that?" Randy held up his beer can. "I got a beer, and fif—*five* dollars in my pocket, and Vince is letting me sleep in his car."

"About that, stud," Vince said. Randy felt a sinkhole

open up in the bottom of his stomach. "Can't have you sleeping in the car no more, Randy Dandy."

Randy started to ask why, then decided what the hell. Vince Colletti had spoken. And when Vince Colletti speaks . . . Randy had a vision of a roomful of ears all turned toward Vince Colletti. He would have laughed, except he was afraid he might cry.

So what was he going to do now? What the hell was he going to do?

His old man wouldn't let him come home. He felt queasy just thinking of the past few weeks—his old man blamed him for Davy getting killed. Blamed him for leaving the kid on his own, although dear old daddy had been doing just that for years. The real truth of the matter was that it was easier to blame Randy than himself, easier to say, "It's *your* fault, you fuckin' killer! You killed him! You get the fuck out, you fuckin' child killer!" The truth of the matter was that dear old daddy was right. It *was* his fault. He shouldn't have left Davy and gone off with his good friends here. He should've waited on the kid, taken him through the House, taken him home . . . Home. What a joke. Maybe Davy boy was the lucky one.

"Whoa, what have we here?" Vince drawled the question, at the same time applying his brakes in a slowdown that was somewhere between giving his passengers whiplash and hurling them through the windshield.

Randy sat up, interested in spite of himself in what could have caught Vince's attention strongly enough to make him stop in the middle of the highway. Vince rolled down his window, leaned out to look at something they'd just passed. Randy and Buddy rolled their windows down

as well, Randy leaning out while Buddy swung his body
up to perch in the opening and survey the scene over the
top of the car.

A car traveling in the opposite direction whizzed by
them. Headlights picked out a form trudging along the side
of the road, then whisked on past. It was the old drunk
PoJo, Randy saw, plodding down the side of the highway
with the steady gait of a man who knew where he was
going. For a moment Randy felt the bitter taste of envy
rise to his mouth; he crushed it, took a swig of beer.

"Hey, PoJo, want a lift?" Vince started backing up the
car in little spurts and jumps, driving one-handed, all the
while leaning out the window and looking back at PoJo.

Randy thought: If something comes up fast enough on
our rear, it'll be all over. Somehow the thought didn't
scare him like it should have.

"Hey, PoJo!" Buddy punctuated his echo of Vince with
a giggle. "Come on, we'll give you a ride."

Randy took another swallow of luke-cool beer and looked
out again. PoJo was still shuffling along beside the road,
hands stuffed in the pockets of his coat, collar turned up
against the windchill. It was as though he didn't see or
hear them. He just kept plodding along toward town. He'd
probably caught a ride out to the C&P for a bummed
dinner and was having to walk back. Or maybe he'd
walked out too. There was something about him that resisted most labels you might attach. Like maybe he was
the one doing you a favor, could even make you go out of
your way to let him do you the favor of springing for a
meal or slipping him some cash—or giving him a ride.

The old man drew nearer, still ignoring their presence.

If he'd been looking for a lift into town, he'd have been on the other side of the road with his thumb stuck out. Randy shook his head. It was a good five miles to town.

Vince had stopped the car again, letting it idle. Periodically he revved the engine with a crackling roar.

"Hey, PoJo," he called, his voice soft and enticing, "why don't you get in? We'll take you wherever you're going."

For a moment Randy didn't think the old man was going to respond, then he began crossing the road toward the car. Randy had already moved over in the back seat, making room for the old drunk to slide in beside him, when he heard Vince chuckle under his breath. He wanted to say, "No, Vince, don't do anything, don't screw with the old man, give the old guy his ride, for Chrissake," but by then the ragged old fool was at the car, reaching for the back door handle.

With a squeal of rubber and a burst of laughter, Vince gunned the car forward and roared off down the highway, leaving the old bum standing there with his old bum hand stretched out to empty air.

Randy didn't look. He just rolled up his window, leaned his head against the seat, and closed his eyes. He didn't want to see PoJo standing alone in the middle of the road, looking after them, maybe waving his fist or shouting a string of curses. Most of all, Randy didn't want to see PoJo just shuffle back to the side of the road, picking up his steady gait where he'd left off, the steady gait of a man who knew where he was going—and would keep on going despite the Vinces and Buddys and Randys the world threw at him.

"Didya see the old fart? Didya see him?" Buddy chortled, breaking into peals of stinging laughter, bouncing back down into the front seat, turning around to share the great joke with Randy.

Vince slowly rolled up his own window, peering at Randy in the rearview mirror, his face a rictus of delight at the joke he'd pulled.

And with the cold wind blasting his face from Buddy's open window, and the bile rising in his throat from the burning in his gut, and the sting of tears pricking against the inside of his vision, Randy found that he, God help him, was laughing too.

Ted Nathan glanced around the Jaycee meeting room, searching for an empty seat. It seemed he was the last to arrive, though the general chatter indicated that Zack Dalton had not yet called the group to order. As their attorney, Ted tried to sit in on some of the meetings for general purposes, and specifically when he had business, like tonight.

Several heads bobbed a greeting as he scanned the room, one of them Samantha's. He felt a mixture of warmth and caution as he returned her greeting with a nod—no more, no less than he was giving other friendly faces—and spotted an empty seat behind Tank Worley and L. J. Hopkins.

Ted's divorce had become final just a few months earlier and he wasn't yet ready for a new commitment. Not that he was still in love with Monica—he wasn't, and wondered if he ever really had been. Yes, he decided, he had been, although not to the depth and breadth and height a soul can reach, as the poet would have it. The cool nonchalance with which Monica had dismissed their marriage had surprised him, and it hurt to discover that you could share almost seven years of your life with someone, yet know her so minimally. He'd suspected she wouldn't want to leave the Atlanta scene for a little town in North Carolina she'd never heard of, especially as he wouldn't tell her why he was so determined to do just that. He just hadn't suspected how easily she'd send him off without her—or for that matter, how easily he'd go.

He traded hellos with Tank and Dood, trying not to wince from the eardrum-shattering effect that was Tank Worley on audio, and slipped into the empty chair behind them. As he sat down, his gaze again swept the officers' table at the front of the room.

Samantha was deep in conversation with Paul Oliver, secretary of the Jaycees, seated on her right. Paul Oliver, a bachelor in his early thirties, a bespectacled, slightly rumpled high school English teacher, headed the more conservative element within the chapter. *A voice of reason crying in the wilderness?* thought Ted a bit cynically. He was aware that Zack Dalton and his majority of supporters referred to this moderate minority as the wimp attempt.

Next to Paul, treasurer Phil Handy sat doodling on what looked like a ledger sheet.

On Samantha's left lounged J. T. Hunsinger, vice-president and one of Zack Dalton's pet peers. J.T. was something of a wastrel, but since his father owned Hunsinger Textile Mills, he could no doubt afford to pursue his ambition of spending his life on the golf course.

Then came Jaycee president Zack Dalton.

Ted didn't like Zack Dalton—didn't like his attitude,

didn't like his opinions, didn't like his style. He kept it to himself because such hearty dislike was unusual for him, and because he knew himself to be in the minority on this; Zack Dalton was something of a folk hero around Merrillville, which he supposed had to do with the championship football team he'd captained.

Zack still wore a team uniform, in a sense—the uniform of the assistant police chief of Merrillville's small local force. He had it on tonight, had probably just come off duty prior to the meeting or was scheduled for it right after. Instead of the regulation headgear, Zack Dalton favored a scruffy black baseball cap with a panther on it—symbol of the Merrillville High School varsity football team.

Ted studied the younger man a moment. He supposed Zack Dalton would classify as attractive, even very attractive. He kept himself in good shape, seemed able to maintain a tan year-round, had a ready smile and a cheerful laugh; a regular blond-haired, blue-eyed, all-American boy-next-door. And underneath the twenty-four-carat charm . . . what?

No, I don't like Zack Dalton, Ted thought, moving his gaze to the left, to Samantha. *Is she part of the reason?* Possible—quite possible, Ted admitted to himself. He knew about Samantha and Zack, the on-again, off-again relationship that had spanned better than a decade. There was always someone eager to fill in a newcomer on all the town gossip, whether he wanted to hear it or not. In this case Miss Bessie Beaufort was the culprit, had seemed to think it her particular duty to inform him of Merrillville's history, scandals, and secrets. He'd indulged her garrulousness partly because he felt her need to communicate, her delight with a new ear to bend, and partly because he *was* interested in learning about the town and its people, for good or bad, though he still made his own judgments.

He watched Samantha Evers carry on an animated conversation with Paul Oliver. She talked with her hands, punctuating her speech with a little wave or gesture, a flip of the wrist. Occasionally more voluble movements would accompany the conversation, and sometimes Ted could almost tell what she was saying, even from across the room.

Right now, he thought she was telling Paul about the feature story she was writing for her "Stuff 'n' Nonsense" column on the wayward puppy who'd wandered into the newspaper office and been adopted. Both hands had flown to her head, one up, one folded half over, in mimicry of the puppy's ears, which were, as she'd told Ted at lunch recently, a case of flip and flop. Paul was laughing, as Ted had done himself, and again Ted felt the warmth Samantha evoked. She was vivacious, with a wholesome attractiveness stimulating to be around. Nothing fragile about Samantha Evers, nothing calculating.

Of course there were qualities some might term debits: Even in the short time he'd known her, he'd realized she was impulsive, headstrong, and plainspoken. And the history of her relationship with Zack Dalton indicated there was a fairly strong possibility that the future might see them together again. Perhaps that one thing above all others made Ted approach their friendship slowly. She could no doubt cause a man his share of headaches, Ted decided, but of one thing he felt reasonably certain—she would never bore him to death.

With a sudden bolt of insight, Ted realized what it was he'd been trying to put his finger on since the breakup of his marriage, what it really was that had kept the situation well this side of traumatic for him: he'd been bored. Bored with his job in Atlanta, bored with the life they were leading, and most of all bored with Monica. Could anything be more insidious?

"Ted?" L. J. Hopkins had twisted around in his seat and was leaning toward him.

Ted leaned forward, eyebrows raised in query, at about the same time Zack Dalton stood up and began calling the group to order.

"Talk to you after the session?" Dood asked.

Ted nodded and they both sat back in their chairs, Ted reaching to pull some papers out of his briefcase and a pad and pen to make notes, if necessary. This done, he turned his regard to the head table, his eyes just happening to fall once more on Samantha Evers. She was looking at him. For a moment automatic caution took hold, then he smiled, and felt a pleasant warmth slip by his reserve as she did the same.

Vince slowed the car down as the highway began its circle around town, around by The Manse. Randy avoided looking at the house that he felt looming up on their right, and the spot he knew was coming, the spot where Davy had been killed.

He thought about the house, and Davy's death, and not for the first time wondered if there had been a subtle connection between the two. No one else had made a connection, not really, and he'd waited for someone to do so, waited to see if someone would say, "I'll bet something in that house drove the kid out in front of that truck to get hit and knocked fifty feet and torn all to pieces." They said Davy's neck had been broken, his body a mass of cuts and slashes. They said it was a tragic accident. How sad for a small boy to start out for a night of fun and end up dead. How unfortunate.

Randy felt The Manse crouched there on his right, crouched like a giant crab with invisible pincers reaching out across the space between them, reaching through the trees and air and car to grip him around the chest and tighten until he felt his heart begin to pound and his breath cramp within his lungs. He rubbed a hand across his chest, just below the breastbone, trying to loosen the constriction that shouldn't be there, feeling his heart jump against the inside of his skin.

He hated the house up there on that hill. Hated it! There was something in that house that didn't belong, something he didn't understand. He knew it sounded crazy, sounded like something from TV or out of a horror comic. It was nothing he could prove, nothing he could even give a name to . . . but Randy knew there was something wrong at The Manse. It scared him shitless.

That was why he'd not thought twice about leaving with Vince and Buddy the night Davy died. When Vince said, "What the fuck are we doing at this kids' crap, let's get the hell outta here," he'd jumped at the excuse not to go through the house full of horrors, and left his seven-year-old brother to face them alone.

His memory fell back to Halloween the year before, and the fountain in the back garden, the fountain that had been covered with swirling mist. The mist had looked like it was trying to form into something, trying to move, reach out, *something*. There had been a moment when he thought he'd seen a face on the mist, eyes glowing to life. A shiver spasmed Randy's body. The memory made his flesh creep. It had even shaken up Vince, though he was first to laugh it off and they eagerly followed his lead, of course. Yet underneath the laughs and jeers and logical explanations, Randy had always suspected that something not quite sane had happened to them that night in the back garden of The Manse.

And Davy had gone out that way.

"Wonder how long it'll take old PoJo to walk all the way back here," Vince mused aloud as they drove past the old Beaufort estate.

"How long, how long," chirped Buddy, well on his way to drunk.

Randy found that he was not exactly sober either, though his was an internal drunkenness rather than the splotch of beer-silly intoxication that frothed out of Buddy.

"Get out of my face," Randy murmured.

Vince, apparently not hearing him, said, "He sleeps up there, you know."

"Up there, up there," parroted Buddy.

"Up there" meaning The Manse. Randy knew.

"Bet he sleeps all warm and nice and dry," Vince continued, as he looped the car in a U-turn and headed back the way they'd come.

Bet not, Randy thought, as yet unaware of where this

was leading. Bet he sleeps with both eyes open and his
breath clogged in his throat.

"Bet he wouldn't mind sharing his free motel," Vince
stated blandly.

The implication hit Randy at the same moment that his
eyes met Vince's in the rearview mirror. Vince knew!
Knew Randy was scared shitless of that old house. Randy
saw it in his eyes, saw it in the smile that curled his big
lips away from his teeth.

Now was the time to break away from this torment and
treachery and force-fed pain. Now was the time, if there
was ever going to be a time, to say fuck you and stop the
car, to get out and walk away and never look back.

Randy felt his hands compile into fists. All he had to do
was say no.

"What'sa matter, Randy Dandy?" Vince's voice curled
from the front seat like thin steel wire. "Scared?"

A corner of Randy's mind registered that the car had
slowed, had inched over to the right-hand curb just across
from where the driveway to The Manse bled into the road.
As Vince stopped the car, Buddy turned around in his seat
to look at Randy, and then Vince did the same. All Randy
had to do was say one word, make one offhand gesture,
even, to break the rope of thin steel threads that bound him
only because he'd tied it there, only because he held it to
him with both hands. Just one word, just shoot Vince the
bird, then get out of the car and walk away.

Maybe if Buddy had giggled or Vince had offered one
more searing taunt he could have done it. But they only sat
there, silently watching him, evaluating, as if they sensed
he was at a cross-point . . . and if there was a certain rabid

glitter in the eyes locked on him, only the darkness knew
. . . for Randy's eyes had closed.

"No, I'll bet old PoJo wouldn't mind sharing at all,"
Randy heard himself say, and immediately sensed the two
bodies turn to the front again. The car swung to the left,
crossed the road, and headed into the drive of The Manse.
It rolled to a stop at the gate that topped the driveway and
the engine was cut off and he had missed his breakaway
and would have to do like Vince said and go into the house
that made him want to puke with fear because

Where else did he have to go?

". . . and it's my goal to see that we make the 13th
Annual House of Horrors so terrifying that paramedics will
be standing by to administer CPR—in fact, that might be a
good gimmick!"

Zack Dalton's sum-up of his enthusiastic plans for the
next House was met with general laughter and a basso
profundo "Here, here!" from Tank Worley. Ted noticed a
few Jaycees around the room who didn't seem to share
their president's enthusiasm. Paul Oliver for one. Paul
raised his hand for recognition in response to Zack Dalton's call for comments.

Paul got to his feet as Zack, tossing an expressive look
at his front-row cronies, conceded the floor.

"I'm a bit concerned," Paul began, "with some of the
feedback I've been hearing on this past House. There's
been talk by the parents of a few of my students, and
believe it or not from some of the students themselves,
regarding a feeling of"—Paul paused, as though carefully

choosing the next word—"discomfort at certain points throughout the tour."

"Discomfort?" Micky Wainwright spoke up from the front row. "You mean they got scared? Awwww . . . and we try so hard to keep from frightening anybody."

Laughter skipped around the room.

Paul smiled faintly. "Perhaps I was a bit too tame in my choice of words. Perhaps I should have said 'alarm' or 'malicious intent' or even 'viciousness.' Some people won't be coming back to future Houses. Several mentioned certain . . . encounters, shall we say, that didn't sound like anything on our list of scenarios, things that honestly frightened them. What I want to know is, did anyone get carried away and branch out on their own?"

"You know that's against policy," Zack stated. "We develop the scenes, scale them out, vote on them, practice them, and present them as planned. No embellishments."

"Nevertheless," Paul countered firmly, "these people talked about seeing things that were not on our schedule—"

Several vehement denials cut across Paul's comment and almost drowned out Tank Worley's "Hey, I remember something like that happening last year . . ." Ted heard it, and so did Dood Hopkins, Ted noticed as he saw him snap a sideways look at Tank.

"Okay, people." Zack Dalton rapped his gavel on the table and rose, bringing the group back to order. "We have a suggestion from Paul that perhaps someone has been moonlighting during the House." He put up a hand to stem the tide of groans, and sobered his own expression. "That would be a serious offense. Anyone want to own up to it?"

Silence met the offer. No one raised a hand.

"I didn't think so," Zack stated. "In that case, let me just reiterate policy regarding the staging of our scenarios so that in the future there'll be no misunderstanding: Once a scene has been developed and accepted by majority vote, there can be no changes made without a second vote, and only the approved scenarios will be staged in the House. No free-lancing. Understood?"

A chorus of verbal agreements and nods answered him. Zack Dalton turned to Paul. "Satisfied?"

Paul shrugged, clearly not satisfied but faced with the impasse of no confessions and not enough evidence to support a specific accusation.

"Anything else?" Zack prompted when Paul remained standing.

"I would like to suggest that we tone down our House next year, make it more what it started out as—a fun house for kids."

Zack nodded solemnly. "You're exactly right, it did start out that way. And since that time we've developed a successful program that not only keeps the kids coming back but draws in adults as well—by giving them something to sink their teeth into. They're the ones we're making our money off of, they're the ones who pay full price, and tell their friends, and drive from as far as a hundred miles away to go through our Houses." Zack transferred his gaze to the room at large.

"This event is becoming a big deal—not just locally, but all over this part of the state. We're seeing hundreds of people nightly and expanding our presentations with every House. More people attend each year. If we stop giving them substance, they'll stop coming." Zack flashed a politician's smile to the room. "My opinion, of course. As always, each one of you is invited to present an idea for our scenarios, which can be anything you wish, from grotesque to completely innocuous. Whatever the majority votes for is what we present, just like always."

Zack turned his smile back to Paul, inviting further comment.

Paul Oliver took his seat.

So much for the wimp attempt.

"I think you all realize, in light of the treasurer's report given earlier," Zack continued, "that our 12th Annual House was our biggest money-maker to date and the most elaborate—until next year, of course. The net proceeds will more than fund all of our charity commitments, including the Children's Burn Center donation we voted in last meeting. And we've got enough left over to hire a live band for the New Year's Eve party"—whistles and light applause met this—"so we must be doing something right." Zack laughed. "The worst thing that happened on the debit side was Tankenstein breaking a window."

Crowd laughter joined his, Tank's just this side of a sonic boom.

"A little boy got killed. That was worse."

The bare statement came from L. J. Hopkins, and immediately wiped the laughter from the room.

Ted looked at the rigid set to the shoulders of the man sitting in front of him. He knew from Samantha that Dood Hopkins had taken the little Dawson boy's death somewhat personally.

"Dood, man." The smile had melted from Dalton's

face, and Ted was surprised to see something like understanding float into its place. An honest emotion? he wondered. Maybe. But he had a feeling Zack Dalton could don an emotion as easily as he put on his scruffy cap.

"We know how you feel about the Dawson boy's accident," Zack sympathized. "We all feel bad about it. But really, it had nothing to do with the House. I did the accident report myself. The kid had been gone from the house for twenty minutes before the accident occurred. He wasn't even coming from the house itself, but out of the woods up the street. He'd probably been playing around there while waiting for his brother."

"In the dark?" Dood remarked. "That kid was afraid of the dark."

"Maybe he was and maybe he wasn't. And maybe he was playing chicken with the traffic that passed by. Kids do that, you know. Caught a three-year-old at it once—a *three*-year-old, f'Chrissake—being egged on by a couple of older playmates.

"Look, the driver said the kid was running down the road toward the truck. We'll just never know what was in the boy's mind, but one thing we do know is that we're not responsible for the accident. Our attorney has confirmed that." Zack's gaze fell on Ted.

Ted shuffled the papers in his lap, crossed one leg over the other, and returned Zack's look. "There was no culpable negligence or incurred liability on the part of the Jaycees," he agreed, then added, as Zack started to dismiss the matter, "There is, however, enough indication that the boy's state of mind might have been influenced by his tour of the House to evoke moral responsibility in the matter."

The smile hardened on Zack Dalton's face and a glitter sprang to his eyes that Ted had no trouble recognizing as animosity. He had a potential enemy in Zack Dalton.

"And is that a professional judgment, Counselor?"

Ted felt a smile tug at the corner of his mouth. He wasn't interested in a verbal sparring match with Zack Dalton. "Strictly a personal opinion. I sometimes offer them in lieu of legal advice. Seems friendlier, and much less expensive."

Laughter rustled across the room. Ted hoped he'd gotten his point across and that Zack would now let it alone. Zack, however, refused to let it lie.

"Any more friendly opinions for us, Counselor?" Zack asked, an exaggerated smile pasted on his face, along with a look of challenge. Ted wondered if anyone else noticed it.

"Tone down the House of Horrors," Ted said quietly, his eyes never wavering from Zack's.

Zack was the first to look away. "Thank you, Counselor. We certainly appreciate knowing where you stand." Zack smiled, glancing at his supporters in the front row.

Ted had no trouble reading the glance, nor the shared smiles that followed. He'd just been sorted, cataloged, and stamped a new member of the wimp attempt. He shook his head slowly as Zack called for the next order of business. He suddenly felt infinitely older than these overgrown boys playing their games. With the feeling came a sense of thankfulness and, oddly enough, a twinge of regret. Sighing, Ted pulled the Beaufort-Jaycee lease from his briefcase.

*   *   *

Vince Colletti vaulted over the waist-high swing gate and began making his way along the path that led around the west side of The Manse. The pale moon shed enough light to see by. He didn't turn around to check if the others were following; he didn't need to. A smile slit Vince's face. They always followed.

The air hung still and breathless, rimed with the penetrating dankness that always seemed layered here. It belonged; long ago it had staked out a claim. The old cold walked hand in hand with the old darkness this place harbored night and day. Vince didn't like it here, a fact he would admit to himself and no one else. He smiled again. Neither did Randy Dandy.

"Hey, Vince, wait up!" Buddy called.

Vince obliged.

He took the opportunity to look up at the big dark house, wondering how it would feel to be in there by himself, to spend the night in there. A flicker of something like nervousness slid through him. He didn't much think he'd want to try it. And nobody would make him. Nobody.

Buddy and Randy reached him, and Vince began walking again, on around the house, toward the back. He didn't want to fool around in front if he could keep from it, on the off chance that someone passing might see them. The car was pretty well hidden by the trees, but the front of The Manse offered less camouflage.

"There's got to be a way in," Vince said, gesturing the trio to a halt at the back corner of the house where an outside stairway led to the basement. "PoJo gets in somewhere, and it ain't the front door."

He looked at Randy, who seemed to be staring out toward the back garden, a pasty look on his face. ''Why don't you travel on down those steps there, stud, and check out the door to the cellar while Bud and I survey the back porch.'' Even in the dim light he could see Randy's jaw tighten; the dimness seemed to emphasize the increasing pallor of Randy's face. *Goddamn, he is scared to death!* Vince felt a little bubble of laughter form in his throat, felt the headiness of being on the edge. He watched Randy turn around, hesitate, then slowly start toward the basement stairs. Vince knew that he had the power. He had the *Power*!

''C'mon,'' he whispered to Buddy, and his voice trembled with the Power.

Together they moved over to stand at the top of the cellar stairs, listening to Randy descend into the darkened pit. After the first couple of steps, the stairwell looked as if it were filled with thick black tar. It even had a sort of tarry smell, a kind of sweetish, overripe smell.

The rattle of the basement door swam up from below, then the rapid tattoo of ascending footsteps. Breathless, Randy started to give his report, ''The door's''—his voice cracked; he cleared his throat, then continued, voice hoarse but steady—''locked up tight. Padlocked on the inside, I think.''

If Vince hadn't heard the sounds that corroborated Randy's statement he might have questioned it, made Randy go back down and try the door again just to be sure. He almost did anyway, then something stopped him, some internal gauge that seemed to measure just how far he could exert the Power.

"How about that window?" he said instead, gesturing toward a small rectangle of glass set into the wall about a third of the way down.

Randy glanced at the window, seemed about to make a claim Vince knew to be untrue, then admitted: "I didn't try it."

Vince felt a smile curl his mouth. "Well, Randy Dandy . . . ?"

"Randy Dandy, Randy Dandy," Buddy chanted. The stairwell gave his jarring voice a hollow sound. Vince cut him off with a casual elbow to the midsection.

They watched Randy slowly descend the stairway, stop at a point in line with the window, and lean over to study the glass-filled opening.

"It opens in," Randy called back to them, his voice sounding relieved. "There's nothing on the outside, no lock, no catch." He started back up the stairs.

"Just a minute, stud," Vince drawled, stopping Randy cold, wanting to prolong Randy's obvious fear of the deep, dark stairwell, wanting to make him submerge in it. "You didn't try it out, Randy Dandy."

Vince enjoyed the way Randy's shoulders slumped, enjoyed that immensely. "C'mon, Nutty-Butty." He grasped Buddy by the arm and ushered him forward, in front. "Let's give old Randy Dandy a hand, shall we?"

Buddy giggled and started down the steps, but there was something slightly altered about his giggle, something hysterical in the sound, and Vince found himself having to urge Buddy forward a bit more forcefully than usual. He tightened his grip on Buddy's arm and felt a sudden urge to see what it would be like to propel Buddy forward, off the steps, off into the nothing that ended at the concrete bottom of the stairwell.

"Vince, let go my arm," whined Buddy, breaking whatever spell had twined itself through Vince's fingers.

"Sure, man, sure," he said, releasing Buddy, allowing him to move on down the steps because suddenly he wanted to get this over with. Suddenly he wanted to be done with it and in his car and away from here because beyond the pleasure that was his payment for orchestrating these little games something not so nice was knocking to get in. He wished he had another joint.

"Go on, try it," he told Randy as he and Buddy joined him, Buddy right next to Randy, himself two levels higher.

Thin moonlight reflected back from the dirty glass, penetrating none of the room beyond, as though the window was a solid barrier. Down here the smell was stronger, rancid now, with a tinge of bitterness that seemed to burn the inside of Vince's nostrils.

"Go on!" he ordered when Randy kept hesitating, an edge of panic undercutting his words. His earlier high had deserted him.

Randy raised his hand toward the window, moving like a slow-motion scene from a grade-B horror flick, the kind that is so hilarious when shown on *Saturday Afternoon at the Movies*, but metamorphoses when viewed alone in a dark room at midnight . . . and then Randy's hand was on the window, flinching back as fingertips touched cold glass, then pressing against it once more, giving a little shove—

The window popped open, moving inward at the bottom with a rasp of rusty hinges. The *skreek*, like chalk across a blackboard, caused a shudder to erupt at the base of Vince's spine and climb toward his neck, bringing with it the prickly tingle of an army of ants crawling beneath his skin. It ended in a shiver that Vince attempted to turn into a shrug of nonchalance. He needn't have bothered. Randy and Buddy were staring at the loose basement window.

"Piece a cake." Vince laughed a bit too loudly, trying to cover up the slight tremor he'd heard in his voice. He wondered if the others had noticed it.

But Randy and Buddy were just standing there, staring at the window, saying nothing, not even a singsong "Piece a cake, piece a cake" echo from Nutty-Butty. For a moment, Vince felt an insane desire to turn around and run. But what would that do to his status? What would they make of it? Leader turns chickenshit. What would they do to him then? He'd lose the power. The Power. He pulled it to him.

"Fuck this," Vince spat, and took one step down. "You girls got a problem?"

The taunt seemed to break through the restraint that had bolted Randy and Buddy in place—at least for Buddy, who started in with his giggling again.

"Problems, problems, I ain't got no problems," sang Buddy, but his voice sounded maniacal. "What about you, Randy Dandy? You got problems?"

Randy said nothing.

"Well, Randy Dandy," said Vince, "there's your home away from home. Everything but the red carpet laid right out for you—and I bet it's upstairs in one of those posh bood-wahs. Why don't you go see? Just step right in and enjoy a real class setup, and all for free."

Vince moved a smile onto his face, felt it contort, applied the force required to keep it there. This scene was taking on nightmarish tones. He felt a wave of dizziness pass over him.

And then Randy turned around, turned to face him, looked toward him with the refracted moonlight splashing his ghost-white face and oh, his eyes, the look in Randy's eyes—a look that held traces of awareness and acceptance and despair and stark, reeling terror and a deep glimmer of hatred, all frozen there in Randy's eyes. But most of all Randy's glassy, staring eyes looked already dead—they looked already fucking dead!

Somehow Vince maintained his position on the step. Somehow he kept from the ultimate disgrace of chicken-shitting it out of there.

Randy, thank God, was turning back toward the window, moving closer, pushing the window inward with another shrill scream of hinges, mumbling something to Buddy, who reached over to hold the glass open. Randy climbed in, one arm over the sill, then a leg up and over, then his head, the other leg, and now only one arm and a gripping hand hooked the windowsill.

"Can you feel the floor?" Buddy asked, his voice a whisper as though he shouldn't disturb anything sleeping inside, in the dark.

Randy didn't reply, but slid farther down until only his hands were holding him to the sill.

"Drop, for Chrissake!" Vince shouted above the thudding of his heart. "It can't be more than a few feet." He felt sweat pop out on his forehead and upper lip, raised a fist and swiped it hard across his mouth several times.

And Randy dropped.

"Randy, you okay?" Buddy called softly through the open window. "Randy . . . ?"

A moment of silence.

"Sure," Randy's voice filtered up to them. "Just fine and dandy. Dandy Randy, that's me." The voice was Randy's—and not Randy's. It sounded different, somehow. Altered. Dead. Already dead.

Vince wanted out of here, just get the hell out of here. "He's okay, let's go," he said in a rush, hearing the beat of his own heart pounding in his ears, feeling sweat breaking out in other places now, a trickle running down his neck, under his collar. And then the smell hit him.

A sour smell, strong, acrid, coming from the cellar, pouring through the window that Buddy, unbelievably Buddy, was still holding open like his hand was welded to the frame.

And Vince wasn't going to stand here and take any more of this; he wasn't going to stay here anymore. He was leaving no matter what Randy and Buddy thought or said or did, and then the sound came, from the basement, from inside the basement a little "Oh." Nothing more, nothing less, just a little sound. It didn't convey the prevailing emotion of the sounder; that one small word that could indicate surprise or fear or pain was offered in a tone that indicated none of these, a blank tone, a nothing tone, a tone already dead.

"Vince." Buddy's voice was a tiny pinprick in the darkness, an infinitesimal sliver of such compressed terror that Vince felt himself seized and held motionless, his whole body suddenly immobilized despite the screaming orders from his brain to *run!*

He couldn't run. He couldn't move. He could do nothing but watch as something began to crawl from inside the cellar. *JesusOhGodJesus!* It looked like the darkness itself was crawling from that window, it looked like snakes of darkness slithering out of the basement, hands of darkness, fingers crawling.

OhmyGod! crawling up Buddy's arm, twining around Buddy's fucking arm!

"Vince . . ." Buddy's voice was a falsetto of fear. "Vince, Vince, Vince . . ." Cracking, breaking, brittle chokes of terror thrown at Vince.

But Vince was backing up the stairs, slowly so as not to stumble, his brain finally getting the order through to move, to get out of there. He started shaking his head. No. No, I can't help you. No. The tentacles of darkness were coiling over Buddy's shoulder, around Buddy's neck.

"Vince! Vince! *Viiiinnnn—*"

Just like the snap of a finger, the cry cut off. The flicking of a light switch. Vince felt a sting of pain, something warm flooded his mouth. He realized he'd bitten through his lower lip. It was funny. He started to giggle.

His right foot reached the top step. Still he stared at the basement window as he slowly backed away. Buddy was being dragged through the window and into the cellar by the arms of darkness. Buddy's head disappeared into the dark like it had been—go on, think it—swallowed. Buddy's legs twisted and jerked in silent rigors of convulsion, as they were pulled upward with infinite leisure, disappearing slowly into the maw of the basement.

With a sudden spasm Vince tore his eyes away from Buddy's twitching legs, swung around, and started to run, stumbling once, scrambling to his feet, feeling the darkness closing around him as though trying to hold him back. In a desperate parody of his earlier, cocky action, he vaulted across the swing gate and crashed against the side of the car. Then he was scrabbling at the door handle, fumbling the door open.

Inside the car. Start the car. Back out. Not too fast. Don't hit a tree—*for God's sake don't get stuck.* Okay. Now into the road. That's right. You can do it. Nothing coming. Shift into first. Move forward. Slowly, slowly. Right on Main. Down into town where there's light—*light*, for Chrissake. Okay. Fine. Calming down now. Calming down. Nothing happened. Mind playing tricks . . . tripping out . . . bad weed . . . Or— Randy! Sure! It had been Randy pulling Buddy inside, of course. Randy. That's it. They thought they'd have one on me. Have one on the old Vince—not bloody likely. Just wait till tomorrow. Just wait till those assholes come looking me up tomorrow. I'll show them. Yeah. Show them a fucking thing or two . . .

Vince wheeled his car in beside the Merrillville Coffee Shop, parking it directly under the glowing streetlight. Maybe a cup of coffee or a soda—

"Shit," Vince mumbled under his breath as he remembered he didn't have any money for coffee or a soda. "Why didn't I get that other five dollars from Randy before . . ."

Somehow he couldn't finish the sentence.

* * *

"Getting the Beaufort Twins to sign our lease renewal before the spring thaw is a five-star coup," Tank Worley chortled, ostensibly to Ted, but loudly enough for the random ear to pick up—as far away as Charleston. "They usually make us wait until the last minute, hoping something will turn up to keep their precious house out of our evil clutches. Ya done good, Counselor!"

Ted smiled and nodded his thanks, then watched Tank turn and lumber over to Micky Wainwright, wincing when Tank slapped a huge hand onto Micky's shoulder, glad he'd missed out on that particular familiarity.

So perhaps we wimps have our uses, after all, he thought with amusement, slipping papers back into his briefcase. Of course what they didn't know, and he was not at liberty to tell them, was that the Misses Beaufort had signed the lease renewal agreement now in an attempt to thwart the plans of Peter Beaufort, their nephew, only relative, and sole heir to The Manse.

A shrewd businessman involved in land development, Beaufort wanted to raze The Manse and build condominiums on the property—a plan that horrified his aunts and one they totally opposed. Now Peter was trying to have them declared legally incompetent so that he could take over their affairs—and their property.

Although the Twins had helped raise Peter after the untimely death of his parents, there seemed to be no real affection between them and him. Miss Bessie had summed it up once: "Peter was always such a little prick." Ted's mouth quirked up at the memory.

Ted was representing the Beaufort sisters on this and

was determined to do all within his legal power to help
them, even though he personally wouldn't have minded
seeing that old house razed and even though their case
didn't look promising from a legal standpoint. For all Miss
Bessie's glibness, the encroachment of senility was upon
her, could be seen from time to time by even the untrained
eye, and would be an easy thing to embellish in support of
Peter Beaufort's claim. As for Miss Florence Beaufort . . .
Ted didn't think she'd spoken half a dozen words in all the
times he'd visited: a faint smile, a soft "Good day." She
seemed removed from the world, and was thought by some
of the staff at the retirement facility to be dysphasic.

In all honesty, as he had recently told the sisters when
they signed the Jaycee lease renewal, Ted thought the best
he could do was stave off the inevitable. But he would do
that as long as possible.

"Ted?"

Ted looked up to see Dood Hopkins waiting for him,
remembered that Dood had wanted to speak to him about
something. His eyes momentarily slipped past Dood to
Samantha, who had neatly avoided being intercepted by
Zack Dalton and was now coming toward them through
the clot of Jaycees grouped about the room. Ted looked
back at Dood.

"You had something to talk to me about?"

"Yes, but not here. Got time for a cup of coffee?"

"Sure." Ted snapped his briefcase shut, lifting it from
the seat of his chair as Samantha joined them, an expectant
look on her face.

"I want Samantha in on this, too," Dood said. "If you
don't mind."

Ted's smile came easily. He looked at Samantha. "Not at all."

They left the meeting room and headed down the street toward the Merrillville Coffee Shop.

"What's this all about, L.J.?" Samantha queried as they walked. Ted was also wondering what Dood wanted, but experience had taught him all questions would be answered in their own good time.

"I'm not really sure," Dood said cryptically, lighting a cigarette, "but I've got to talk to somebody . . ." His words trailed off and they walked on in silence, even Samantha's typical impatience dampened by the strange tone of Dood Hopkins's voice.

Ted felt the coolness of the night gather around them, heard their footsteps echo hollowly down the dark, empty sidewalk. He glanced toward their destination, seeking the light of the coffee shop window like a moth searching for a flame. He noticed a car parked under the streetlight outside the door, with someone sitting behind the wheel, then his glance moved on down the street and across the highway to where an old house waited, out of sight in the darkness. For a moment he seemed to feel something reaching out from that darkness, something that brought a constriction to his chest. He touched his torso, rubbing gently just beneath the breastbone.

The roar of an engine starting up drew his gaze back to the coffee shop. The car was pulling away from the curb, coming down the street toward the three pedestrians, headlamps bright. Ted glanced at the driver but did not recognize the boy at the wheel; he followed Dood and Samantha inside the coffee shop, dismissing the incident from his mind. He did take a moment to wonder, however, why the kid was driving with his interior lights on.

Slipping into the back booth Dood had chosen for them, sitting opposite the pair, Ted waited while the waitress served a round of coffee and moved on to another table. Just before Ted thought he was going to have to prod him, Dood spoke, pulling no punches:

"There's something fishy going on up at The Manse and it ain't Charlie the tuna."

"What?" Samantha exclaimed, producing a little laugh that seemed singularly devoid of humor.

"What are you talking about, Dood?" Ted felt a small frown knot his brow.

Dood sighed and sat back, playing with his coffee cup. "I don't know. I honestly don't know. But there's something . . . *wrong* up there." Dood shook his head.

"Come on, L.J." Samantha shoved her cup aside. "What are you trying to say?"

Dood leaned forward, voice pitched low. "I'm trying to say that maybe we ought to stay away from The Manse, maybe we ought to call a halt to these Halloween Houses."

Ted's frown deepened. "Do you know someone who's branching out, as Paul Oliver suggested? If so—"

"Not some*one*," Dood interrupted.

Ted felt puzzlement edge out the frown. "I'm not sure I understand."

" 'There's trouble up there,' she told me, 'all the trouble you could ever nightmare up.' And dammit! I'm beginning to believe her."

"Her?" challenged Samantha. "Dood, you're talking in cryptograms."

"Pearl Rollins. You've seen her around town—she's a small, old black woman. She stopped me on the street one day, laid that warning on me. And I know it sounds hokey as hell coming from me, but if you'd heard her say it, seen her eyes . . ." Dood's gaze momentarily clouded, recalling the scene. "I asked around, found out she used to work up at The Manse, years ago. She was the housekeeper; her husband was the butler. When he died, she left and never went back. Lately I've noticed her standing on the street over there, watching The Manse, sometimes even at night. Word is she can *sense* things."

"Really, Dood," Samantha muttered. Ted thought she sounded slightly embarrassed.

"Oh, not see the future, or tell your fortune, or do parlor tricks for a couple of bucks," Dood insisted stubbornly, with an offhand wave, "but *feel* things."

"What sort of things?" Ted asked, his voice calm.

"I can't tell you. I've tried to get her to talk again, to explain." Dood shrugged. "She just walks away."

"Then I don't see what we—"

"Dammit, man!" Dood hissed. "I'm not weirding out on you here. I'm telling you there's something strange going on at The Manse! I've felt it myself."

"That's absurd, Dood," Samantha stated flatly, but Ted saw a contradiction in her eyes.

"Is it, Samantha?" Dood gave her his full attention. "What about Paul Oliver's report? And Tank said something similar happened to him last year. You felt it, too, that day down in the basement."

"Give me a break, L.J.," Samantha mumbled, turning

her head, unwilling to meet Dood's gaze, reaching for her cup of now tepid coffee. She took a swallow and grimaced.

Dood looked back at Ted. "You?"

Ted held Dood's look a moment, steady, evaluating. There was something chillingly sincere in Dood Hopkins's eyes. Logic, however, was not something Ted easily put aside. "What can I say?"

Dood maintained their eye contact another moment, then relaxed back into the booth. "Nothing, I guess."

"Look, L.J." Samantha swung toward Dood, placing a hand on his arm. "It's not that I don't believe you—at least, I believe that you believe—"

"Yeah," Dood said cynically. "I wouldn't want to believe me, either. It's okay, Freckles." Dood managed to grin as he saw her look of distress, softening the moment. "Forget I said anything. A momentary aberration. I mean, really, can you see me in one of those ghostbuster suits?" Dood feigned a fastidious shudder. "Not a fashion risk I'd care to take."

They all laughed mechanically, and by unspoken agreement stood to leave.

Dood laid a couple of dollars on the table, saying, "My treat, kiddies. You'll get stuck with a bigger check."

They left the coffee shop, Samantha saying she had some despised clerical work to catch up on at the newspaper office, voicing a perfunctory complaint about having to be all things to all jobs on a small-town paper, Dood saying he'd walk her there since his video store and his efficiency apartment, above it, lay in the same direction.

Ted said good night and headed across and up the street to his office where he'd left his car, not sorry to be on his own for the moment. It had been a strange evening, one that provoked an unusual sense of disquiet in Ted—he didn't know why. Maybe it was just tiredness making him more susceptible to the oddly compelling look in L. J. Hopkins's eyes. Ted had a suddenly overwhelming urge to glance up toward The Manse, an urge he gave in to, reluctantly, stopping on the sidewalk in front of his office to stare blankly at the old house sitting quiescent on the hill.

A car sped through the nearby intersection, following the highway loop through town. Its lights arced across a segment of Main Street, illuminating shop fronts and side-walks, streaking past a single, solitary figure standing motionless in the mouth of an alleyway. The old woman, dressed in black, stood rigid, statuelike, staring up at The Manse.

Ted blinked against the sudden return of darkness as the car moved on, preparing to go back across the street toward the solitary figure standing watch. Another car fled by, lights sweeping the corner of Main.

The woman was gone.

============================== Chapter 11 ======

The Merrillville day was crisp, bright. It was the last day of the year, December 31, New Year's Eve day . . . the kind of day that should have been a beginning, not an ending, the kind of beautiful, clear, sunny day that seemed to say: "Enjoy me to the fullest."

So why, then, thought Ted Nathan with an ironic grimace, *am I following three people who are quite obviously in the late stages of insanity, into a musty old house that I don't particularly like, on what can only be called a wild-ghost chase?*

Ted shook his head slowly as he ascended the front porch steps and stood quietly while Dood Hopkins fit key to lock and unbolted one side of the double front doors to The Manse.

Admittedly, Ted harbored an unnatural dislike for this

place, something he couldn't explain except by seizing the perfectly legitimate excuse that this old house simply held no particular appeal for him. From the first time he'd seen it perched here on its hillock, staring up Main Street, he'd thought it ugly, graceless, and haughty. Lately it had seemed almost to hover over the town, watchful, vulturelike.

Ted was aware of the slight emotional shift that affected him here. It had happened again today, a feeling that moved onto him when they'd driven up the driveway and refused to be banished, as if they'd passed through an air lock separating unequalized pressures. The air seemed heavier here, the sun not quite so bright. A fanciful sensation, certainly, perhaps even mildly irrational, but not in the category L. J. Hopkins was propounding. Nowhere near.

If it wasn't that Ted always tried to bend over backward toward open-mindedness—and his growing involvement with Samantha—he wouldn't even be here today, would have laughed off the whole charade the night that Dood Hopkins invited him for coffee after the Jaycee meeting and ended up giving him ghost stories.

Ted had wanted to laugh off Dood's tales, to accuse Dood of trying to set him up for one of the industrial-strength jokes he was known to pull from time to time. Samantha had done just that, inserting all the proper protests in all the appropriate slots; somehow Ted had been unable to do the same. But now things were getting a bit out of reason.

For Dood the situation had escalated in the past few weeks with news of the disappearance of Randy Dawson and Buddy Grey. The two boys had last been seen heading for the old Beaufort estate in the company of Vince Colletti.

The initial police inquiry soon turned into a "missing persons/presumed runaways" report after information surfaced that Randy had been set adrift on the world by his own father a few days previously, and Buddy's mother appeared glad to be rid of her son—she hadn't even questioned his absence for nearly a week. Colletti had dropped off both boys at The Manse after Randy insisted he was going to sleep there, even if he had to break in to do so. According to Vince, Buddy had elected to go with Randy; Vince himself had refused. It was Colletti's opinion that his two friends had simply skipped town the next day and were by now headed south or west or wherever the grass smelled greener.

Since there was no evidence of foul play and nothing disturbed at the house, this theory was held probable—except by Dood Hopkins, who seemed to think that something had happened to Randy Dawson and Buddy Grey that night at The Manse, something impossible by rational standards. And there was nothing either Samantha or Ted could say to dissuade him from this line of thought.

The caper they were currently involved in was the next logical step in proving Dood's theory—if you were prepared to accept the completely illogical conjectures on which it was built.

Ted studied the elderly black woman who was today's feature attraction. Pearl Rollins was a petite whisper of a woman, dressed almost exclusively in plain black garments, a prim black hat perched atop hair barely gray, an old black pocketbook clutched tightly in two gnarled hands whose skin stretched like parchment over bone. She was

somewhere between seventy and a hundred—Ted doubted
even Pearl knew her age for sure.

In the past few weeks, Dood had paid several visits to
the woman at her small, neat home on a Merrillville back
street, talking to her about The Manse, revealing his feelings and suspicions, trying to discover hers. She'd told
him nothing, but when he'd finally asked her to come here
with him, surprisingly enough she'd agreed.

Ted found it difficult to believe he was really involved
in this ghostbusting jaunt. If it wasn't for Samantha . . .

Ted's eyes shifted to her, standing just behind and to
Dood's left. Could she really believe all this nonsense? He
remembered thinking that with Samantha, life would never
be boring.

Ted had a sudden urge to put out his hand and give a
small tweak to a wayward curl that had refused to be
smoothed into place, a playful whim. He didn't do it, of
course. Playful urges were foreign to Ted; he didn't really
know how to deal with them, so they rarely went beyond
the musing stage. He thought about the Jaycee New Year's
Eve party tonight. She'd asked him to go, and he'd agreed.

The dull click of tumblers falling into place dispelled the
momentary lightness of Ted's mood and reminded him of
the activity at hand. Dood Hopkins swung the door inward, then stood back to allow his companions to enter.
Samantha led the way, glancing back at Ted with a smile;
behind her, Pearl Rollins walked resolutely, looking neither right nor left. Ted followed them in, then turned to
close the door behind Dood.

The entry hall was brushed by softly muted light seeping
through the thin windows on either side of the double

doors and the lead-paned fanlight above. Dust motes swam
and danced in the diffuse rays. A musty smell pervaded
the house, slightly sour, but being inside wasn't particularly oppressive. Ted realized he'd been expecting oppressive.

"Cold in here." Samantha crossed her arms and rubbed
them briskly, a gesture Ted was coming to recognize as
characteristic. She strode over to the light switch and
flicked on the hall lights. The residual gloom immediately
fled.

"Feel warmer now?" Dood quipped, trying for chipper,
and they all laughed on cue—all but Pearl Rollins.

One by one, Ted, Samantha, and Dood fell silent, their
attention drawn to the small, dark face, a face set in the
mosaic of time and the pattern of listening.

Pearl had moved only a few paces inside the front door,
as though she had gone as far as she intended going. She
stood framed against the heavy wood, bound by the slivers
of light on each side and the fan above. Her slight body
was taut.

"Mrs. Rollins." Dood took a step toward her. "Pearl?"

Ted and Samantha traded glances, Ted unable to read
Samantha's face and knowing his own was no less confused. The mood had become suddenly tense, and he
didn't understand why.

"When first I came here as a young girl bride," Pearl
Rollins began speaking, her voice soft and lyrical, with an
overlay of rich southern dialect and an underlying tenacity,
"I felt something gathering about this old house. Not
already in it, mind, no restless spirits here then, no demon
magic or possession, no age-old evil to be put down . . .

but something growing. I felt a stirring in the under space, a movement as though something here was being summoned up in some way. A coming together, but slow, so slow, like an egg lying quietly in its mammy's womb till it's seeded, then growing slow toward life.

"For a long time I said nothing; I felt no evil present, no really bad thing, just a weak sense of fear now and again. But it still lay nesting in its womb and gave no threat to me and mine. Then something happened, and I sensed hatred, violence, and more fear. And I could feel this thing begin to grow, take shape, moving like a sickness nursing its blight, feeding off what happened here."

Pearl Rollins took a small step forward, an earnestness in the action, pocketbook gripped in front of her like a shield.

With a start of surprise, Ted realized his body had become rigid during her tale, fingers curling tightly into palms, breath coming more rapid and shallow as she spoke. He relaxed his stance, smoothed out the slight pucker he felt pinched between his eyebrows. Her words seemed to have woven a silken thread around them all, holding them almost mesmerized. He glanced at Samantha, then Dood: their bodies stood as still and hushed as his own.

"I told my man what I sensed here," Pearl Rollins continued, "told my Rollie. He paid me no nevermind, feeling nothing himself, though he didn't laugh, didn't mock my gift. From then on he'd soothe my fears when they came rushing at me, and never once admitted he might have felt them too, not until the day he died. Then he told me, 'Pearly, you leave this house now if you want. You leave and don't come back.' And then he died, and I left, and I never set a foot back on these floors until this day.''

Pearl Rollins fell silent, and her silence left a void in the hall. Ted wanted to feel an amused tolerance for this time-embellished tale of superstitious nonsense, wanted to shake his head in disbelief, but something in the shadowed wraith of a woman standing pat at the threshold of this old, disquieting house belied the humor, belied the denial that lay in his mind.

Samantha was the first to speak: "Are you telling us, Mrs. Rollins, that you believed The Manse was haunted?" It was the kind of question a news reporter would ask, but the voice that asked it fell just this side of hushed.

Pearl Rollins smiled. "No, child, not haunted. The Manse wasn't haunted. I couldn't have lived here if that had been so, not even with my Rollie . . .''

"Then—" Samantha's comment was cut off.

Pearl Rollins spoke again as if she hadn't heard the interruption: "No, child, The Manse wasn't haunted . . . not then. But it was becoming haunted.''

"What do you mean, *becoming* haunted?" Dood asked. "What is it you feel here, Pearl?"

The old woman hugged her purse to her, leaning forward so that the top half of her body bent slightly over it. "Fear, young man. I feel fear. And what *is* fear, boy? What does it do? Where does it go? How is it spent? There's been lots of fear in this house, on these grounds—''

"That can be said of most old houses," Samantha interrupted stubbornly, and was silenced by a look.

"Yes, child, there's some in all old places." The old woman raised her eyes upward, looked around. "But it's harbored here, been nurtured. In times past by the usual routine of things that go bad, in my day by something I won't tell you about, and in past years by you people here, you and your scary shows. Been a lot of fear deposited in this one place.''

"And that fear is . . . what?" Ted found himself asking, his rational mind telling him this thing was getting out of hand, moving into the absurd, yet some prick of irrational fascination urged the question.

Pearl Rollins turned toward him, and he could see glittering aliveness in the age-old eyes.

"That fear, young man who don't believe, is supping on these happenings, building shape here, drinking in vitals, becoming . . ." Pearl hesitated.

". . . alive?" murmured Dood into the silence.

They all turned to look at him.

Ted broke the paralysis. "Mrs. Rollins," he said, his voice strong and firm, "I certainly don't wish to insult your beliefs in any way or offer you any hint of disrespect, but what you're saying is clearly impossible." He turned to Dood and Samantha, who he could see were caught up in the emotions of the situation, so much so that their judgment was at the moment questionable. "You'll have to forgive me. I simply can't go along with this any further. Now, what I suggest is that we all go get some lunch, and then I have to get back to the office." Ted felt that he had to get this thing back on the grounds of sanity before they all made fools of themselves.

For a moment he wondered if Samantha and Dood were going to join him in reality or just continue staring at him with a mixture of suspicion and uncertainty. If they didn't, he knew, if they tugged even slightly on the tenuous bond that had woven itself around them all, he might himself waver.

Then Samantha spoke. "Yes, let's get out of here."

Ted sighed in relief. He moved over to the door, opened it, and stood back. Samantha walked out briskly, not looking left or right as she passed through the doorway. Ted glanced toward Dood.

For another moment, Dood hesitated, returning Ted's look with a blank stare that obviously reflected his internal conflict.

"Come on, Dood," Ted said softly. "We'll talk about this."

Dood nodded once, went over and gently took Pearl Rollins's childlike hand. "Thank you, Pearl. Thank you for coming, for talking to us."

Pearl hushed him with a look, then studied Ted in the doorway and Samantha, who stood waiting on the front porch. For a moment her eyelids squeezed shut, as if she were resisting something or straining to catch the last nuance of a sound. Then they blinked open again, and slowly, with the infinite gesture of the enlightened for the ignorant, she shook her head once, only once. It was enough. Ted felt a sudden chill hone the air.

Without a word, Pearl allowed Dood to lead her through the door and out onto the front porch. Ted started to follow, grasping the doorknob perhaps a bit harder than absolutely necessary to pull the door closed behind them, when suddenly Pearl stopped walking and turned around.

Her sharp eyes darted over the house, a searching gaze. "I'm glad I came back," she hissed, as if to the house itself. "I said I never would, knowing what I did, sensing what was here—but I'm glad I came back one more time."

Her gaze fell on Ted, who at that moment seemed to feel something in motion around them, a ripple in the fabric of the world that warned of unseen things beneath. A shiver slid up his spine.

"Yes, I'm glad," Pearl Rollins murmured, reclaiming Ted's attention, her eyes dark crystal orbs in the ancient face. "Because I can tell you now, young man who don't believe, it's getting stronger."

A pall clung to Samantha's mood, blunting the brilliant afternoon and emphasizing its chill. She swung her VW Rabbit right, off Main Street and onto the highway loop, heading out of town toward the Country Manor Retirement Home and her hastily set up visit with the Beaufort Twins.

The events of this morning had left her with nagging doubts, worries about things that were the stuff of nightmares. Though Dood had told her and Ted what he was planning when he'd asked their participation, what Pearl Rollins had said was an experience unanticipated and unprepared for. The small black woman had spun a tale that seemed drawn from some madman's dream. It had no place in the real world, yet, looking into those onyx eyes, listening to that soft voice, Samantha had found herself inching toward belief, confused, uncertain, and afraid.

Samantha had fastened onto the one point of factual reference that she might be able to confirm: Pearl Rollins's comment that something had happened at The Manse during her time, something she couldn't, or wouldn't, tell them about. It had sounded significant.

At the best of times, Samantha's job at the newspaper meant a lot of legwork, paperwork, and deadline pressures—of that, she had no illusions. And a small-town press rep would never O.D. on hard-nosed reporting. But Samantha held on to her slightly ambitious vision of doing more than feature articles and her "Stuff 'n' Nonsense" column and all the other little sundry chores that employment with the *Merrillville Weekly* dictated. Dood was prone to baiting her with Lois Lane jokes; he didn't realize that they held just enough validity to make them honest.

So despite the Twilight Zonish aspect to the morning, and the residual taint it had lent to the afternoon, Samantha's professional snoopishness was aroused. If Pearl wouldn't talk, maybe Miss Bessie would. So Samantha was on her way to see the Beaufort sisters.

"Something happened," Pearl had said, then: *"hatred, violence, fear."* What could she have meant? A number of the tragedies connected with The Manse fit that description; the Jaycees often based several of their scenarios on the old tales. But they were all well-known stories, liberally told and retold over the years. There had been reticence in Pearl's voice when she spoke of this particular occurrence, reticence and finality; enough to suggest a hidden truth, a secret kept. Samantha wanted to know what that secret was.

She braked for the turnoff to the retirement home, avoiding a glance at the neighboring skilled-care facility where four years ago the grandmother who raised her had gradually forgotten everything but how to die. Samantha still felt the wrench of being alone in the world. Perhaps that was why she kept clinging to Zack. She closed her mind to that thought.

Turning into the circular drive that wound up to the minimum-care residential complex, she inched past a trio of elderly residents out for a nice winter day's stroll, and pulled the Rabbit into the visitors' lot. Gathering up the paper-wrapped bunch of cut flowers she'd picked up at the greenhouse, Samantha slid from the car and walked briskly up the drive to the attractive one-story building.

A sleepiness pervaded the home this afternoon, a sort of lazy-day-summer attitude that cast a stillness over the building. The reception parlor was empty. Samantha resisted an urge to tiptoe down the hall to the Beaufort Twins' suite, but did walk as quietly as possible. Afternoons, residents at the Country Manor napped or followed other leisurely pursuits, while the staff chatted over coffee or attended meetings.

At the Twins' door Samantha stopped and knocked lightly. A woman's voice said, "Come in," and Samantha stepped into the comfortably furnished sitting room of the two-bedroom suite, beaming a smile at the two little old ladies enthroned in their usual spots. Fraternal twins, the pair were nothing alike in looks or temperament.

"Ah, Samantha dear," Miss Bessie trilled, lifting her small plump form from her favorite overstuffed wing chair to come toward Samantha, hand outstretched.

"How are you, Miss Bessie?" Samantha placed her long slender hand in the short plump one, glancing at the other twin. "And how is Miss Flossie?"

Florence Beaufort, seated in her customary rocker drawn

up to the room's only window, did not acknowledge Samantha's entrance in any way. Samantha wondered if she was even aware of the intrusion.

"She's having one of her quiet days," Miss Bessie said sotto voce, then continued, "Aren't you, dear?" in normal tones, flashing a smile at her sister and nodding affirmatively. Miss Flossie kept on rocking, silently.

A made-for-TV movie Samantha had seen recently sprang to mind: an Agatha Christie Miss Marple mystery starring Bette Davis and Helen Hayes. Grandmotherly little Helen Hayes as Miss Marple could have been cloned from Miss Bessie Beaufort, twinkly and chatty and sharp as a tack. And Bette Davis . . . tall, aloof, willow thin, showing the effects of illness yet still carrying that regal bearing, that quiet dignity that categorized Florence Beaufort.

"Come in, come in, my dear." Miss Bessie drew Samantha farther into the room, closing the hall door. "What a nice surprise your call was. It's always such a treat to have you visit, and what lovely flowers!"

With a start, Samantha realized she'd forgotten the flowers clutched in her other hand. Grinning, she extended them. "To brighten a winter's day, though it's so pleasant out you'd hardly recognize December."

Dropping Samantha's hand, Miss Bessie claimed the bouquet, childlike in her eagerness. Samantha made a mental note to be more frequent with little presents.

"Oh, they are lovely," cooed Miss Bessie, burying her gray head in the colorful blooms. Her bright button eyes sparkled with delight. "Aren't they lovely, Florence?" She turned toward the rocker, extending the flowers for

her sister's inspection, head bobbing agreement, though
Miss Flossie made no move to look her way.

"I'm glad you like them," Samantha said as Miss
Bessie cradled the blossoms, "and I do appreciate your
seeing me on such short notice."

"Quite all right, my dear. We enjoy your company
anytime, don't we, Florence? Of course we do."

Samantha couldn't help smiling at the way Miss Bessie
kept assuming her twin's part in the conversation, though
it bothered her that Miss Flossie seemed all the time more
removed from the world. Not for the first time Samantha
wondered if Miss Flossie might be an undiagnosed victim
of Alzheimer's disease, the same insidious syndrome that
had consumed her grandmother.

Of course, Florence Beaufort had always been some-
what detached, somehow sad, as though something had
long ago touched her life with lasting pain. Could some
past tragedy, perhaps Pearl's "happening," have left a
permanent mark on the woman? Was this increasing senility simply the normal encroachment of age, or was it the
natural progression of a weaker twin's personality being
absorbed by the stronger sibling? Sometimes Samantha
wondered what Miss Flossie's life had been like before she
came to the home.

"I take it there is a special reason for this visit." Miss
Bessie's plump features suddenly froze. "Oh, I do hope
there's nothing wrong at the house?"

Samantha quickly shook her head. "No, no. I should
have said—everything's fine at The Manse. I'm sorry if I
worried you needlessly."

Miss Bessie visibly relaxed, reassuming her cherubic

expression. Samantha spared a hope that if anything ever
did go wrong at The Manse she wouldn't have to break the
news. The welfare of that house was an obsession with
Miss Bessie.

"Then . . . ?" Miss Bessie left the question hanging,
delicately, but obviously prompting Samantha to get on
with her business.

All at once Samantha was uncertain just how to proceed. Sudden doubts assailed her regarding the tactfulness
of this visit. She'd decided not to mention this morning's
escapade; Miss Bessie might not take kindly to it. But she
hadn't given a thought to the judiciousness of asking point-
blank about an event in The Manse's past that might have
painful associations for the Beaufort sisters—she'd just
smelled a spicy story brewing and followed her nose.
*Good job, Lois; and where's a convenient phone booth
when you need one?*

"I'm thinking of doing a full series of background
articles on The Manse this year," Samantha hastily impro-
vised, liking the sound of the idea even as she ad-libbed it.
"A lead-up to the Halloween House. This will be our
thirteenth year and something special seems to be in order.
What could be more appropriate than delving into some of
the house's unlucky events?"

Miss Bessie's round features tightened sharply, a look
of speculation driving the childlike innocence from her
twinkling eyes. "What events did you have in mind,
dear?" Miss Bessie's tone held distinct chilliness.

Oops, thought Samantha. Backtracking, she said, "Oh,
a few of the old legends and stories—like the young man
who's supposed to have drowned in an old well on the

property, and the gardener who went berserk one night with an ax. As you know, we've based several of our scenarios on occurrences at The Manse, and I think my readers would be interested in the true stories behind them. I hoped you might be able to give me some background information; family knowledge, so to speak." Samantha wondered if she'd poked a raw spot; the sharpness had eased from but not left Miss Bessie's face.

"You know, dear, I've never been too fond of your group using my home for its theatricals. I feel it may irreparably tarnish the house's historical significance and lessen its value to restoration societies."

Samantha understood this sentiment all too well; Miss Bessie expressed it often. The Jaycees knew they were being granted their lease on sufferance only. "All the more reason to expel the more lurid myths surrounding these events," Samantha offered, trying another tack while ignoring the thought of Zack's probable reaction to a series of articles expunging the horror from several of their best scenarios. "It might even provoke new interest in preserving the scene of such, uh, stimulating folk tales."

"You may be right." Miss Bessie pondered a moment, then her face cleared. "I see no harm in discussing a few of the old tales. My father was the one who dispensed with the gardener, you know, after the man killed two of the servants. Florence and I were just children, but I remember how we and our brother Avery clung together in terror for hours while that madman stalked the premises. And that poor boy who drowned—he was courting one of the serving girls, I believe the story goes, meeting her in the back garden at dusk. That happened before we were born, of course. The fountain was built where the well used to be.'' She shuddered delicately. ''It was all so long ago, I'd almost forgotten.''

Samantha nodded dutifully, but had her doubts that Miss Bessie would ever forget anything connected with The Manse. That old house had been, was still, her life.

''Why don't I get something for these lovely flowers, dear, then we'll sit down and have a nice coze—if you can endure an old lady's prattle.''

''Love to,'' Samantha said with a grin. ''Oh, just a minute.'' She plucked a bright yellow chrysanthemum from the bouquet, then gestured toward Miss Florence. Miss Bessie nodded and beamed like a happy parent as she started for the other room, presumably to fetch a vase.

Carrying the flower, Samantha approached Miss Flossie gently, stooping beside the rocker to smile into the thin gaunt face. ''Miss Flossie . . . ?''

For a moment there was no response, then the rocker slowed, almost imperceptibly, and Miss Flossie's eyes focused on the chrysanthemum. Florence Beaufort lifted a hand that was skin-coated bone, took the flower so lightly Samantha feared she might drop it. Angular features smoothed as the old woman gazed at the bright flower; the film of disinterest cleared from deep hazel eyes.

''He always liked yellow,'' Miss Flossie murmured, so softly that Samantha had to lean forward to hear her.

''Who, Miss Flossie?'' Samantha's tone was also hushed. Her forehead wrinkled in a slight frown.

With the stately manner of a queen conferring a benevolent gaze on one of her subjects, Florence Beaufort slowly turned her head and met Samantha's look. The hazel eyes had warmed; a smile gentled the thin, pale lips that whispered, "You wouldn't know him."

Puzzlement silenced Samantha for a moment, then the sound of Miss Bessie bustling back into the room caused her to glance away. When she looked back, Miss Flossie had returned to her faraway vision, eyes staring through the window at their own private world.

"Now, dear, isn't that nice?" Miss Bessie set an exquisite cut-glass vase, filled with flowers, on the table between wing chair and rocker so that both she and Miss Flossie could enjoy them. "See, Florence? Don't they look lovely in Grandmother's vase?" She acknowledged herself with a nod, continuing to arrange the flowers.

Now, thought Samantha, *is the time for an offhand:* "Oh, by the way, I met a former employee of yours recently."

"Really, dear?" Miss Bessie spoke without looking at Samantha. "And who was that?"

"Pearl Rollins."

Miss Bessie's darting hands grew still. "Oh? And how is poor Pearl?"

Scary. "Fine." *Poor* Pearl?

Miss Bessie turned around, cherubic smile regretful. "Such a pity about poor Pearl. We had to let her go, you know. She was always spreading such fanciful gossip, and after Rollins died— her husband; you remember Rollins, don't you, Florence?—she seemed to become quite unhinged, frightening the other servants with her mumbo-jumbo talk. Did she say anything strange to you?" Miss Bessie eyed her curiously.

Did she ever. "I didn't talk to her long," Samantha

prevaricated, uncertain now if she'd let this morning's episode run away with her imagination or if Miss Bessie really did have something to hide. A problem to sort out later. "We just met in passing."

Miss Bessie's smile brightened. "How nice. I'm glad to hear she's doing well. I always liked Pearl."

She went back to puttering with the flowers, then excused herself, telling Samantha, "Please, dear, do have a seat. I'll just be a moment."

Samantha drew up a small Nantucket rocker upholstered in faded rose damask and moved it to a spot between the sisters' chairs. As she passed Miss Flossie, she thought she heard the old lady whispering something. She bent down.

Miss Flossie's words were timed to the rhythm of her rocker, back and forth, over and over, a whisper-thin phrase: "Oh no you didn't, Oh no you didn't, Oh no you didn't . . ."

The Jaycee New Year's Eve party was pushing toward the midnight countdown with all the finesse, style, and grace of a Sherman Tank Worley—a roaring success, literally. The party roared around the small corner table where Samantha and Ted, and Dood and his lady, Jill Willis, had set up camp.

Dood and Jill were dancing; Samantha toyed with the gin and tonic she'd been sipping for the past hour or so, rubbing a sliver of lime back and forth around the rim of her glass. The ice had long since melted, making the drink a facsimile of the tart highball she'd started out with.

"Freshen that?"

Samantha looked up into Ted Nathan's quiet gray eyes,

realizing he'd been watching her. She smiled and shook her head. She'd had enough, enough of it all, actually— the liquor, the noise, the forced gaiety that she'd tried to uphold all evening. The episode at The Manse this morning hung like a rain cloud over the balance of her day, dripping omens at every turn. She'd been pulled around in circles, by Dood, who appeared totally convinced that Pearl Rollins's farfetched horror tale was truly happening; by Ted, who was equally convinced they were crazy to even entertain such a notion; and then by the Beaufort Twins, who had somehow merged with the enigma.

"Samantha?" Ted's voice probed gently.

"Ted, would you mind terribly if we got out of here?" Samantha heard the strain in her voice. She hated it, hated being like this tonight when she'd so looked forward to this party and to sharing it with Ted. But, dammit, she wanted to go home!

"I don't mind at all," he told her, standing, smiling down at her as the music from the rock group on the dais blazed around them, drowning out further attempts at conversation.

Samantha picked up her evening bag and was in the process of rising when Dood and Jill returned to the table. Dood's expression looked like Samantha felt, and Jill seemed slightly bewildered. No doubt she was; she'd listened to some pretty wild speculation tonight, and Dood had been more interested in trying to sway Ted's opinion and secure Samantha's support than attempting to explain this fixation to his date. Samantha felt a little sorry for Jill. Dood would sure owe her one after this evening.

"We're gone, L.J.," she said as Dood looked at her, his eyes a question. "I've had it for this year."

He nodded, not trying to dissuade them, and after a round of murmured good-nights, Samantha and Ted threaded their way around the edge of the dance floor and out into the lobby of the private club. Ted went to get their coats from the serve-yourself cloakroom to the right of the entry, and Samantha slipped outside, finding the cold night air like a draft of cleansing water. She turned her face up to the night, drinking in the biting air, blowing her breath like smoke, trying to pick out Orion or the Big Dipper among the glittering maze of diamond brilliants scattered across the almost-midnight sky.

The crunch of footsteps on the gravel drive alerted Samantha that she was not alone. She looked toward the parking lot and the pair coming toward her: Zack and a rather tipsy J.T., brown bag stuck under one arm—probably white liquor from a local moonshiner. The boys were getting down to hard stuff now. Zack was drunk. Very drunk, Samantha saw as they came nearer. Of course with Zack it was hard to tell; he rarely displayed the overt symptoms that usually came with the condition, but she'd had some experience judging the depths of his inebriation.

Samantha put up her hands and absently rubbed her arms just above the elbows. All at once the night didn't seem so clean anymore. She moved away from the club-house door, wishing Ted would come on out, hoping Zack and J.T. would just go on in.

She didn't get her wish.

"Where's your date, Sam?" Zack remarked caustically as he stopped beside her. His ice-blue eyes seemed to glitter ominously in the swath of yellow light coming at them from the ornamental fixtures on either side of the clubhouse doors.

"Leave me alone, Zack." Samantha was suddenly incredibly tired and didn't want a confrontation. She started to turn aside, to walk toward the parking lot.

"What do you see in that dipshit Nathan, anyway, dammit!" Zack's voice was contemptuous as he moved around in front of her. "Just tell me what the hell you see in him?"

J.T. muttered, "C'mon, now, Wolfman," from the background and was ignored.

"I asked you a question, Sam!" Zack moved closer to her, raising his hands as if he intended taking hold of her.

"Ready to go, Samantha?" Ted's quiet voice was a safety line.

She grabbed it eagerly, stepping backward out of Zack's reach, pleading silently with whatever power might be listening that the man standing frozen in front of her would let them go their way in peace. But then Zack turned toward Ted, arms taut at his sides, fingers curled, his body poised on the cutting edge. *Oh, God,* the thought raced through Samantha's mind. *Oh, my God, he's going to start a fight. Zack's going to start a fight with Ted and try to kill him and he just might do it and J.T. can't stop him and where the hell is Tank.*

And then she realized Zack had broken off the gaze he'd locked with Ted, was stalking away from them, going into the clubhouse. J.T. followed along in Zack's wake. Ted had turned to watch them go, and there was something about the set of Ted's body . . . Samantha wondered what exactly Zack had seen in Ted Nathan's eyes that made him walk away, and then wondered if she really wanted to know.

She moved toward Ted, came to stand beside him as the clubhouse door swung shut on Zack Dalton and J. T. Hunsinger. She started to put a hand on Ted's arm.

"I find it hard to believe you were ever involved with Zack Dalton," Ted murmured, almost to himself.

The relief Samantha had been feeling fled. Anger took its place. She felt her eyes blaze with anger, her stomach contract with it.

Whirling around, she began walking briskly toward Ted's car, hearing him come after her, sensing his puzzlement. She knew she was overreacting, her logic center already chastising her for excessive behavior based on the perverse "I can call him a jerk but you'd better not" theme. But she'd taken the comment like a slap in the face, seeing it as criticism of Zack, certainly, but more specifically criticism of *her*—a slur on her judgment, her taste, even her emotional stability. While Ted might be right, he didn't have any right to say that. Not to her. Not yet.

She stopped at the car, stood by the door as he unlocked it, then held it open for her to slide in. She saw him look at her quizzically, but he said nothing, thank God. At the moment she was beyond putting any response into words. She just wanted to be away from here, away from Zack, even away from Ted.

Ted got in, started the car, and drove in silence to her home, an apartment in one of Merrillville's converted Victorian houses. She was already getting out as he stopped the car, leaving him to park. He called out as he came up the walkway.

"Samantha, wait a minute!"

She doggedly pulled her keys out and unlocked the front door. He was right behind her now, she felt him there, saying nothing but clearly determined. Well, she was just as determined. She opened the door, stepped inside, and turned around.

"Good night, Ted," she said, trying for firmness and coming off shaky.

He slowly shook his head. "No. Not like this."

Then he was inside too, closing the door gently, moving to stand beside her in the middle of the living room. Only the small lamp on the corner table was lit, like a candle in the darkness. Samantha felt her breath coming in quick, deep spurts.

"Now, what is going on between us?" he asked, his voice still quiet, but with no weakness in it.

Samantha felt tears prick the insides of her eyelids, felt her raging anger move toward a torrential release.

"Look, dammit," she said stiffly, "I lived with Zack Dalton for a year and a half. We were lovers! Even before that, we were lovers. Do you hear me, Ted? But now it's over. And if Zack can't accept that fact, then fuck him!" Samantha moved a step closer to Ted, her body trembling now. "And if *you* can't accept that fact—then fuck you!"

For what seemed an eternity, Ted stood quietly, making no reply, no move toward or away from her. Samantha felt her chest heaving, like she'd been running hard and hadn't had long to rest.

The sound of her breathing, heavy in the silence, was

suddenly eclipsed as her grandmother's old antique mantel clock began chiming the hour. Midnight. A new year being heralded in.

Then Ted was closing the space between them, was slowly putting up a hand to touch her face, the tips of his fingers barely brushing the edge of her chin as he guided her lips to his. "Yes, please," he whispered.

And then he was kissing her, gently, deeply, and Samantha wondered why she had ever thought tenderness couldn't be equated with passion.

Chapter 12

The young nurse's aide at the call desk was finding the late January day a bit of a bore. If it hadn't been for the typical midwinter conditions outside, she would have found the afternoon unbearable. As it was, the cold drizzle and icy wind whipping it up out there made her shift easier to bear.

The phone buzzed with an incoming call. She laid down the romance magazine she'd been reading, picked up the receiver, and pressed the button, hoping it wasn't her boyfriend calling to cancel their date tonight. She'd be in the mood for some warming up by then.

"Country Manor Retirement Home. Good afternoon."

A brisk, masculine voice said, "I'd appreciate being put through to my aunt, Elizabeth Beaufort, with as little delay as possible. This is Peter Beaufort, calling long-distance."

The aide put the call on hold and buzzed the Beaufort
Twins' suite.

No answer.

She buzzed again, holding the button down for several
extra seconds, knowing the sisters were both in; she'd seen
them go down the hall shortly after lunch.

Still no answer.

No doubt Miss Bessie, who was rather deaf, had her
television set or her personal stereo on full-blast. The
young aide giggled as she always did when she thought
about an eighty-year-old plugged in to a portable radio—
and she listened to rock music too. Unreal.

Wondering if a boom box might be next on the old
fossil's list, the aide reopened the line to Peter Beaufort.
"I'm sorry, Mr. Beaufort, but your aunt's not answering.
I'll have to go get her. I know she's in her room." Her
tone was respectful.

"Please do so." His tone was clipped.

The aide rose and walked quickly down the corridor to
the bed-sitter occupied by the Beaufort Twins.

With only a halfhearted knock at the door, she entered
the small sitting room. "Miss Bessie, you're wanted on
the phone," she called out, seeing the old lady in her
overstuffed wing chair in the corner of the room, feet
propped on a chintz-covered footstool. The culprit earphones rode firmly in place.

Miss Bessie lifted one side of the earphones. "Yes,
dear?"

The aide pointed toward the room phone, in its place on
the small round table next to the wing chair. "Your nephew's on the phone."

A shadow seemed to dart across Elizabeth Beaufort's face, then she said, "How nice," laid aside the stereo, and reached for the telephone. About to pick it up, she hesitated, glancing at the aide. "Anything else, dear?"

The young woman shook her head, aware that the old lady wanted to be rid of her before taking her nephew's call. The aide left the room, glad to be away from the depressing atmosphere of gray hair and wrinkles and lemon verbena sachet. She returned to the desk, noting that the blinking light which had announced Peter Beaufort's call was now on constant. She wondered what Miss Bessie had to talk to her nephew about. Then she noticed that she'd left the line open when she went to get Miss Bessie; she hadn't pushed the hold button.

Carefully, very carefully, the young aide sat down and picked up the receiver. That Peter Beaufort had sounded kinda sexy, in a mature way. Like some of the men in the stories she read—arrogant, strong-willed, dangerous. A delicious shiver traveled up her spine. She wondered what he looked like. She put the phone to her ear:

". . . and the provisions of the will give me peremptory right of access," Peter Beaufort was saying in that commanding, masterful voice.

His aunt interrupted: "Peter, my attorney assures me you are enjoined—"

"I know my limits, Aunt Elizabeth," he responded. "I'll be bringing a surveyor and architect to the property soon." The line went dead.

The nurse's aide started to replace the receiver, then paused as she heard Miss Bessie murmur:

"Peter is determined to pursue this thing." The young

woman could picture Miss Bessie absently holding on to
the receiver, talking to her sister, or perhaps to herself.

"He thinks he can do this to us," Miss Bessie continued
harshly, unaware of her extra audience, "but I'll see him
in hell first."

The aide smothered a giggle with her free hand. Imagine
that prim and proper old lady using such language. She
almost dropped the phone when the intercom buzzer suddenly sounded. Choking back a laugh, she punched the
lighted button. "Call desk."

"This is Elizabeth Beaufort, dear," came the old lady's
apple-dumpling voice, quite a contrast to the tone she'd
used with her nephew. "Would you please see if you can
get me that nice young man in Charles Hamilton's office,
that Mr. Nathan?"

"Sure, Miss Bessie. Buzz you right back." She pulled
out the Merrillville phone book, thumbed up the number,
and put through the call, remembering "that Mr. Nathan"
from his visits to the Twins. She'd also seen him around
town, though they'd never been properly introduced. He
was good-looking enough to catch your eye, though he
seemed sorta quiet; not in the same league as a Zack
Dalton, say, but she wouldn't turn down an opportunity.

"Mr. Hamilton's office." The aide's fantasy bubbled
away.

"Miss Elizabeth Beaufort calling for Mr. Nathan. Is he
in?"

"I'm sorry, Mr. Nathan is out of town. May I have him
call Miss Beaufort next week when he returns?"

"Just a moment. I'll check." The aide put the outside
line on hold and buzzed Miss Bessie on the intercom.

"Sorry, Miss Bessie," she said as the old lady answered. "Mr. Nathan's out of town until next week. He can get back to you then."

"I suppose that will have to do. Please leave the message that I'd like to see him at his earliest convenience." The line went dead.

The aide made a face at the phone. It would seem their resident dear old lady had a bit of her nephew's abruptness.

She returned to the secretary, passed on Miss Bessie's message, then hung up and reached for her romance magazine, slightly bored with the whole thing. Real life just didn't begin to compete with fiction.

A week later, the normal fifteen-minute drive from Merrillville to the Country Manor Retirement Home took better than half an hour. February was coming in white this year. A gentle snow had begun in the morning and now promised to last throughout the day and into the night. It was already sticking to the roads, and though it didn't yet pose a real hazard, it did tend to slow traffic.

Samantha glanced at the man behind the wheel of the midsized, steel-gray Buick. A feeling of warmth stole over her. She felt completely safe with Ted Nathan, and not just because of his snow tires and his careful attention to the road, but because of his air of self-reliance, of having the ability to deal competently with whatever situation might present itself. If she'd been with Zack today, in the old four-wheel-drive Bronco, she'd have been scared to death.

"Warm enough?" Ted's question broke into Samantha's reverie. She was suddenly annoyed with herself. Would there ever come a time when memories of Zack would no longer intrude on her life?

"I'm fine," she said with a smile, reclaiming the special warmth she'd felt earlier. Ted smiled back, not taking his eyes off the road as they made the turn from the highway onto the retirement home's drive.

"I'll let you out at the door," he said, carefully navigating the circular driveway that took incoming vehicles through a covered portico at the front entry.

"Can't you just leave the car here?" Samantha remarked absently, unfastening her safety belt.

Ted shook his head. "Might be in the way of an emergency vehicle."

"Of course. How stupid of me." Samantha wrapped her wool scarf tighter about her neck and got out. "I'll wait for you inside."

Closing the door, she watched him ease back out from under the portico and drive toward the almost empty visitors' parking lot. Samantha hurried into the neat brick building.

Samantha was glad she and Ted had been able to combine their visits. She'd almost postponed hers due to the weather, then he'd called and offered her a ride. She hadn't even known he was planning to come out here until then, though they'd been together last night. Samantha smiled. Her relationship with Ted had been a smooth progression since the clock had chimed 1986 into 1987 that night in her living room.

Apparently Ted was handling some ongoing concern for the Beaufort Twins. He rarely mentioned the legal matters he was involved with, a direct contrast to Samantha's habit of prattling on about whatever current thing she was writing, but she knew of his periodic visits to the sisters and that more was involved than just Jaycee business.

"Samantha, my dear."

Turning toward the voice, Samantha saw one subject of her recent thoughts bustling toward her: Miss Bessie Beaufort, all pink and round and beaming a smile of welcome.

Samantha felt herself immediately responding in kind. "Miss Bessie, you look positively fetching today. Is that a new dress?"

The old woman absolutely radiated pleasure, preening just a bit and waving a plump hand over the pink, lace-trimmed concoction that looked like it was designed for a Barbie doll. "Oh, this old thing? I've had it for ages, but you're such a dear to comment on it." Her old eyes twinkled merrily.

"Now, you wouldn't be all dressed up in honor of a certain young man's visit, would you?"

Miss Bessie leaned closer, placing a hand on Samantha's arm with a gesture of conspiracy. "Well, I won't say I did, and I won't say I didn't, but I will say one thing . . ." She darted her eyes past Samantha for a moment, then gave Samantha's arm a little squeeze. "I believe I'd have my work cut out for me if this is the certain young man to whom you're referring."

Samantha glanced around to see Ted standing just behind her, pulling off his gloves and reaching to smooth down the collar of his overcoat, which he'd raised against the wind. A smile hovered around the edges of his mouth.

Samantha turned back to the old woman in front of her,

giving her a look of wide-eyed innocence. "Why, Miss Bessie, whatever do you mean?"

Miss Bessie just chuckled good-naturedly, and releasing Samantha's arm, went over to greet Ted. "I do appreciate your coming, Mr. Nathan, and in such weather too."

Ted responded typically: a warm smile, a nod, a simple "Miss Beaufort" as he clasped the small plump hand she proffered, but evidencing the understated charm Samantha thought would no doubt appeal to anyone from the age of birth to a hundred.

Linking an arm with Ted, who had to bend slightly to accommodate her, Miss Bessie smiled back at Samantha. "I'm afraid I must claim your young man all to myself for a little while, dear, but I promise we won't be long."

"Take your time," Samantha replied, "but please go easy on the charm. It would break my heart if you steal him away, Miss Bessie."

Like a young girl, Miss Bessie giggled with delight. "My sister will be chaperoning every moment, Samantha dear," she said, and drew Ted off down the corridor toward her rooms, chattering away to him as they went.

Samantha shook her head in amusement. Shrugging off her coat and scarf, she hung them on the stand beside the door. Stupidly she hadn't worn gloves, winding up stuffing her hands into her pockets in search of an elusive heat. She blew onto her chilled fingers.

Retrieving her small portable tape recorder from a coat pocket, she went to curl up on one end of a couch to wait, deciding not to remove the old Merrillville Panthers toboggan pulled down around her ears. She had a fair idea of how her hair would look after being stuffed up under the cap.

The building was quiet. Samantha rechecked the batteries in her recorder for want of something better to do, then reached for a nearby magazine, leaned back, and began idly flipping through it. Not by nature a patient person, despite her protestations to the contrary, Samantha hoped Miss Bessie would be true to her word and not keep Ted long. Although anxious to continue the project that brought her here, with the weather kicking up outside it might be best to come back one day next week. After all, the series of articles on The Manse wouldn't be scheduled until mid- to late summer, depending on how many installments she finally ended up with.

The idea to do this series, publishing one a week during the five or six weeks leading up to the 13th House of Horrors, had begun that day with Miss Bessie, the same day Pearl Rollins had hinted at some untold truth. Samantha had visited the Beaufort Twins several times since, recording subsequent sessions for dissection at her leisure. So far, nothing had surfaced to strongly support Pearl's allegations. Still, she was getting some interesting bits and pieces for the projected series, so it wasn't a total loss.

Most of what she'd gotten predated Pearl's tenure at The Manse and fell into the category of selective reminiscence rather than outright fact. But the facts could be exhumed from old newspaper files, and what she was getting would make better copy for feature work, particularly if she contrasted it with the old news accounts.

As expected, Miss Bessie proved adept at steering their conversations into channels that suited her, whitewashing anything that might stigmatize her cherished home. She minimized the number and severity of unpleasant events,

maximized the elements of chance and rampant sensation-
alism, and never missed a chance to plug her restoration
hopes. She barely touched on anything that might have
been Pearl Rollins's cryptic happening, glossing over the
only two fairly recent incidents that fit the category of
traumatic: the accident that had claimed the lives of their
brother Avery and his wife; and the death of Edward, the
young man she'd once been engaged to, of pneumonia.

Miss Bessie had been understandably reluctant to discuss these tragedies, and Samantha had not insisted. She
had, however, looked up the newspaper account of the
more recent of the two events—Avery and Susannah Beaufort's accident—and found that the couple had fallen down
the main staircase at The Manse. Susannah had been killed
outright; Avery died several days later. There had been
some mention of a possible argument between the pair
prior to their fall, though the deaths had been ruled
accidental.

Thinking this might be a promising clue, Samantha had
sought out another source; but her attempts to interview
Pearl Rollins had met with stony silence and a softly
closed front door. Dood had refused to intervene, becoming a little miffed when he learned Samantha's objective
was commercially motivated, even though she assured him
she had no intention of exploiting Pearl Rollins in any
way. He'd wound up giving her a token lecture on the
respect of privacy. Since then he'd turned clam on the
subject, which, she supposed, was less unnerving than his
hoodoo routine of before. A shiver darted through her
body. Why was it she could joke about Dood's fixation
and still not find it funny?

"Your turn."

Samantha gave a startled jump at the sound of Ted's voice. She looked up at him, saying, "You know, you've got to quit sneaking up on me like that or I'm going to hang a bell around your neck. You keep surprising me."

The faint smile of amusement that Samantha was beginning to know so well softened his face. "Indeed . . ." An eyebrow lifted slightly.

Samantha found herself blushing. She pulled her gaze away from those steady gray eyes and rose, tossing the unread magazine back on the table, picking up her small tape recorder. "I won't stay long." She glanced outside. "In fact, if you think this weather's going to be a problem, we'll leave now. I can come back anytime, there's no real urgency to what I'm doing."

Ted shook his head, moving around the couch. "I think we can allow a bit longer before we risk getting snowed in. I'll wait for you here. I've got some notes to go over."

"Okay. But if I get too involved with Miss Bessie . . ."

"Understood." Ted smiled again.

Samantha headed down the corridor toward the Beaufort Twins' suite, glancing back at the man who had tossed his coat over the back of the couch and folded his lean body into the corner she'd vacated.

As she neared the bend in the corridor, a rather flashy-looking teenage girl passed her, headed toward the front room. The girl was carrying a steaming coffee mug in one hand. Samantha smiled. Somehow, she knew it was meant for Ted.

The cold midnight wind careened around the small frame

house, whistling a tuneless dirge as it tried to penetrate old boards and find loose windowpanes. Failing for the most part, the wind contented itself with whipping the falling snow into swirls and drifts and sending them against the obstacle in its path as though a feud were being waged with the small house. Occasionally the wind would moan its frustration, a mournful song to the darkness—and to the old woman lying awake and fearful in her bed.

Pearl Rollins lay as still as the death that steadfastly kept refusing to claim her, watching the snow rush by her bedroom window, each individual flake picked out and emphasized by the corner streetlight. It was as if a vengeful god had swung a powerful fist and shattered the day into a million tiny pieces, allowing them to fall onto the night. Often, Pearl lay awake in her bed and wondered if another day would greet these tired old eyes, wondered if the night demons would gobble her up with the sun and spit her out in hell. Lately it had been worse, because of what she knew, what she sensed coming.

There would be a reckoning. Pearl had felt it the moment her foot touched the tainted soil that day. She'd sensed it lying in wait.

Sudden tears stung fearful old eyes, blurring the snow-drenched window. Soon, there'd be no more waiting.

Chapter 13

Dood Hopkins followed his last customers to the door, shut and bolted it firmly behind them, then flipped the sign that hung midway down the glass to "Closed." It had taken his best effort to appear to be the friendly, joking Dood his video store's patrons expected, difficult to conceal his impatience as they dawdled over the shelves of tapes.

For weeks a plan had been fermenting in Dood's brain, a plan now aged and ready for taste-testing. *Tonight*, Dood told himself. *It would have to be tonight.*

Flicking off the showroom lights, he noticed it was already fully dark outside although five o'clock had just rolled in; the consequence of a late-February evening. Outside, a gusting, bitter wind sped by, giving the window a shake. Weather forecasters were predicting an ice storm for later; from the look of things it was already getting under way. A sudden spatter of rain mixed with sleet beat a quick tattoo across the glass. Dood retreated from the window.

Chain-smoking, he busied himself for a while, clearing away the miscellaneous clutter that had accumulated on the counter during the day. Dood knew he was simply marking time, putting off what he'd planned for tonight, postponing a solid commitment to his decision. It was not something that appealed to him—spending a night alone in the old Beaufort house—not something he wanted to do at all; but until he got some sort of hard, irrefutable evidence to support his claims, there'd be no convincing anyone of anything. Hell, if he couldn't convince Samantha and Ted, his closest friends . . .

Taking a deep breath, Dood went over to the cash register and punched "No Sale." When the drawer slid open, he lifted the money tray and removed a set of keys from among the checks and larger bills. It had been a good day for rentals, no doubt because of the impending storm that threatened to keep Merrillville homebound for the weekend. At the moment, however, Dood wasn't interested in his cash flow. Setting the tray back in place, he closed the drawer.

The idea had first occurred to him while visiting Pearl Rollins, when he'd asked her to come "feel out" The Manse. He'd spend the night inside the house, just barely inside the house, right up next to the open front door, in fact; no sense in pushing this thing *too* far. But something very strange was happening up there, of that Dood was certain; something not normal. He wanted to know what.

From its hiding place behind the counter, Dood took the box of equipment he'd assembled days ago, admitting that he wanted the answer for himself as much as for the others. Despite his big talk to Samantha and Ted, one small, nagging part of him still kept taunting: *Dood, boy, you've gone over the edge, here. You've finally blundered across the boundary and started seeing boogeymen.*

Dood freely acknowledged the bit of remaining doubt, the .001 percent of him that was laughing up a blizzard at what he was about to do, calling him twenty-seven kinds of crazy. Which is why he was going to The Manse tonight, armed with his portable video camera, prepared to confront things that go bump in the night.

The rest of him, the other 99.999 percent, was fucking scared to death.

Frigid wind, thin winter-steel blades, sliced up the alley between the back of Lawson's Real Estate and the west side of Gibson's warehouse and into the old packing crate where PoJo huddled miserably. Crumpled newspaper stuffed into the crate's many holes and seams did little to block the chill. PoJo stared dismally at the meager remains of his last bottle of rye. Only one good swallow or two half nips were left in the fifth that had gone so quickly on this brutal afternoon—remnants of warmth that would never see him through the night.

Already the storm was attacking PoJo's grizzled old body with a ruthless knowledge of his physical weaknesses. There was no more daylight to temper the harshness, no more newspaper to stuff in the cracks, no more rye to keep his blood warm and flowing against the bitter cold. PoJo

knew he had to move to get inside somewhere if he wanted
to wake up tomorrow. For a moment he pondered this
question, considered its options, turned it over in his mind.
Then, as he had before, the few times this particular
musing took him, he decided that yes, he did want to wake
up tomorrow.

Nesting his bottle into the pocket of his tattered pea coat,
PoJo carefully crawled out of the crate. *A fine place, that,*
PoJo thought to himself, looking back at the wooden
packing crate. *Gave a person some independence, some
space of his own.*

PoJo didn't like sleeping where other people slept, not
even on the road. He'd always gone off by himself—just
him and the night in an abandoned barn at the end of some
dirt road, or an empty train car down to the railroad yard
. . . or an old packing crate in a small-town alley. Of
course, there were a few places around town where PoJo
could go when rain and cold and ice storms drove him
indoors. Like the back storeroom out at the C&P, and the
rooming house over on Tate Street, and even the town jail
if it came to that. But the C&P was too far to walk this
night, and the rooming house lady had tried to rip him off
last time, and they'd gotten where they expected you to do
something wrong before they'd let you in down at the jail.
There was nothing wrong that PoJo wanted to do.

But there was always The Manse.

PoJo levered himself upright, feeling the protest of cold
bones and old muscles as they unfolded. He stretched his
arms and legs to get them moving like they ought, then
reached back down into the crate and pulled out a handful
of crumpled newspaper. This, he stuffed inside his shirt as

extra protection against the furious wind. Crimping up his collar, he stuck his hands in his pockets and headed down the alley at his usual shuffling gait. Better to face the elements now, while he still had some staying power, than later, when they'd get the upper hand.

As he rounded the corner of Lawson's Realty and stepped out onto the sidewalk, PoJo felt the first icy needles of rain sting his face. He'd been better sheltered in his alleyway than he'd suspected. Shoving gloveless hands deeper into pockets, PoJo bunched his arms together, forcing the pea coat tighter around him. Missing buttons were an open invitation to the searching wind. Head bowed, shoulders hunched, PoJo turned and started walking toward The Manse, glancing up now and then to take a bearing on his destination.

The old house looked stark and cold, strangely foreboding. Glimpses of it, slotted in between slim black tree trunks, reminded him of a row of tall, marble-white cemetery monuments standing silent and aloof from the coming storm. It should have drawn him with a promise of shelter and protection, but instead it seemed to repel him slightly, look angrily at him from its dark, lead-paned windows, glazed with ice.

Stinging rain was fast becoming sleet as the dropping temperature kept pace with nightfall. PoJo's joints felt stiff and frozen, his feet thick and numb in their paper-lined shoes. Only the tiny explosions of pain that greeted each step continued to assure him they were still alive and walking.

His shuffling gait became a jerky quickstep as he reached the intersection and cut a diagonal path across the street, bypassing the concrete stairs that led up to the front yard of The Manse. PoJo never used those stairs. He always went around by the side driveway to avoid the risk of being seen by anyone on Main Street. Of course there was no one out tonight to see an old bum trespass forbidden ground, but the habits of time run deep.

Up the long, winding drive. PoJo dipped his head against a sudden blast of arctic wind that went tearing across the open space at the top of the hill. He moved on forward, around the wooden swing gate, on toward the side of the house, pushing through the wind that seemed bent on attacking him. Somewhere a loose shutter was banging a discordant rhythm against its wooden facing. Behind him a muttered creaking moved with the wind through the trees, leafless branches rubbed and scraped against one another, an abrasive, whispery sound. Sleet pelted the rooftops and gravel driveway around him—a dull, crackly noise. It was like swimming through a bowl of Rice Krispies.

The earlier rain had become a thin overlay of ice, giving a dark sheen to the grounds and paths. PoJo moved as swiftly as possible toward the back of the house. Something in the air made him want to slip in unannounced, get away from the murmuring trees and lead-paned eyes. For a moment he almost turned around, almost let himself fall prey to the prickle of disquiet that moved across his shoulder blades. But now the wind was at his back, urging him toward the cellar stairs, making him almost run to stay with it, and he didn't have the strength to fight his way back through that again.

And then he was gazing down into the abyss where the

flight of steps dropped away like a narrow chasm slashed in stone.

PoJo couldn't see the bottom landing, could barely make out where his window indented the left-hand wall. It had been a while since he'd come here, he realized. The last time had been about the time those kids disappeared. PoJo recalled some talk they'd been here that night, maybe broken in. But nothing had turned up to prove it, and the talk had died away. It was possible, though. What PoJo had found could be found by others. They might have discovered this entry to The Manse. PoJo wondered if he might find it closed to him now, wondered if he'd be forced to go somewhere else, after all.

Remembrance flashed: the last time he'd spent the night here, something about being uncomfortable—not hard-floor, too-cold, sore-bone uncomfortable, but the restless, uneasy kind, the kind made of bad dreams and murky thoughts that left a sourness coiled in the pit of your stomach like yesterday's dinner gone bad.

PoJo sloughed the memory aside.

Withdrawing his left hand from the pocket of his coat, he carefully balanced himself against the house, aware of the potential treachery of ice-slicked steps. Firmly placing his feet, PoJo began his descent, feeling immediate relief as he moved into the house's protection, a windbreak against the gusting storm. The feeling moved with him down the stairs, giving him a false sense of warmth, making him feel safe. Walking across the grounds of The Manse, he'd felt exposed, defenseless . . . and painfully cold. All he wanted now was to get inside the house, away from the sounds of the night and the storm, burrow himself into a silent room, and sleep away the hours of darkness.

PoJo reached for his window, placing his stiff hand against it with a quick shove. The window refused to budge. PoJo saw that ice had formed a seal around the window frame. Bringing his right hand up to reinforce his left, he began rapping sharply at the thin coating of ice, moving along the windowsill as it cracked apart and fell away. Small jagged shards of ice shattered on the concrete steps with little tinkling sounds like slivers of dying crystal. When he'd finished going all the way around the window, PoJo placed both hands against it and again gave a quick, hard shove. The window popped open.

Immediately PoJo noticed the smell. Sour. Rotten. A dead smell. Something had gotten trapped and died inside this cellar, was decomposing in there. A cat, maybe. PoJo wrinkled up his nose, hesitating.

Like a banshee, the wind howled above him, curling through the upper air with a wail that stung his ears the way the freezing rain was stinging his face and gloveless hands. PoJo shrugged and began lifting his body up onto the window ledge, anxious to get inside the house. He could stand the smell. He'd smelled worse.

For the past two weeks, Dood Hopkins had been on caretaker duty up at The Manse. For the past two weeks, the keys and general checkout responsibilities had been his. And for two weeks, he'd been planning his pajama party.

Each day for fourteen days, Dood had told himself, "Tonight's the night." Each day for fourteen days, he'd planned to head on up to the old Beaufort house sometime after dark and settle in for a night of wait-and-see that he half hoped, half feared would become show-and-tell. And each night, for thirteen nights, he'd chickened out.

Tonight was his last chance. Tomorrow the keys to the kingdom would be passed on to the next Jaycee in line. Thirteen down and no more to go. Dood picked up his equipment, turned off all the inside lights, and headed out the door.

It had to be tonight.

PoJo stood inside the basement. The blackness around him was total, thick almost to the point of making it difficult to breathe. Above him, the cellar window was lost in darkness, giving no indication of its existence.

Bitter cold clogged the cellar; a tighter cold than outside, a slab of solid cold, thick like the darkness. PoJo's whole body was becoming numb with it, a dull, aching sensation like he'd traveled long and hard with a dead carcass flung across his shoulders and draped down the length of him.

Gingerly, PoJo began to feel his way across the cellar floor. He thought he was moving toward the stairs that would take him up into the house proper, but he could find no reference point, no familiar guidepost. The table that usually stood midway between the window and the inside staircase had apparently been moved—or maybe he'd passed it without knowing. Disorientation crawled around the edges of his mind.

Something skittered across the floor to his right—a rat? —and was gone. The silence was almost as thick as the cold and darkness. The distant moaning of the wind and the muffled *ka'thump-a'thump* of a loose shutter sounded hollow and illusive, giving no indication of which way was right, which left.

PoJo stumbled against something, reached out and felt the broken remnants of a chair. He grasped it firmly, a buoy to hold on to for a moment, get his bearings. The brief stirring of fear receded. PoJo moved on.

His body was becoming sluggish now, his feet leaden; he had difficulty picking them up and moving them forward, like trying to walk underwater. A languor invaded his steps, his thoughts, almost as though he were caught up in one of those dreams where you keep trying harder and harder to go forward, to get away from something coming after you.

Air lapped against him, thick, heavy with the undercurrent of his passing. PoJo felt as though he were swimming across the room, triggering ripples and waves that went spreading out toward the corners to lap against the surrounding cellar walls. He could almost hear the vibration of their movement, hear the undulation of the cold, dank air. PoJo shivered as a tickle, like the delicate touch of a woman's finely shaped fingernails, slid up his back and onto his neck, making the stubble of coarse hairs spring apart on the grizzled nape.

And suddenly PoJo felt the fear that had touched him earlier take hold again, making him feel something he'd felt before—once when he'd thought himself alone in a railroad car and had almost given himself up to the vulnerability of sleep; once when he'd crawled into an old tobacco shed somewhere in Virginia to nurse off a

drunk—*eyes!* Stabbing into his back, pinpointing him like
a target on a carny's shooting gallery! It almost knocked
him over with its intensity.

PoJo whirled around, slinging his gaze left and right
across the blackness that surrounded him. Rawness gripped
his throat. He swallowed painfully. There was nothing
there. Nothing!

Lunging forward, PoJo crashed across the cellar, raking
obstacles from his path until at last he stumbled against the
stairs. Grappling blindly, he found the wooden handrail,
welcoming the pain as splinters of wood dug into his palm.
He climbed as quickly as he could. Below him the darkness
had begun to eddy, forming a whirlpool to suck him back
down. Grasping the banister with his right hand and brac-
ing himself against the wall with his left, PoJo forced his
body up the stairs, fighting for each step, pulling against
the undertow trying to claim him.

*Hurry, hurry, get up the steps, get up the steps before
something starts coming up after you, before something
gets close enough to twine cold fingers around your ankles
and your throat and pull you down—*

PoJo could sense the darkness reaching for him, feel a
mist of cold, fetid breath swirling about him like a cloud,
coming up behind him.

The storm was coming, no doubt about it. Dood hugged
his parka tighter, pulling at the drawstring that held the
hood snugly around his face. Sleet continued to fall, harder
now, little stinging pellets that grazed his cheeks every
time he glanced up.

The box under his arm was proving a bulky encumbrance. He wished he'd left it back at the store. What did he need camera equipment for, anyway? Taking home movies of The Manse's resident ghost? *"That's it . . . smile . . . no, a little more to the left . . . Got it!"* Stupid.

Dood thought about another stupid piece of equipment he'd tucked into a corner of the box and brought along for the ride: a little blue and white plastic dashboard saint, bought recently on a whim, and because the store was temporarily out of wooden crosses. Had he really thought the $2.49 petroleum by-product made in Taiwan might protect him? He'd just as well have stuffed his pockets with garlic.

"Dood, my man, you've popped your cork and the wine's gone sour," he murmured to the icy wind, feeling its cold and discomfort roam every part of his body. With an ironic shake of his head, he began to whistle the lilting refrain of "I don't care if it rains or freezes, long as I've got my plastic Jesus . . ." trudging on down Main Street, moving firmly on the salted sidewalks that fronted business doorways, stepping more carefully over the icy in-betweens, threading an obstacle course.

He hefted the box of equipment more firmly under his left arm. Wouldn't do to drop it now. Might break something vital, and that would mean he'd have to abandon this night's work, think of another way to make an ass of himself.

He didn't want to do this, he decided.

"I don't want to do this," he muttered as he inched across the next slick spot. Still, he continued to move along the sidewalk, a cold, frightened man travelin' on down the road.

"Lay down, music . . ." Dood breathed out the chorus of a Dead Red Sampson blues song between frosty puffs of air. *"Lay down, sound . . ."* He heard the quiver in his voice, the slightly off-key pitch. *"Lay it down on de nightnin' time, where da blue notes can be found."*

He stopped singing. He'd reached the end of Main Street.

With a reluctance that exceeded anything he'd ever experienced before, Dood slowly lifted his face to the punishing night and stared across at The Manse . . .

With a jolt that wrung a tight, thin cry from his gut, PoJo slammed into the inside of the cellar door. Grappling for the doorknob in a frenzy as new to him as the feeling of killing fright exploding his insides, he twisted at the handle. Then he was bursting through, into the hallway, slamming the door behind him, stumbling along the corridor that led to the front entry hall of The Manse.

The huge double doors loomed up in front of him, the pale black fan above and twin strips on either side framing them and providing an immediate touchstone. Breathless with exertion, sweat pasting his clothes to his body and streaming down the sides of his face, PoJo scrambled into a corner of the entryway and sank down beside the double doors, his back to the walls, sliding slowly to the floor. At some point during his headlong flight, the sound of his own heartbeat had eclipsed the thumping of the broken shutter.

PoJo listened to his heartbeat, marveling at what had just occurred. Never in his life had he experienced such . . . panic? Was that the word he was looking for? Was

that what had just happened to him in the cellar? Had he
panicked in the dark, like a greenhorn kid on his first rail
ride?

PoJo leaned back against the wall and closed his eyes.
Panic. He studied on the word. *A strange feeling, that.
Allays good to have a little fear about you. Keep you
sharp. Keep you ready. But this here panic . . .* PoJo
shook his head, tried to think some more about it, then
merely shook his head once more.

Calm was easing down on him again. The pounding in
his ears had quieted, the jumping in his chest stilled. Black
wasn't the only color he saw. He could make out forms
and shapes around him, outlined by the hint of light seeping in through the windows here and in the large room to
his right. The curtains must have been left open to catch
what daytime light and warmth would come in. Though no
moon shone this night, streetlights in the town below were
lit, and some of that light, however diluted, was falling on
the front of The Manse and seeping in. It helped to steady
him.

As though waking from a nightmare, PoJo realized he
had begun to shiver with hard, jolting spasms. He couldn't
control it, couldn't hold himself still—

Exposure!

The word shot across his mind with a searing flash of
alarm. Years on the road had conditioned his body to all
sorts of hardships—hunger, weather, pain. You learned to
endure such things. But there was a boundary, a fine line
of survival, and PoJo was well aware that exposure was a
chief killer of street people like himself.

He started to get up—and felt panic return when his

body at first refused to obey. He waited a minute, then slowing his actions down, tried it again and managed this time to regain his feet.

Holding on to the wall for support, he stood there surveying the situation. His body was shaking violently now, rigors of involuntary tremors rolling over him. Was he going into shock? He needed to get warm, had to get warm.

Build a fire, that was it. He could make it to the room with the fireplace, find something to burn. He had matches. *Allays* had matches on the road.

Abandoning his corner, PoJo inched along the wall to his right, moving toward the arched opening that led into the large front sitting room. He knew the layout from previous visits, was sure he'd find some ready kindling in the woodbin. He thought the Jaycees sometimes used this room for club doings.

Around the arch and along the inside wall. PoJo patted the wall with his left hand in front of him, trailing his right along beside him for balance. Hand met brick. The fireplace. PoJo patted his way across the opening to the other side where the fire bin was. There. He patted his hand inside the hole set into the brick wall. Wood. Small and midsized pieces, dry as old bones in the desert.

PoJo withdrew several of the larger sticks, tucked them into the crook of his left arm, then scooped up some kindling. He moved back to the fireplace.

At the end of the room, two long windows shed just enough diffuse light to see by. As PoJo had suspected, the curtains were open. He'd have to close them to keep this fire from being seen—but after, *after* he'd built it, not now. PoJo didn't want the total darkness back again.

Kneeling on the cold tile hearth, PoJo laid down his armload of wood, opened the flue, and began pyramiding the kindling, breaking a couple of smaller sticks to lay beneath the teepeed structure. Once he had this little fire going, shedding some light, he'd go close the drapes, then lay the larger wood across the dog irons.

PoJo worked in silence, shivers periodically racking his wizened body. The convulsive shudders of moments before had receded. Being up and moving had brought enough warmth to his old bones to stave off shock.

All at once he remembered the remains in his bottle of rye. He started to pull it out, amazed that he'd forgotten it till now. It should have been the first thing he'd thought about when the shivering had taken him over. His hand stopped only a couple of inches away from the pocket where his bottle nested. Maybe it was better to get this fire going first, get some warmth on him before taking some inside.

Soon the fire was laid. PoJo got out a match, struck it against the rough brick, and held it to the chips of kindling. In moments, a small flame began dancing and crackling its way up the steeple of sticks. PoJo waited until he was sure it had lit, then struggled to his feet and loped over to close the curtains. Wavery light cavorted along the hardwood floor and rippled up the wall in front of him, sparkling off the ice-glazed windows that looked out on the front yard of The Manse. PoJo hurried, fearful his firelight would be seen even in a town snugged in by the storm.

The small fire was blazing merrily now. PoJo banked a couple of larger logs across the dog irons and watched the flame leap up and around them. He couldn't let it get too big or they might see the light in town, even through the curtains. He was taking a chance on the chimney smoke, but with the wind and sleet and darkness, it should be okay.

The dry wood caught quickly; PoJo added two more sticks and sat back on his haunches, letting the glow of the fire spread warmth and light over his thin, cold body.

Wouldn't be like this in Flarida, nosir, thought PoJo as the fire began to counteract the frigid air. *Be sun allays shinin', that. Just like little Jenny's pitchurs, be sun allays shinin'.*

It was time to move on. Always when he stayed a spell somewhere, he ran the risk of getting cornered in, getting bit by the stayin' bug. Wouldn't do to sit down on a spot too long, might get your tail in a crack, sprout out a root or something. But no matter how long he stayed somewhere, PoJo seemed to have a knack of knowing when leaving time had come.

Tomorrow, next day for sure, PoJo knew he'd be hitting the road again, heading on south. Things had changed here lately, got . . . different. Things wasn't comfortable no more.

PoJo wiped the sleeve of his coat across his nose, which had begun to run as the warmth of the fire bathed his face. *Time to move on, yessir. Git on down to Flarida.*

Taking the almost empty bottle of rye from his coat pocket, PoJo sat back, started to screw off the cap, then instead stretched himself out lengthwise in front of the

fireplace, just at the edge of the hearth. Hugging the bottle
to him, he stared into the dancing flame. He might have a
wee sup in a minute, but right now he was content to just
lie here holding it, watching the fire, feeling its warmth
creep up the length of him. *A fine feeling, that, to be safe
and warm . . .*

Sleep took him, a dream-hazed semiconscious reality
where thoughts and memories and fancies raced by, yet
where he still felt the hard cold floor beneath him, the
warmth of the flickering fire. He saw his Marlie, with
baby Jenny at her breast, saw the tired brown eyes, the
sadness; he saw another Jenny, his little Jenny, little laughing girl, running toward him with her hands stretched up,
chubby hands that would pat the stubble on his face when
he caught her to him. He saw the woman he had slept with
once in Pittsburgh, he didn't know her name; saw the body
of the kid who'd tumbled from a moving train. He saw it
all, and more; and through the visions watched a man
grow old with life and fate and wondered why it seemed
not sad to him, but good . . .

Dood Hopkins was colder than he'd ever been in his
life. Sleet beat down on him and wind tore around him like
he was a personal vendetta to some celestial malevolent.

"Did I ask for this?" Dood murmured, glancing up at
the pitch-black heavens, a mistake made evident as a piece
of sleet struck him in the left eye. "Shit!" Dood swiped at
the eye that was already tearing from the bitter wind.

It was going to take every ounce of will he possessed
not to turn around and go home, to make himself step off
this curb and walk across that street and climb up those

stairs and go into The Manse. For just a moment, earlier, he'd thought he'd seen light flickering up there, *two* lights, in fact, like two bloodred eyes blinking open in a pale white face. For just a moment the house had looked like a huge, misshapen head, a monstrous head trying to come awake, heavy eyelids twitching open. It had stopped him cold. But then the illusion had vanished, and it was just a house up there, just a big old house waiting for him to come see what was what. An enigma, it stood there now— silent, dark, a challenge to innocence.

Dood felt his jaw tighten; he straightened his shoulders. This was something he had to do, tonight, something he was damn well going to do. With narrowed eyes, clenched teeth, and sleet raining down around him, he stepped off the curb . . .

Movement woke PoJo. The sensation of being in motion. His eyes flew open, and he stared at the wall. Somehow he'd twisted himself around sideways while asleep; his body lay perpendicular to the fireplace now, head farthest away, feet up close. He seemed to be moving— very slowly, but moving—sliding across the floor. He could feel a gentle pull on his left leg.

With the absolute caution born of too many precarious encounters on the road, PoJo began to raise his head for a look-see. Strangely he wasn't afraid, merely curious. Around him the firelight seemed to be festering with an eerie, luminescent quality, a whiter, harsher light than the golden twinkle of before or the burnished red gleam you'd expect from dwindling embers.

Slowly PoJo lifted his head, craning his old neck side-

ways and into position for a look down the length of his
body. Apparently his waking up hadn't alerted whoever
was pulling him—he was still in motion, could feel the
steady tug against his leg, though he didn't feel a hand.

A quick whistling sound, like pressure being released
from a vacuum seal, split the silence as PoJo sucked a
lungful of air through his teeth. What he was seeing, what
he was looking at, couldn't be real—*it couldn't be real!*

PoJo's eyes were riveted on his left leg, lids freezing
open, pupils dilating to stare wildly at the coil of blue-
white flame encircling his foot. Slowly, inexorably, a
tentacle of fire was coiling around his ankle—and pulling
him toward the fireplace!

Several abstract observations stood out against the single, impossible scene confronting him:

One: The fire was burning brighter now, glowing with a
crystal whiteness that looked icelike rather than molten;

Two: There was nothing to support it, fuel it, the wood
he'd stoked it with was gone; and

Three: There was no sense of heat, no warmth, not in
the air, not on his face, not against his ankle where the fire
had hold of him. There was *fire* wrapped around his foot,
but he wasn't being burned!

A soft growl eased out of PoJo as he levered himself up
by his elbows, an animal sound that came without being
called. He placed his hands on the floor to anchor himself
against the pull, realized his bottle of rye was still clutched
tightly in one, and stuck it in his pocket. His left foot had
reached the edge of the tile hearth now and was completely
wrapped in flame; a rope of fire had begun curling up his
leg.

Experimentally, PoJo gave a quick tug; the pressure on his leg increased. Bending his right leg, he tried to flatten his foot against the floor, get some leverage to push against. Using his arms and hands to reinforce the effort, he jerked his left leg back . . . once, again . . . then harder, alternately kicking out and pulling against the thing that held him.

Somewhere in the back alleys of his mind, PoJo wondered if he might be still asleep, might be dreaming up this nightmare, though he couldn't begin to fathom the well it might have sprung from. Little grunts punctuated his efforts. Little puffs of breath condensed on the cold, dank air.

In a burst of frenzy, PoJo strained and jerked against the horror that had him by the leg, the thing that was pulling him in. He was halfway across the hearth now, inching ever closer to the gaping, grinning fireplace. His right foot managed to get a toehold on the inner edge where brick met tile, but kept slipping when he shoved his weight against it.

Thrusting himself to a sitting position, PoJo started kicking at the coil of flame, scraping his right shoe down across his left calf and ankle in an attempt to dislodge the fire-demon. But it kept spreading around his leg, slithering past his knee, spiraling up his thigh like the glowing tongue of some hellish giant whose mouth was the open, gaping wound of the fireplace beyond.

Suddenly PoJo felt a rage of searing, blinding fury explode inside him, erupt out of him with a cry of savage ferocity! "Damn you! Goddamn you to hell! You sonuvabitch ain't going to have me! I'll fight you, *fight you plenty, fight you down!*''

He screamed his fury at the hungry fire, eyes flashing hatred into the glowing white maw that had opened in front of him.

With a burst of strength that might have been a memory pulled from younger times, PoJo engaged the fire in battle. Grimly he struggled against the hand of flame that held him, rocking his body from side to side, clawing at the floor, the hearth, his pants leg. Still the fire-hand pulled him in, new fingers of it stretching, coiling, completely encircling his leg. And now a little offshoot had jumped across to the right leg, was snaking its way upward there . . .

Tears of anger swelled in PoJo's burning, glittery eyes. He felt them break away and run down his face, shook his head violently to be rid of them. There'd be no tears for this—not from anger, and goddammit not from fear; he wouldn't have it! He'd done with fear, used it all up down there in the basement. This thing could have his anger, but it wouldn't get his fear!

PoJo saw his left foot enter the glowing maw. For a moment he stopped his struggle to marvel at the sight. Piece by piece, bit by bit, his foot began to disappear. Still there was no pain, but PoJo knew his foot was gone. It was as though the fire was eating him!

A snarl of frenzy tore loose and broke away, peeling lips back from clenched teeth in a feral grin that convulsed PoJo's face into a rictus of ferocity. ''You sonuvabitch, *you goddamned sonuvabitch!*'' he gasped through gritted teeth, fighting with a renewed fury that demanded every inch of him, every molecule and atom . . .

He felt the floor beneath him change, felt smooth, cold tile slide under him. The fire held both legs now, firmly, inescapably. His left leg was gone up to the knee, and as PoJo watched in horror, his right foot slipped into the maw. Now he felt pain intrude—but not from his legs! The pain was in his hands and fingers, where he'd beat and scraped them raw. In frustration he'd been pounding his fists against the hearth.

The fire had him up to the thighs now. He heard a low keening fill the silence and realized it was seeping out of him. Dizziness spun his head, a swimming sensation like standing up too fast after drinking rotgut. But he couldn't stand up—his legs were gone—the sonuvabitch had eaten his legs!

Light blinded him, brilliant like a welder's arc. He felt himself spinning into a void, slipping down into a tunnel of light. The top rim of the fireplace loomed in front of him. Like a drowning man, he grabbed hold of the edge, digging raw fingers into brick, discarding the protest that screamed through his hands and arms. The pressure against him increased—demanding, pulling—and now there *was* pain, gushing up through his groin like stabs of lightning. It was tearing him apart!

PoJo felt his teeth grind together as he hung on to the edge of the fireplace. Tears seeped from his tightly shut eyes. He tried not to think about what was happening, tried to shut it out.

He remembered his bottle.

Anchoring his right hand and arm more firmly on the upper ledge of the fireplace, PoJo clawed the bottle from his pocket. With his teeth, he unscrewed the cap, a ragged

laugh punching through the grunts and gasps of effort. All
at once the cap came off in his mouth. He spit it at the
fireplace, and with a cry of triumph held the whiskey aloft,
shaking the bottle at the flames that steadily continued
sucking him in.

"Here's to Joe Clark!" he screamed at the blinding fire.
"Here's to old Joe Clark!"

With a jerk of his arm, PoJo gulped down the rye. Raw
liquor coursed inside him, an avalanche of burning warmth
and comfort, just like always. For a moment he savored it,
cherished it, held it to him.

Then, in a final act of anger and defiance, PoJo flung
the empty bottle into the midst of the flames.

There was no sound of breaking glass, no explosion of
fragmenting bottle against brick fireplace, only a brief
flicker of blue-white light at the center of the flame,
quickly gone. And with its going, something flowed out of
PoJo, leaving him stranded and uncertain on the brink of a
glowing pit. He felt his grip on the fireplace ledge weaken,
felt the sudden tearing pain of rending muscles and broken
tendons as his arm was pulled away. Hands grasped and
clawed at the brick trying to hold on, but there was
nothing left to cling to, nothing left to hold. He felt the
well opening beneath him, saw a swirling brightness . . .

Like a ghost, Marlie's sorrow-scarred face flashed by
him; he saw his little Jenny's chubby, reaching hand, tried
to grab hold . . . but he couldn't do that, couldn't take her
down with him! Then it was gone; a dream-vision of white
sand and dazzling skies sped by . . .

From some unknown depth within him a cry welled up,

a final, screaming curse of despair and helplessness thrown out into the darkness and the night.

From the house in front of him Dood heard the beginning of a cry—a low wailing sound, a moan, barely human, riding on the wind. He froze, staring up at The Manse, feeling that keening wail creep into him, squirm beneath his skin like thousands of crawling ants until he thought he would scream with the invasion.

He took a step backward, hardly crediting what was beginning to happen, what was taking shape across the yard. An unearthly glow had begun to rise amid the surrounding whiteness, as though some unholy parody of life was returning to a corpse. There was no mistaking the sudden gleam of eyes this time, the sudden awareness—hollow, sunken sockets being filled with sight; rabid, virulent hunger focusing; his incarnate nightmare coming to life in front of him, screaming to be fed, *trying to be born!*

And it was looking at him—ChristJesus—*it was looking straight at him!*

Dood didn't feel the box tumble from beneath his arm as he stumbled backward—faster, faster, turning to plunge back down the cement stairs, tumbling down the last few to the street below. Then he was picking himself up, running across the street toward the safety of town, casting little panicked glances over his shoulder as he ran, slid, grappled his way across the icy pavement.

He heard the horrible cry choke off; he saw the gleaming eyes dim across the darkness.

Another cry split the night—his own—he couldn't seem to stem it.

Dood looked around frantically as he ran, searching the empty sidewalks, the streets devoid of traffic. "Don't you see what's up there?" he screamed at the dark and empty businesses he passed. "Can't you fucking *see*?"

Past Tully Ryerson's photo shop he ran, past the Merrillville café . . . everything was closed and dark, everyone was gone. "Is nobody going to see?" Dood flung at the silent town, hearing tears of fright diluting and choking his voice, feeling them freezing on his face as finally, *finally*, he reached his own dark and empty window.

Hands shaking almost out of control, Dood managed to get his key, unlock the door, and throw it open. He fell into the room, slamming his body against the door to close it, flipping on the inside lights, sinking down into a sobbing pile of terror on the floor beside the door.

Outside, the wind howled as it raced past the window; sleet beat a staccato pattern across the glass. Dood flung his head from side to side, tears streaming down his face, heart pounding against his chest and in his ears.

"Can't anybody out there fucking see . . . ?" he whispered to the empty room.

Chapter 14

"**P**eople are *disappearing*, for Chrissake!" Dood shouted, banging his fist down on the table in front of him, causing heads around the Merrillville Coffee Shop to turn toward him.

Samantha reached out and placed her hand on Dood's tightly clenched fist. "Calm down, L.J. You're going to get us thrown out of here."

For a moment, Dood seemed about to rebel, then the hand under hers went limp and his taut body slumped into acquiescence. "Okay, okay." His other hand stubbed out a cigarette in the overflowing ashtray, then darted across his mouth and chin, a spasmodic little act of nervousness—involuntary, and completely uncharacteristic.

What's happened to him? Samantha looked across the table at a man she hardly recognized. Gone was the natty

dresser, the immaculate, urbane L. J. Hopkins of before.
Gone was the casual elegance, the carefree nonchalance,
the offhand wit. Dood was crumpled, lackluster, and needed
a shave. He looked like he hadn't eaten a good meal in
days or slept well in weeks. And Samantha knew from talk
around town that his video store was staying closed more
and more of the time.

The beautiful late-March day stared in through the window of the coffee shop as though trying to understand why
these people were huddled inside instead of out enjoying
the bright morning sunshine. Coffee and Danish were
hardly a choice prize with spring up for grabs.

Samantha removed her hand from Dood's and sat back,
taking a moment to gaze out the window. Instead of easing
her disquiet, the brilliance of the day merely seemed to
underline the darkness of her thoughts. *Get hold of yourself, Samantha*, she took herself sternly to task, turning
back to Dood.

"All right, L.J. *Who's* disappearing?"

Dood gave a derisive little snort and shook his head.
"Can't you see what's happening? First it was those two
kids, Buddy Grey and the little Dawson boy's older brother;
now PoJo's gone." He pierced her with a look. "There
may even be others we don't know about, runaways,
transients—people disappear all the time these days without question. We simply shrug them out of existence!"

Samantha nodded in agreement, punching down an ici-
cle of doubt, keeping her movements slow and steady, her
words logical and calm. Dood seemed right on the verge
of explosion. "I know, L.J.—the invisible people that
walk among us. I did an article on them once, remember?

But there's no evidence of any other disappearances, and the three you mentioned can be explained."

"Yeah, sure." Dood flicked his lighter, held a flame to another cigarette, and inhaled deeply. "Two teenage runaways and a broken-down hobo who decided to go south for the winter. But there's no proof that that's what happened."

"There *is* proof," Samantha interrupted stubbornly, hearing doubt roughen her voice. "PoJo's been talking about going to Florida for years, and Vince Colletti said—"

Dood had started shaking his head from side to side the moment she began this recital, and now he cut her off: "Vince Colletti! I wouldn't believe that smart-mouthed little bastard if he was strung up to a lie detector and shot full of sodium pentothal."

Samantha felt her calmness slipping away, felt the cold sliver of fear inching upward. She leaned forward, anchoring her arms on each side of her empty coffee mug. "Well, what happened to them, then? You tell me."

"The house got them." Dood shook his head. "God, I know that sounds ridiculous!" He jammed his cigarette in the ashtray and leaned toward her, lowering his voice to a hiss. "But it's there, Samantha. It's there. I saw it."

"You saw *what?* C'mon, Dood, give me specifics!"

"I don't know. Eyes . . . *something!* It was looking right at me!"

Dood shuddered with the memory, and Samantha felt her body echo the movement.

"Believe me, Samantha, it's there." He dropped his forehead down onto his raised fists, talking to the tabletop. "It's there."

Samantha clasped her hands together and brought the gathered thumbs to her mouth, expelling breath as if trying to warm them. She was aware of Dood's nighttime foray up to The Manse several weeks ago, aware something had happened that scared him badly. She and Ted had talked to him several times since then; he'd been vague about specifics but almost frenzied in his warnings to stay away from the Beaufort estate. Ted thought Dood might be bordering on some sort of mental breakdown. Samantha didn't know what to think, but something in Dood's voice today, something in his eyes, was wreaking havoc with her common sense. She didn't want to believe him, *couldn't* believe this madness might be real—yet his words reached down and gripped the seed of doubt that lay at the pit of her stomach. A sudden gut-level fear wrenched at her self-control.

She replaced her folded hands on the table, clasping them tightly, unwilling to see if they would betray her by trembling. "Okay, it's there. What do you think it is?" Her voice held the tremble.

Dood raised his head slightly; his gaze locked on her hands. He reached out a tentative finger as though to touch them, drew it back without doing so, then lifted his eyes to hers. "Do you remember what Pearl Rollins told us? Remember what she said?

" *'There's been a lot of fear in this old house,'* she told us. *'A lot of fear deposited in this place.'* And it's true." His eyes narrowed slightly as they bored into Samantha's. "You know it's true. Not from just what we've been doing for the past twelve years with our haunted house routine, but from way before that, right from the beginning. It's there in those stories you've been getting from Miss Bessie.''

Samantha nodded slowly. For months now she'd been visiting Miss Bessie, listening to the history of The Manse, hearing about its triumphs, but between the lines, learning more about its tragedies.

Samantha shivered. She could still remember the chill she'd felt that day Miss Bessie had chattered on and on about the little girl who'd been trapped in the basement during the house's construction and spent three days in cold, dark terror before being found, alive but permanently insane.

Yes, The Manse had its share of tragedies.

"But those were all perfectly explainable occurrences, L.J.," Samantha insisted, as much for herself as for him, "spanning several generations. If there's a common denominator, I don't—"

"Fear!" Dood interrupted. "The common denominator is fear! Pearl Rollins asked us, *What* is *fear*? Remember, Samantha? *What does it do? Where does it go?*"

Dood ran a distracted hand through his unkempt hair. "What if this fear, this *aura* of fear, is growing stronger with each event? What if it's—I don't know—being fed by these incidents? Intensified somehow? Maybe even instigating or encouraging them?" He pierced her with a look. "Don't tell me you haven't noticed how oddly people behave up there—like normal reactions are being stimulated into some sort of exaggerated emotional high."

Dood brought his hands back to the table, laying them out before him, palms up, as though in supplication. "Could this intensity, this emphasized emotion, concentrated each

year by our House of Horrors, added to what's already
been deposited there . . ."

He stopped speaking, staring at Samantha with a look
that seemed to ask, *Do you want it all? Do you want to go
over the edge with me and see what's there?*

She nodded, once.

"What if it's evolving into something *alive*?"

They stared at each other as though neither of them
could believe what Dood had just said. The silence stretched
until Samantha felt she would scream with the tension.
"Look, L.J., there've been people up at The Manse since
your—" She waved her hands, searched for a proper
word, and finally settled for "encounter." "I've been on
caretaker duty myself—"

In a sudden frenzied motion, Dood's hand clamped
around her wrist. "Don't go in that house, Samantha!
Stay away from there! Promise me you won't go back
inside—promise!"

People were turning to look at them again.

"L.J. . . ."

With a quick oath, Dood released her and stood up.
"It's there, Samantha," he said quietly, looking down at
her upturned face, his voice growing dull, lifeless. "Believe me, it's up there." Without another word, he strode
from the coffee shop.

Samantha took several deep breaths, absently rubbing
her abused wrist. Confusion held her, logic pulling one
way and instinct another. She almost found herself believ-
ing Dood; after all, he was her *friend*, and he seemed so
certain. But what he'd told her was absurd. Wasn't it?

She sighed. Maybe Ted was right. Maybe she ought to try and convince Dood to see a doctor.

"More coffee?"

Samantha jumped, casting a startled glance at the waitress who had appeared at her elbow, pot in hand.

She covered the top of her mug. "No, no thank you. I've had enough."

The waitress smiled down at her. "Don't blame you," she remarked in a low voice. "It's been sitting there awhile, now, just getting stronger and stronger."

Samantha returned the smile and the waitress walked to another table. Pulling out her change purse, Samantha laid a dollar on the table and started to get up.

Like an echo of a dream, a memory came flooding back—Pearl Rollins:

I could feel this thing, she'd said, *feel it beginning to grow, take shape—like an egg in its mammy's womb.*

And something else she'd said, standing outside on the porch: *I'm glad, glad I came back one more time, because I can tell you now . . . it's getting stronger . . .*

Samantha left the coffee shop with this refrain spinning in her mind, thoughts more tangled than ever. The harder she tried to sort them out, the more jumbled they became. "Later," she murmured, taking a deep breath of the spring-sweet air. "Think about it later."

Keeping to the west side of the street, she headed on down Main toward The Manse. Her gaze moved past Tully Ryerson's photo shop—*was that Zack just going in?*—and zeroed in on her destination. The Manse stood placid and whitewash clean in its gently budding surroundings, the first soft brush of spring beginning to lay a greenish tint to its framework.

She hadn't told Dood she intended going to The Manse this morning, hadn't wanted to mention it, even when he'd almost forced the issue by trying to make her promise not to. Samantha was currently pulling her two weeks of caretaker duty, and today she wanted to check the attic to make sure the cobwebs weren't getting the upper hand. At the last meeting, Janet Weims had mentioned them being a problem during her duty stint. A lot of their props were stored in the attic, and clots of spiderwebs would prove a nuisance come October.

There *had* been some talk by some of the Jaycees about an odd occurrence or two at the house lately, but Samantha and a couple of draftees had been up there twice in the past week and a half, doing general cleanup chores, and they hadn't experienced anything unusual. Well, maybe Teresa had been a bit more hyper than usual, and Martha some-what less cheerful, but Samantha had noticed nothing out of the ordinary. Was she getting used to the house's aura, or being brainwashed by Ted's down-to-earth logic? Still, these past couple of visits had been routine.

As today's would be, she was sure.

Resisting the impulse to glance through Tully's window as she passed, Samantha looked across the street toward Charles Hamilton's office, although she knew Ted was out of town. Some sort of legal snarl he was handling for the Beaufort Twins seemed to be coming to a head. She wondered briefly, as she always did when the thought occurred to her, just what it was he was doing for the

Misses Beaufort, then put the thought aside. She was more
interested in Ted's personal affairs than his legal ones.

A smile claimed Samantha's face, wiping away any
residue of the frown that lingered from her conversation
with Dood. Not that she was dismissing her concern over
L.J., but at the moment she was baffled as to what to do to
help him.

Thoughts of Ted were more relevant on this beautiful
morning. Their relationship seemed to be gliding swiftly
over the early-stage rough spots and slipping into an intimacy they both cherished. Their lovemaking was a natural
high of compatibility and exploration. Their quiet times
were comfortable, punctuated with long walks, good conversation, and honest sharing.

She had begun, hesitantly, to talk of Zack, feeling the
first faint stirrings of catharsis; he had told her of his
ex-wife in Atlanta. They had laughed and loved together in
a myriad of ways, and were finding that their respective
quirks and differences merely added to the bonding.

In a recent revealing conversation, Ted had told her why
he'd come to Merrillville, shared with her what he'd never
shared with anyone else, not even his wife: Theodore
Hamilton was his father.

Ted's mother had been a legal clerk with a law firm in
Charlotte, North Carolina, and during a case handled in
conjunction with the Hamilton firm, became involved with
the elder, married, Hamilton. Finding herself pregnant,
she moved to Atlanta, created a fictitious dead husband,
and devoted her life to raising the son she loved dearly.
Though she never touched a penny for herself, for Ted she
accepted the financial help Theo Hamilton provided through

a blind trust, which continued even after he died. It put
Ted through law school and provided him a start in his
career. Ted had been Theo Hamilton's only child.

After the death of his mother, Ted received a visit from
Charles Hamilton, who spent several days and quite a bit
of emotion telling Ted about his real father. A bachelor,
now without close family, Charles Hamilton asked Ted to
consider coming to Merrillville and becoming part of the
family law firm. Ted took time to think it out, but knew
almost from the first that this was what he wanted to do.
With certain conditions—anonymity being the foremost—
Ted agreed to Charles's request and made the move, losing
his wife in the process. But as he told Samantha frankly,
perhaps she had already been lost.

A car horn brought Samantha back to Main Street
Merrillville. She absently waved at the driver, a friend
from work, glanced right and left for other traffic, then
dashed across the intersection to the steps leading up to
The Manse. Flashing a smile of irony at the sunny spring
morning, she realized that she'd traveled almost the length
of Main Street in some sort of romantic daze.

"Better watch it, Samantha," she warned herself se-
verely. "You're going to get hit by a—" A sudden vision
of little Davy Dawson caused the word "truck" to lie
stillborn on her tongue. The vision destroyed her smile,
and for a moment Samantha smelled the dank, stale chill
of an open grave.

All at once, she wanted to get done with this job and on
to other things. Running lightly up the cement steps, she
hurried across the yard, digging out the house keys as she
went. She made a mental note to remind Tank, who was

next on the caretaker list, that it was time to start mowing again.

The front door opened easily, well-oiled hinges performing their duty in flawless silence. Then she was in the dusky entryway and heading for the main staircase, her soft-soled shoes making no sound on the hardwood floor.

Was it the silence? Was it the unsettling conversation with Dood? Samantha seemed to feel some small something in the air this morning that hadn't been there the past couple of visits. Of course, she hadn't been alone those times . . .

A small shiver climbed her spine as she made her way up the dusky staircase, the staircase down which Avery and Susannah Beaufort had tumbled to their deaths. *Why hadn't she taken time to flip on the downstairs light?*

Reaching the second floor, Samantha immediately rectified this problem, wincing slightly at the weakness of the forty-watt bulbs they'd been using in the ceiling fixtures to help save on the power bill. She hurried past the dark corridor that angled off to the family bedroom wing on the right and moved briskly down the left hallway toward the recess where the narrow attic door was located. A gaping sense of aloneness walked with her down the corridor, a view of this solitary chasm filled with muted light, hollow footsteps, and eerie thoughts.

Had that been a sound? A sudden draft? A door opening?

Samantha hesitated, lifting an unsteady hand to rub her arm, listening to the house around her. She didn't hear anything. *No, of course not.* She shook her head and continued down the corridor.

Did the air seem to be getting heavier all of a sudden,

thicker as she neared the small door set into the wall beside the back stairs? Or was it just her imagination?

It was bloody cold up here. Too cold. Also too silent, too alone. Samantha's heart began to thud; breath constricted in her chest.

Maybe this wasn't such a good idea, after all. Maybe she should table the job until later, come back another time . . .

She stopped, stared at the small, uninviting attic doorway and the gaping dark hole beyond where the small back staircase descended, then turned around and retraced her steps. Yes, she would come again another time, come again with someone else, not alone. She avoided looking at the dark branching corridor that led to the bedroom wing, avoided glancing down the snaking passageway that seemed ominous and threatening all of a sudden—

Was that a footstep?

Fear gripped Samantha, an almost frantic feeling of being watched, a panicky sense that she was no longer alone in the house. Biting her lip against the scream bubbling up inside her, she quickened her steps, slinging out a hand to grasp the banister as she reached the main staircase.

Something icy cold touched her shoulder!

Samantha started violently, swinging her head around toward the empty corridor, poised at the top of the stairs. She was shoved, hard!

Her body lurched sideways, sickeningly off balance. She felt her feet slide out from under her, felt the banister being torn from her grip. It happened so fast she hardly had time to gasp in surprise as she launched into the fall.

Then hands grabbed her, roughly yanking her back, jerking her to safety.

Her fingers clawed desperately at the bands of steel manhandling her body, dragging her away from the stairs. Her feet stumbled back onto the landing, found purchase, and began to support her once more. Breath that had snagged in her throat came out in ragged little spurts, a sound that was half laugh, half sob of relief.

For a moment she thought she might black out; waves of dizziness bombarded her, sending little sparkles of light dancing across her vision. Then the vertigo began to recede. Her gaze, locked in horror on the floor below, turned slowly toward her rescuer. And only then did she realize who was holding her.

"What the hell are you trying to do, kill yourself?" Zack Dalton demanded harshly, his expression a match for his tone.

"I . . ." Samantha heard the tremble in her voice, swallowed firmly in an attempt to control it. "I was going to check the attic for cobwebs . . ." Her voice trailed off as her eyes locked with Zack's.

His look was intense, fierce; she became aware of being held tightly in his arms, and for a moment felt the giddy rush of adrenaline it always triggered.

Then she remembered the push on her shoulder, the shove that had started her fall, and went cold. She stared into the eyes that she had known for so long and felt a small flicker of fear. That *had* been him in Tully's; he'd seen her, followed her here.

Could Zack Dalton have pushed her?

Something must have shown in her eyes. She felt the

hands encircling her upper arms tighten, felt the heat of them, saw Zack's eyes narrow.

"What is it, Sam?" His voice was soft, silky. "Afraid?" He smiled, a slow, lazy smile that sent chills rushing up Samantha's arms. "Afraid of being in here alone, with me?" His gaze shifted to her mouth. "Afraid of betraying your own emotions?" His head began to slowly descend.

It would be so easy, so easy to lean against him, give in to the truth that she was far from over Zack Dalton. But suddenly she was afraid—of him, of *something*.

"Did you try to kill me, Zack?" Samantha's voice was trembling with a mixture of emotions she didn't begin to want to define. "Did you try to push me down the stairs?"

Her words seemed to impact on him with the suddenness of a thousand volts of electricity jolting through a body strapped in a chair. He froze, head poised inches above hers. The cloudy passion left his eyes and a hard glitter replaced it. He said nothing, and silence stretched between them.

Samantha's heart began to pound again, she could hear it echo in her ears. Her breath hung midway to her throat; she suddenly felt like she was smothering. There was danger here, all around her, stalking her. Looking at her from ice-blue eyes? *Had* Zack Dalton pushed her . . . ?

A strange opaqueness suddenly moved into Zack's gaze. She couldn't read it, couldn't identify it at all; but she knew one thing—she didn't like what she saw.

Zack's hands began to slide tightly up her arms, releasing their grip only enough to allow movement, not enough for her to get away. Samantha doubted she could have run if she were free; her body felt nailed to the landing.

Slowly, Zack's hands climbed to her shoulders. She winced as the heat from his palms seemed to sear her naked throat.

With renewed alarm, Samantha realized Zack's hands were closing around her neck. Fear leaped up from the pit of her stomach to the lump of breath caught in her chest—slowly, almost caressingly, Zack's hands were encircling her throat, were beginning to apply pressure, contract, squeeze until the scream that exploded in her emerged as a whimper.

"Kill you, Sam?" Zack said, and his voice fell whisper soft and feather light on the silence. "Is that what you think? That I'd push you down the stairs? Has it come to that between us?" The words came rhythmically, almost lyrical in their evenness, like a funeral dirge. "If I can't have you, no one can—is that it? And at the last moment—what? Did I change my mind, decide not to deny myself the pleasure of a more personal touch . . ." The hands around her throat squeezed a tiny bit harder. "Like this . . . ?"

Samantha saw blackness move back in around the edges of her vision, blackness filled with those little sparkles of brilliant light.

"If I were going to kill you, my love," Zack continued with chilling deliberation, his words beginning to echo inside her head, as though she were slipping down into a tunnel, "I wouldn't push you down the fucking stairs . . ." The choking hands gave her a little jerk. "I'd simply break your neck."

Samantha's eyes had blurred with tears of fright, matching the blur in her mind as it fought to retain sanity. *This couldn't be happening—not with Zack, for God's sake!* She heard a ringing in her ears. Her chest felt ready to explode. Like a dream vision, the scene clouded, became two ghost people, grappling at the top of the stairs, shrieking, falling, locked in eternal torment . . .

Hardly able to move her lips and totally unable to make even a strangled sound, Samantha forced her terrified eyes to lock on his, forced her mouth to form a word—his name.

And suddenly the pressure on her neck was gone, his hands simply falling away as though their strength had been spent. She slumped against the wall, pressing her body against it to keep from crumbling to the floor, gaze still joined with Zack's. For a fraction of a second she thought she saw uncertainty in his eyes. Then his face closed down.

"Get out of here," he said, the words clipped. "Just get the hell away from me"—his eyes blazed with sudden violence—"until you're willing to stop playing these goddamned games and admit what we both know. You belong with me, Sam, and there's nothing, and *nobody*, that's ever going to change that!"

Turning, Samantha ran down the stairs, stumbling blindly in her haste, hardly caring if she fell or not. A sob broke from her as she dragged air into her tortured lungs, her hand grappling with the banister.

She reached the entry hall, pulled open the front door, rushed out of the house and toward the street, some semblance of rationality seeping back into her numb body as she fled. *Had Zack tried to kill her—not once, but twice?*

Dammit, no! Zack could be a bully, and a thin wire of meanness was threaded beneath the boyish charm, but murder? She remembered his look of shock at her accusa-

tion, that quick glimpse of pain. *No!* She couldn't—
wouldn't—believe that of him.

Yet someone had pushed her at the top of the stairs.
She'd felt the hand on her shoulder, and Zack was the only
one there.

That hand had been like ice. Zack's had been hot,
burning hot. Not Zack. Then *who*?

Samantha came to a dead stop at the bottom of the
cement stairs. Or *what*?

Chapter 15

"Come in."

Elizabeth Beaufort affixed a bright smile to her pink and white face, plump hands folded primly in the lap of her pale lilac afternoon dress, and fastened her eyes on the door. She willed strength into her eyes, attempting to banish the pinprick of fear she felt.

The door swung open. Ted Nathan took one step into the small sitting room. He seemed to fill half the room, to tower over her, though he was barely inside the door. His expression confirmed her dread.

"I'm afraid it went against us, Miss Beaufort." He spoke softly, his words small hot knives of pain. "I am sorry."

Elizabeth Beaufort held her smile in place only by the rigid discipline that was the mainstay of her life. She felt, rather than saw, her sister, Florence, cease her continual rocking and turn to stare at them, felt that penetrating look. She did not look back.

"I appreciate your coming personally to tell us, Mr. Nathan," she said, pleased that her voice was strong and firm. "I must admit I feared the worst when your secretary called to say you'd be stopping by, but I do appreciate your courtesy and thoughtfulness in coming."

"I only wish there was something more I could have—"

"Nonsense!" Elizabeth Beaufort waved his apology aside. "You did more than enough. It was not your failure, but ours. I'm afraid that interview with the court-appointed doctors went rather badly"—she allowed the merest sideways flick of her eyes—"in view of dear Florence's disinclination to respond to their questions. And I . . ." She hesitated, then continued almost matter-of-factly, "I, of course, must share the responsibility. When . . . ?"

"We have retained partial aegis through the end of this October, concurrent with the Jaycee lease agreement." His voice was matter-of-fact now, the attorney-to-client voice. "Your nephew will assume total control November first."

A twinge of burning hatred lanced through Elizabeth Beaufort. "At which time he'll no doubt begin tearing down my heritage!" She heard the edge in her voice, felt her control beginning to slip. With a little shake of her head, she calmed herself.

"It's all right, Mr. Nathan. We did what we could." Somehow she managed to smile once again. "I do hope you'll understand and forgive my rudeness if I ask you to please leave me—*us*—alone now."

"Of course. I'll be in touch." He turned to leave,

grasping the door handle to pull it closed behind him. "Good-bye, Miss Elizabeth, Miss Florence."

"Good day, Mr. Nathan," Elizabeth replied for them both. "And again, thank you."

He nodded once and quietly shut the door. The room immediately resumed its former spaciousness.

For a moment, Elizabeth could do nothing but sit there, staring at the inside of the door, unmoving, almost unearthly in her calmness.

So . . . dear Peter had won. Treacherous, greedy little bastard!

Elizabeth felt her jaw tighten as she clamped together teeth that were still her own, despite her years. She was fond of responding to questions about her age with: "I'm as old as my tongue and a little older than my teeth," a vintage saying, but one that always drew a laugh of amusement from those who hadn't heard it. Elizabeth Beaufort was proud of her good, strong teeth, her excellent eyesight (no glasses for her, not even for reading), and her robust health in general. In fact, the only thing that seemed to be weakening with age was her hearing, and she vigorously disdained wearing one of those unbecoming aids. Elizabeth knew that if she had been the only one on trial, she would have breezed through that interview session, easily shown those *leeches* the perfidy and unjustness of Peter's claim.

But dear Florence . . . Something inside Elizabeth cracked, sending a surge of bitterness bubbling up in her. Her hands, in her lap, tightened into little balls, nails digging into palms.

It was all dear Florence's fault . . . all of it! She swung around to glare at her twin, pushing her bitterness and fury at the one who deserved it.

Clear, watchful eyes met Elizabeth's, eyes full of the awareness Florence seldom showed anyone these days, even her own sister. It made Elizabeth's rage even greater.

"*You,*" Elizabeth hissed, feeling heat spill onto her neck and face. "You did it on purpose! You helped that Judas of a nephew win his case, played the fool and lost us everything! He's going to tear it down, do you hear me? Tear it down to build his filthy tenements"—Elizabeth twisted her plump body toward her sister, leaning over her doubled fists—"and it's *your fault!*"

The sisters' eyes clashed in silence, fury confronting *something.* Elizabeth found she couldn't read Florence's look, couldn't decipher just what emotion held her sister in thrall. It was rather disconcerting.

Then a smile began to form on Florence Beaufort's face, starting at her mouth and easing over her features like the flow of honey across warm bread.

For just a moment, Elizabeth Beaufort saw again the quiet beauty that had belonged to a younger Florence, saw the depth of loveliness so often missed by others at first or even second glance, overlooked in the light of another, more demanding personality, another's vivacity and eye-catching prettiness. But not always overlooked . . . no, not always . . .

Memory fanned Elizabeth's rage, burning like acid against the fury that suddenly exploded as she read the truth in her sister's eyes.

"You're *glad*!" she hissed, and the sound of her voice was like the sizzle of that acid. "*Glad* I've lost. After all these years, you dare oppose me? I'll show you—and I'll show Peter. I'll show you all just like I showed Avery and Edward!''

Elizabeth broke off her tirade. Florence's smile had suddenly vanished, her eyes widening. *What had she just said? Something about showing Peter—and what else?*

Elizabeth's rage melted away. Had she said a bit too much? Could stupid, weak-willed Florence at last suspect?

As suddenly as it had opened, Florence's face shut down. As quickly as the sparkle of awareness had brightened it, the light went off. The eyes Elizabeth now looked into were dull, colorless orbs; the face long and thin, devoid of knowledge. Like an automaton, Florence slowly resumed her rocking, turning her head back toward the window to stare, unblinkingly, at the darkening sky. She'd retreated into her jar, into her sealed world where intrusions could not enter.

But what did she take back with her? Elizabeth wondered, a prick of alarm chafing her turbulent thoughts.

As usual, Ted Nathan arrived late at the Tuesday night Jaycee meeting. He slid into a back-row seat, trying not to disturb the proceedings, exchanging smiles with Samantha, across the room at the officers' table.

Samantha was vice-president now. She'd surprised Ted by changing her candidacy status prior to the election, a move she explained clearly. She'd judged her odds on beating Zack as slim, hadn't wanted to cause a potential rift in the newly combined chapter, yet was strongly averse at being excluded from the governing body entirely and had correctly guessed she'd have an easy win in the second spot.

Ted had jokingly accused her of playing politics—a fact she readily admitted, adding: "Just wait till next year." What he hadn't accused her of—jokingly or otherwise— was being overly restrained lately in her dealings with Zack Dalton, a fact he doubted she would as easily concede. And maybe he was overreacting to the whole thing anyway, reading unwarranted subtleties into the situation. His relationship with Samantha seemed more firm every day. Still, as on any point dealing with Zack Dalton, he'd been reluctant to probe further.

At the moment, Zack held the floor, not in uniform, but dressed casually in jeans and an old black and gold football jersey, number 11. The ever-present baseball cap rode at a jaunty angle on the back of his head. Ted felt a slight frown pucker his forehead at the thought that he'd never even owned a football jersey and would no doubt feel strange in one. Perversely he reached up and loosened the knot in his tie.

Zack was in the process of setting up committees to take charge of the various rooms in this year's House. The scenarios had been decided on weeks ago; now came the planning and preparation.

From here on the meetings would be taken over with details of the preparations for the 13th Annual Jaycee House of Horrors. Ted thought he would ease up on his attendance during the next few months. In fact, he wouldn't be here tonight but for the report he had to deliver.

". . . and it's going to be the absolute highlight of this year's House," Zack was saying, revving up his audience

like a TV evangelist just before the sales pitch. "Think of
it, people—being *inside* a living, beating heart!"

"Have you got the technicals worked out?" someone
asked.

Zack nodded toward the front row where Tank Worley
was lounging across a couple of chairs. "Tank's handling
that. Want to explain the setup, Tankman?"

Zack flipped his chair around and straddled it as Tank
Worley shifted the toothpick from one side of his mouth to
the other, turned toward the audience, and began speaking.
Ted found himself fascinated by the sliver of wood bobbing up and down as Tank spoke, and the man's apparent
ability to control it with minimum effort. *He'd* probably
have swallowed it by now, or at the least poked it through
his tongue.

"That small, octagon-shaped room in the center of the
house gives us a perfect setup," Tank was saying as Ted
finally tuned in on the conversation. "No outside walls, no
windows. The very things that kept it from being used
before make it perfect for this scenario. We're going to
call it the Heart of the House."

Somehow Tank managed to reverse the toothpick using
only his tongue, flipping it out and around, then working it
back to the other side of his mouth—*look, Ma, no hands*—
as a few murmurs of laughter and comments skimmed the
room. Everyone else seemed immune to the toothpick
sideshow, but Ted found himself enthralled. How did he
do that?

"Sound effects are the key," Tank continued when he
again had the group's attention. "Spectators will go into a
totally dark and empty room. Nothing. No noise, no sound

at all. We're planning to double-pad the walls inside and out to completely deaden any unwanted sound.''

''This'll be a safety factor too,'' Zack Dalton interjected from the head table, probably to forestall a possible complaint from the woman at his side, or any objections from the wimp attempt. ''No way is anybody going to get hurt in a padded room.''

Apparently this tack was effective, as only general laughter greeted the remark. Zack gave Tank a small nod to continue.

''After total darkness and silence for several minutes, a very faint heartbeat will begin. We're going to make an audio tape of an actual heart, starting with the subject at rest, then gradually speeding the beat up through movement and vigorous exercise so that the pace will become faster and more frenetic.''

A few catcalls interrupted Tank, a couple of suggestions regarding what kind of exercise and whose heartbeat they should use.

Zack allowed the group their fun for a minute or two, then rapped for attention and gave them all an exaggerated leer. ''As your leader, I, of course, am prepared to make whatever sacrifice is necessary.''

Groans and hoots greeted this statement, not subsiding until Zack once again rapped his gavel and said, ''Okay, okay, let's get back to business.''

Tank removed the toothpick from his mouth—it must be dead, Ted decided—looked at it, then stuck it behind his left ear to lie in state. It didn't budge, even when Tank swiveled his head around toward the audience again.

''A sound control system will be set up down in the

basement, with the speakers inside that old unused coal furnace. Some of the ductwork is still intact, and we're going to run the sound up to the heat outlet in the octagon room. As we play the recording, we'll increase the volume in conjunction with the beating of the heart. That old metal furnace should give the sound a hollow, echoing sort of amplification as it travels up the duct into the room; we'll probably use an electronic amplifier to beef it up too.''

''Won't the sound bleed through to other parts of the house?'' someone questioned.

Tank flashed the group a mock-sinister grin. ''Yeah . . .''

''And speaking of blood, tell them about the visual,'' Zack prompted amid the several groans and chuckles that filled the room as the thought of a disembodied beating heart in the haunted house took hold of their imaginations.

''We're also going to try and rig a simulation of blood flowing down the walls of the room,'' Tank said over the general noise this time, having no trouble being heard. ''Those novelty lamps that make it look like it's raining indoors—with a red bulb they should produce the effect we're after. We'll control the light with a dimmer switch, enhancing it as the sound increases. Add to that a deadpan voice doing some sort of monologue hype about being inside a living heart and hearts bursting with fright or something—we may even rig some sort of light water spray to shower down from the ceiling like drops of blood— the total effect should be good.''

Murmured agreement came from around the room.

''Hey, Dood man. How about helping Tank out with the sound equipment?'' Zack tossed his question toward the very back of the room.

Ted followed Zack's look and saw Dood Hopkins standing just inside the door, leaning up against the back wall with his hands in his pockets and a look of resignation on his face. There was weariness in his stance, and an aura of being slightly removed from the scene.

"Not me." Dood's voice was as dull and lifeless as his whole demeanor.

Ted stared at him, as did others in the group, hardly crediting the change that had taken place in this man over the past couple of months. He wondered, somewhat uneasily, why Dood was here tonight.

Zack had started to say something else, annoyance in his tone, when Dood continued, overriding him:

"And if you know what's good for you, you'll *all* stay away from the old Beaufort estate." With this, Dood turned on his heel and walked out the door.

For a minute there was utter silence in the meeting room, then a few quiet conversations broke out. Ted glanced toward Samantha; she was staring at the door, a look of dismay on her face. Quickly, Zack picked up his gavel and rapped for attention, resuming control.

Soon the Jaycees had forgotten Dood and his cryptic words. Ted, however, continued to ponder the enigma of a man losing touch with reality, banishing the group around him until his name being called brought them back into focus.

"You have a report for us, Counselor?" As usual, Zack's tone was patronizing.

As usual, Ted ignored it; still, Zack Dalton nettled him. He stood.

"Some of you may have heard rumors about the court

case involving the Beaufort family." *Give it to them short and sweet.* "I'm afraid that the Beaufort sisters, Miss Elizabeth and Miss Florence, have been declared *non compos mentis"—okay, Ted, cut the legalese crap, are you feeling that nettled?—*"legally incompetent by the courts. Control of their affairs will be passing to their nephew, Mr. Peter Beaufort. It is Mr. Beaufort's wish that the Jaycee lease agreement be terminated at the end of this option, which would be 1 November 1987."

A number of astonished faces gaped at him and several "I *knew* something was going on" comments shot around the room. Though Ted had discussed this with no one, not even Samantha, he was well aware of the quality of small-town gossip. With a perverse twinge of pleasure, he noted that Zack Dalton was one of the astonished.

"What are we going to do?" came a pained voice, then another: "It's become a tradition."

Zack ignored the questions, staring at the lawyer with a look of bitter accusation as though Ted was directly responsible for this sudden unscheduled play from the bench. *I'll bet his football coach was glad to see him leave despite the championship*, thought Ted with a glint of insight.

"This year's House won't be affected?" Zack asked, his words tight.

Ted met the narrow-eyed look. "No."

Zack nodded, collecting himself. He still had a touchdown to make. "It's okay, then," he said. "We've got the house for our special thirteenth show and we'll worry about next year afterward. There are other houses . . ."

"Not like The Manse," someone said. Heads nodded in agreement throughout the room.

"I want to see you after the meeting, Counselor!" Zack's voice sliced through the din, for Ted's ears alone, a gauntlet thrown.

And accepted. Ted nodded once, sat down, and tuned out the general chatter, suddenly tired, disgusted with his childish urge to throw spitballs at Zack Dalton, and hungry. He'd missed supper in order to make this meeting after visiting the Beaufort sisters, and he wanted nothing more at the moment than a turkey club at the Merrillville Coffee Shop and a cup of—no, a beer, cold and foamy, and Samantha, warm and soft, beside him.

"Ted?"

Ted looked up at Samantha, startled to see that the meeting was over and people were beginning to leave.

Samantha's hands were pushed down in the pockets of her skirt. A small frown knotted her forehead. "Ted, would you mind if we go see about L.J.?" she said as he stood up. "I'm really concerned about him."

Ignoring the pangs in his empty stomach and elsewhere, Ted nodded. "I've just got one quick item of unfinished business to take care of. Then we'll go. Why don't you wait for me outside?"

Samantha cast a worried glance toward the head table and Zack Dalton. "Zack's very angry, Ted. I don't think you should—"

Taking Samantha lightly by the arm, he steered her through the milling group to the door. "Wait for me outside, Samantha. Please."

She held his eyes for a moment, frown still in place, then turned and left the room with a group of Jaycees that included the boisterous Tank Worley. The level of noise immediately plummeted.

Ted held the door as a final group of loiterers strolled from the room, catching bits of conversations that centtered around the loss of The Manse. He didn't miss the several condemning glances tossed his way, and wasn't surprised. He'd expected some of the Jaycees would blame him for this. Ted reaffirmed his intention of avoiding upcoming meetings; they were sure to be more of the same.

Closing the door, he turned back to the room. He and Zack were now its sole occupants, the latter still sitting astraddle his chair at the head table. So be it. Ted had known for some time that this confrontation was inevitable, that sooner or later this scene would occur, under whatever circumstances, over whatever pretext. It was as unavoidable, as elemental, as the passions seething behind the glittering blue eyes that had fastened on him when he turned around. A confrontation whose time had come.

Ted walked to the head table, meeting Zack's furious regard with a coolly professional look indigenous to the courtroom. He did not intend to pass control of this skirmish to Zack Dalton.

"I'm sure you have questions regarding the termination, which I'll be glad to answer, but if you can drop by my office tomorrow, my secretary should have a report ready that will completely outline the Jaycees' temporary rights to continue— "

With a jarring scrape of his chair, Zack stood and began slowly walking around the table. "You goddamn shyster lawyers, you're all alike. Think being in a little hick town makes it easier to play both ends against the middle?"

"Are you accusing me of malfeasance, Dalton?" Ted watched the younger man round the end of the table.

"If the asshole fits . . ." Zack moved toward him. "Think you're dealing with a bunch of stupid rednecks here who never heard the term 'conflict of interest'?"

"There's been no conflict of interest, Zack, believe me. Talk to Charles Hamilton if you feel—"

Zack walked up to him, stopped, then reached out and grabbed him by the lapels. "I'd rather discuss the matter with you, Counselor," he rasped, punctuating "Counselor" with a little shove.

Ted maintained his calm. He had no intention of allowing Zack Dalton to provoke him into a fight. He held no illusions regarding the potential outcome, and no desire to spend time in a hospital. What would it prove?

"Let go of me, Dalton. I've got someone waiting." As soon as he said it, Ted wished it unsaid. What, in God's name, had made him throw another spitball at Zack? Did he subconsciously want this as much as Dalton?

Zack's eyes narrowed, glancing toward the door then back again. "Sam waiting for you, Counselor? In a hurry to join her?" Sarcasm filled his voice.

Ted felt a small tic begin pulsing at the side of his jaw, realized the amount of tension being held in check. "Samantha—she's what this is really about, isn't she?"

Surprisingly some of the anger seemed to dissipate from the glittering blue eyes. "Is she, Counselor?" Zack's voice was a slow drawl, smooth as silk to match the lazy smile that slid onto his face. "She won't always be there, you know. You'd better make the most of it while you can."

Ted didn't like the direction this conversation was taking. "All right, Dalton, that's enough. Let go of me."

Zack made no move to release his hold. A certain craftiness edged into his eyes, his voice. "Tell me, Counselor, has she made a commitment yet? Expressed her undying affection?"

Ted's jaw tightened.

"She won't, you know," Zack said softly. "Samantha already made her commitment—years ago—to me." The eyes that met Ted's were suddenly assured, explicit, the look of a man who knew he'd won before the game even began. "We were together before you, Nathan, and we'll be together after you. That's the way it is." His smile turned mocking. "Believe me."

Ted realized he'd allowed control to shift sides, realized he was being deliberately, effectively goaded. The fists at his sides confirmed it. "Leave Samantha alone, Dalton! She's trying to get on with her life. Why don't you try getting on with yours?" He vaguely noted the unfamiliar harshness in his voice.

Zack's smile broadened, the self-satisfied smile of a man who'd made his point. Abruptly he released his hold on Ted's jacket, hands smoothing the lapels back into place. "You're used to dealing with facts, Counselor. Why be so obtuse about this one? It's just a matter of time."

Ted watched in silence as Zack Dalton strolled from the room, closing the door softly behind him.

"Son of a bitch!" Ted abstractedly ran a hand through

his hair, taking a deep breath against the incisions this scene had cut in his composure. He felt like he'd just been finessed by a first-year law student.

He stood there a moment, until his breathing slowed and his hands relaxed, moving away from the edge where reason takes a back seat to blind response.

Was Zack right? Would Samantha eventually go back to him? That possibility bothered Ted a hell of a lot more than it had a couple of months ago. *Obviously*, he thought, still reeling from the emotions of the scene just enacted.

Finally feeling some semblance of control return, Ted left the room, wondering if he'd find Zack outside, talking to Samantha. He refused to consider the other possibility: that they'd both be gone.

Night lay balmy and humid on Main Street; clouds hung in tight bunches across the sky. Ted took another deep, slaking breath of the night air as he stepped outside, almost unwilling to look around.

"Ted?" Samantha's voice.

He turned to her; she was alone. Her look was a question, one he was not prepared to answer at the moment.

"Let's go see Dood," he said flatly, reaching for her arm to guide her up the street. She fell into step without a word.

As they walked, calmness began to settle back in place. Releasing Samantha's arm a moment, he shrugged out of his suit jacket, loosened his tie further, then hooked the jacket over a finger and slung it across his shoulder. Taking her arm again, he pushed Zack Dalton from his thoughts.

"It's a shame about the Beaufort Twins," Samantha

finally broke into the silence that had moved down Main Street with them.

Ted looked at her. She was gazing down the street, face patterned by shadows and moonlight. His look softened. "I'm glad you said that."

Samantha glanced toward him, surprised. "Why?"

He turned his eyes forward again. "I'm just glad your first concern was for the sisters and not at losing The Manse for your bloody House of Horrors." The words came out more forcefully than he'd intended, and suddenly Ted realized just how angry he'd been at the response to his report during the Jaycee meeting. "I'm just damned glad somebody thought about *them*, that's all," he remarked, glancing back at her.

She continued to look at him, eyebrow raised, a little smile hovering at the corner of her mouth, and after a moment he added more calmly, "Snapping at you is a hell of a way to say I'm glad you're nicer than the national average."

"You're welcome." The smile had moved into her voice. "But it's not *my* bloody House of Horrors, thank you very much. In fact"—the smile disappeared—"I think I'd like to see the whole thing stop with this year. Or go back to the kids' fun house it was originally meant to be."

She looked down at the sidewalk and Ted's eyes were drawn by the familiar little gesture as she pulled her hands from her pockets, brought them up, and lightly rubbed her upper arms.

His brow furrowed as Dood's cryptic words of earlier returned to the forefront of his mind. Maybe she was right. Maybe it would be better for everyone concerned if the Jaycee House of Horrors ended with number thirteen. Dood's words had held a warning, one Ted somehow couldn't summarily dismiss tonight. It seemed different this time, different from those other times when logic easily negated the absurd. He pondered this thought as they walked on in silence. Maybe it would be better still if the annual Haunted House had ended with number twelve.

"How did they take it?" Samantha asked.

Ted glanced at her, pulling his mind back in line. "The Beaufort sisters?"

She nodded.

Ted faced forward again, momentarily seeing the scene from earlier this evening instead of the sidewalk in front of them. "Elizabeth maintained a rigid control, but I think she was breaking up inside. And Florence . . ." He hesitated, remembering, then said, "You know, for just a moment Florence seemed . . . alert suddenly, acutely alert."

"Why? What did she say?"

Ted shook his head slowly. "Nothing. She didn't say a word. It was just a look she gave her sister." The vision receded.

"How strange. Yet I've sometimes felt Miss Flossie might be a bit more attuned to her surroundings than she lets on."

"Maybe."

They walked on in silence, Samantha with her hands in her pockets, Ted with his thoughts on two little old ladies and the puzzle of Florence's look. It hadn't occurred to him at the time, but if he were now forced to classify Florence Beaufort's expression at that moment, Ted would

say "satisfied." Strange . . . or curiouser and curiouser,
as the story said.

"You know," Samantha said, now pensive, "I've been
visiting the sisters for months, talking to Miss Bessie about
The Manse and its past . . . There was one afternoon, Miss
Bessie got to talking about her fiancé, Edward, her 'young
man who died.' I seem to remember sensing an alertness
in Miss Flossie that day, like she was listening intently to
everything her sister said. And something else. When I got
ready to leave, I went over to her chair to say good-bye
like I always do—she never responds, but I do it anyway—
and there were tears in her eyes." Samantha looked over
at Ted as though requesting an explanation for this unusual
behavior.

"Perhaps she still shares her sister's pain over that
particular loss. Neither of them ever married. They must
be quite close."

"Perhaps."

They fell into silence again, and Ted's thoughts wandered to the contradiction of Florence Beaufort's seeming
satisfaction over losing The Manse, a deep, aching blow to
her sister, and her apparent concern for her sister's long-
dead suitor. And why, if Miss Florence was capable of
coherent thought and action, had she done nothing to
counter Peter's claims of incompetence? Everything concerning The Manse held undertones of mystery.

"The lights are on." Samantha had stopped walking.
They'd reached Dood Hopkins's video shop. Lights blazed
from inside, but there was no sign of movement.

Ted glanced up to the second story where Dood lived.
There, too, lights gleamed from behind curtained windows.

Stepping up to the front door, Ted tried it, found it locked, and rapped sharply against the wooden facing. They stood in silence, waiting for an answer. After a moment, Ted tried again.

There was no response from inside the shop.

Samantha moved forward and banged against the glass window that filled the top half of the front door. "He's in there, Ted, I know he's in there." She stepped back to gaze upward, raising her voice. "L.J.? L.J., will you please come open the door!"

Another moment of silence.

Ted touched her arm. "Come on, Samantha. If he's in there, he obviously doesn't want to see us. Let's just leave him alone."

Samantha stood gazing up at the apartment windows for another couple of seconds. "I guess you're right. Let's go."

They turned to walk back the way they'd come, and Ted felt oddly relieved that their visit had come to nothing. At the moment, he wasn't sure he could deal with another emotional scene.

"It's just . . . I don't know what to do for him," Samantha said tightly, deep concern clinging to the words. "I think he's getting worse. Tonight he seemed . . ." She paused.

"Resigned." Ted's voice was hard, and he felt caution cloud his eyes as he glanced into the darkness lying down at the end of Main Street. "And somehow that disturbs me."

Samantha stopped walking and turned toward him. "Ted, you've been the voice of reason through this; you've been

the one to debunk it all along.'' She laid a hand on his
arm. ''Are you saying now that you think there might be
something valid in what L.J. has been telling us?''

Ted looked at her a moment without speaking, then
said, ''I don't believe in ghosts, Samantha.'' His voice
and eyes were steady, calm.

But she was right. He *was* experiencing a feeling of
unease concerning this upcoming House of Horrors. It was
more than just the emotions of the day.

Slowly he returned his gaze to the end of Main Street,
staring into the darkness where The Manse lay silent,
brooding. From the first, he'd disliked that old house, a
dislike that had somehow gotten buried beneath the weight
of reason he'd used to parry Dood Hopkins's wild claims.

For just a moment, something seemed to span the gap
between fantasy and reason, between logic and lunacy.
Ted felt a coldness ease in at the base of his spine, and a
distinct throb of menace.

''Ted? Say something—you're scaring me.'' There was
a touch of real alarm in Samantha's voice.

He turned back to her, gazing down into the green eyes
that reflected the moonlight and clouds plaiting the night
sky, searching for the words of reassurance that suddenly
were not there.

''What's going to happen?'' Samantha's voice sounded
small and lost, and he recognized a plea for *Nothing, love.
Everything's going to be all right.*

''I don't know, Samantha.'' He answered honestly, and
saw fear etch her eyes, felt it reach into him as well, a
sickle of dread. He reached for the words she wanted to
hear him say . . . but couldn't say them. ''I guess we'll
just have to wait until October.''

Excerpt from *The Merrillville Weekly,*
September 16, 1987, Samantha Evers, Feature Writer:

Preparations continue for the special 13th Annual Jaycee House of Horrors, an event that will this year
expand into a full month of nightly presentations incor-
porating a record number of participants and scenarios. According to the Jaycees, this will be the most
horrifying Haunted House ever.

PART THREE

The Manse: October 31, 1987,
Halloween Night

===================== Chapter 16 ====

It is not a night like any other. There is something heavy
in the air, something that crawls around beneath the skin
and send chills up your arms. Thunderclouds bloat the sky,
sluggish, boiling gray giants hanging in place the way a
harrier jet—or a vulture—will hover above its target. In
the distance, occasional flashes of lightning illuminate the
swollen clouds, spilling out around the edges; not the
jagged, forking type, but sheets, like the heat lightning of
late summer, a flickering glow. The atmosphere is oppressive, not overly hot or cold, but thick, as though the
barometric pressure is dropping. There is a stormy feel to
the early evening, a premature darkness; nevertheless, people are already crowding to The Manse, where the
Merrillville Jaycees have promised a final night of fear
surpassing anything they've ever done before.

*   *   *

Earlier in the day Peter Beaufort had arrived in Merrillville, dropping by to "greet" his aunts (and in the process
completely destroying the elaborate fantasy a certain young
nurse's aide had built up around a compelling telephone
voice and too many romance magazines—for Peter was
nearly fifty, was short, overweight, and balding). To Peter's disgust, his Aunt Elizabeth demanded he meet her at
The Manse later in the afternoon, to remove some personal
contents still in the attic, saying she would never set foot
in the house once it passed from her control.

Toward lunchtime, Tank Worley stopped by Dood Hopkins's video store to pick up another sound amplifier. The
Jaycees planned to make the entire estate "come alive" as
a grand finale to their last House of Horrors at The Manse.
Floodlights and speakers positioned at strategic points about
the house and grounds would give a midnight explosion of
light and sound that should have spectators talking for
years, "with monsters coming out of the woodwork."
Tank ribbed Dood a bit about his dire predictions of
doom—the House had been running for a month now, and
absolutely nothing out of the way had occurred.

Sometime around one o'clock, Vince Colletti finished
packing the last of his belongings into the back of his car
and headed out of Merrillville—for good, if he had anything to do with it. The nightmares were getting worse, the
closer it got toward the anniversary of that night at The
Manse, the night Bud and Randy "skipped town," Vince

told himself for the hundred-thousandth time. Like he was doing now. Just like he was doing now.

About midafternoon, as she passed Dood's video store, Samantha was surprised to have Dood come out to ask casually how the House was going. Delighted at this first indication of normalcy in months, Samantha confirmed Tank's earlier report of nothing unusual happening. Dood then further surprised her by agreeing that maybe he'd been just a bit off the deep end with this thing and perhaps he'd stop by the House tonight for the grand finale.

After leaving Dood, and in a happier frame of mind concerning him than she'd been in a long time, Samantha literally ran into Zack Dalton, who emerged from the Merrillville Coffee Shop. A strange tingle—fear?—spread down her spine as his powerful hands gripped her arms, steadying her . . . but he let her go before she could fully identify the feeling. Tipping the scruffy baseball cap back on his tousled blond hair, Zack treated her to: "Been pushed down any more stairs lately, Sam my love?" before giving her his boyish grin, a grin that didn't quite reach his ice-blue eyes.

At the Country Manor Retirement Home during afternoon naps and a convenient staff meeting, Miss Bessie Beaufort had a close brush with a parked car while backing out an old station wagon "borrowed" from one of the second-shift nurses. Once safely away from the home, however, and on the highway to town, Miss Bessie breathed a sigh of relief and increased her speed to a respectable

thirty-five, going over her mental checklist of things to do:
Arrange to meet Peter? *Yes*. Bring cape? *Yes*. See to
Florence? *Yes*. All taken care of. The sudden blare of a
horn caused Miss Bessie to lose control of the unfamiliar
car momentarily, but she quickly regained her composure,
and the proper lane, and for the rest of the drive concentrated solely on being behind the wheel of a car once
again.

In a small frame house on Third Street, Pearl Rollins
continued her pacing, back and forth, pausing now and
then to stare, unseeing, through her living room window.
The activity had consumed her since the night before, like
the feeling pressing harder and harder against her terrified
mind. Was the waiting over? Was the waiting finally
done?

Just before the first visitors to the 13th Annual Jaycee
House of Horrors arrived to stand in line, Peter Beaufort
entered the house and climbed the stairs to the second floor
where his aunt had arranged to meet him. After an initial
encounter in the front entry hall, his presence went
uncontested—apparently the workers were too involved
belowstairs with their foolish horror show to give him
much attention. As with people the world over, they were
easily manipulated by a positive, aggressive man and a
certain attitude.

At almost precisely the moment the first tickets went on
sale at the door, Ted Nathan decided that tonight, after all
the fuss and finale of the Haunted House, he was going to

take Samantha home for a quiet little late-night dinner, a
special bottle of wine he'd been saving for just such an
occasion, and see if she'd be willing to take a couple of
weeks off, go with him on a cruise he'd been checking
into, see if their relationship was ready to grow . . .

No, it is not a night like any other. There is sometning
in the air, something heavy maybe, like static electricity
. . . and like the thunderclouds, it seems to be hanging
above a certain spot at the north end of Main Street, above
a certain old house on a certain old hill. Darkness begins
to fall. Merrillville comes alive to the evening. Costumed
children dot the streets, holding tightly to their orange
jack-o'-lantern buckets; parents hold close to their children; something uneasy holds sway in the night; and The
Manse holds fast to its fear . . .

========================= Chapter 17 =====

Elizabeth Beaufort felt more alive than she had in years. As the miles slid by, she felt as though time were being shed by the wayside like so much excess garbage picked up along her route from past to present. Elizabeth smiled at the thought, and at the feeling of lightness, giddiness, that seemed to increase with each foot of passing scenery. She felt young again, excited, in total control for the first time in . . . how long? *Too* long. Probably since she'd left her home and moved into that place that now receded in the distance.

She was handling the car quite well now, getting the hang of it with ease as a slightly tarnished talent was re-buffed to a remembered sheen. Florence had shunned learning to drive; Elizabeth had demanded it. In fact, it had only been a few years ago that she finally sold the Edsel to that collector and allowed her driver's license to lapse.

And a good thing, too, thought Elizabeth as she maneuvered the car smoothly into the long, sweeping turn that led into Merrillville by way of The Manse.

Slowing the car, Elizabeth saw the beginning of the estate move into view on her right. The trees looked thicker than she remembered, even with so many of the autumn leaves already beaten off by heavy autumn rains. Dark, tangled branches of oak and hickory reached skyward as though trying to claw past the huge pines that shadowed and surrounded them. In one spot, patches of kudzu vines had begun to climb a rise of ground and take hold of several tree trunks. If left untended, they would eventually take charge, tree by tree, choking life from the very things that sustained them. Elizabeth made a mental note to chastise the maintenance group for their neglect of the outer perimeters of her property. They'd better attend to such things if they wanted their lease renewed for another year.

Elizabeth steered the car around the gently curving road, and suddenly there it was, the house, tall, majestic, an image carved forever on her mind and heart. *You* can *go home again,* Elizabeth thought, tears misting her eyes for just a moment. She blinked them away, carefully edging the car to the right to allow someone behind her to get past.

Slowing down to a crawl, Elizabeth allowed her eyes to roam the scene, bending over the steering wheel to get a better view through the windshield. Dark clouds banked the house, forming a backdrop of charcoal, deep purple, and gray. Though she much preferred fluffy white puffs against an azure-blue summer sky as the ideal frame for

her beloved house, there was something powerful about
these clouds, something intense. They were . . . Elizabeth
thought for a moment . . . *befitting*, that was the correct
word. Befitting. She started to smile in satisfaction, then
noticed something odd gathered at the top of one of the
turrets—a tarpaulin, edges hanging down on either side in
the absence of a breeze. She craned her neck. It was black,
and . . . *a bat?* Yes, yes, it was! A huge bat. No doubt
about it.

Elizabeth darted a glance forward and slowed the car
almost to a stop, frowning. She looked back at the bat, and
then she remembered. Of course. It was part of the theatricals currently being staged at her house, the Halloween
program.

Small, rosebud lips pursed tightly as other incriminating
evidence emerged: a person dressed in witch's robes setting up a ticket booth on the front lawn; a clutter of
costumed children climbing the masonry stairs to the yard;
a huge, grinning jack-o'-lantern suspended by a noose,
desecrating an upstairs window. As a rule, Elizabeth avoided
thinking about this facet of the agreement she held with the
Merrillville civic group. It had been a necessity—a slightly
vulgar necessity—and it had not been particularly gratify-
ing, so Elizabeth had banished the more undesirable parts
of their agreement from her mind.

Now she was confronted with them. She crawled the car
toward the long, winding driveway that led up to her
home, thought about it a moment, then made the turn into
the drive. No one would notice her in the general confusion, and despite her renewed vigor, Elizabeth didn't want
to push herself too far, too soon.

Several vehicles were parked in the graveled area at the side of the house. Elizabeth carefully pulled the borrowed car beside a large blue van where it wouldn't be readily noticed, and cut off the engine. She started to take her foot off the brake, then quickly stomped it again as the car began rolling forward. She'd forgotten to place the gear in park. She corrected this error, pulled up the handle on the emergency brake for good measure, then took a moment to collect herself. Day was waning, and she hadn't much time to waste, but she needed a quiet moment before the coming ordeal.

Actually, Elizabeth found herself rather looking forward to this meeting with dear Peter and was feeling quite satisfied with herself for taking such a positive step. So useless to allow this unfortunate misunderstanding to go further.

Getting out of the car, Elizabeth donned the long black velvet cape that had been the highlight of her twenty-first Christmas and a cherished possession for more than sixty years, kept carefully packed away between layers of tissue paper and lemon-scented moth crystals. The cream silk lining made a delightful swishing sound each time she moved. Plump hands caressed the down-soft velvet; old eyes glittered with remembered parties . . . soirees, the theater. It had been years since she'd worn the cape . . . so many years.

Elizabeth gave herself a little shake, recalling the matter at hand. There would be time enough for reminiscences, time enough for having parties again, new occasions to wear the lovely cape. She would see to it. Christmas would soon be here. She would open up the house, throw a magnificent homecoming party like the county had never seen—

She was doing it again. Elizabeth took herself to task for continuing to waste time when Peter would soon be here—in fact, he might even have preceded her. Arranging the voluminous hood over her carefully chignoned gray hair, she left the shelter of the two vehicles and made her way across the side yard toward the back of the house and the breezeway entrance.

If everything went as planned, she'd blend into the costumed comings and goings around the house. If everything went as planned, she'd make her way through the house and up the stairs to the private meeting with her dear nephew that she'd arranged, a private meeting in the attic. Then there would be time for reminiscence and parties and wearing the cape whenever she liked.

But first she had to kill Peter.

Peter Beaufort looked at his watch for the third time in four minutes. This was absurd. Why had he humored his Aunt Elizabeth by agreeing to meet her here? And it now looked like she wasn't even going to show up—four o'clock had come and gone with no sign of her. This whole idea had probably been no more than a capricious whim of his aunt's to cause him inconvenience. And it had. He should be back at the inn going over the preliminary sketches from his architects instead of bowing to the ridiculous request of an eccentric old lady, a *mentally incompetent* old lady, Peter qualified, savoring the term and what it represented to him.

Peter glanced at his watch once more, a glance that turned into a scowl, then got up from the hard desk chair in his old bedroom where he'd been waiting for his aunt, as requested, and walked out into the hall. He'd always hated that hard, straight-backed chair. "Builds character," his Aunt Elizabeth used to say, he could almost hear her now. Why had he chosen to sit on it?

The premature gloom he remembered so well from his early years had settled in the corridor, seeming to thicken toward the main hallway that gave access to the west wing, servants' stairs, and attic. Peter strode down the corridor, heading in that direction. Maybe his Aunt Elizabeth had forgotten she'd asked him to meet her in his room and had gone straight up to the attic.

Stopping where the corridor met the top of the main stairway, Peter hesitated before turning on the light, glancing at the spot where his parents had fallen to their deaths. He hardly remembered them, though he'd often speculated on the topic of the violent argument Aunt Elizabeth hinted had occurred that day, wondered if the carefully avoided rumors had been true: that his father, in attempting to kill his mother, had been pulled down the stairs with her.

Shaking off the unwanted reminiscence, he reached over and flicked the switch that should have turned on the upstairs hall lights. Instead, the hall was suddenly plunged into a startling tunnel of glowing yellow eyes, hundreds of them.

"Jesus Christ!"

A shiver pricked at Peter's masterful control as for a moment he responded to the eerie scene. Then he flicked off the light switch and watched the eyes disappear into the afternoon gloom, realizing that the group using this house for their Halloween routine had stuck day-glo paint patches all over the walls and replaced the regular bulbs with black lights.

"Jesus Christ," he again muttered, anger resurfacing.

He could hear them downstairs now, laughing, talking, moving things about, though their work crews seemed to be through on the second floor for the moment. He started to go down and ask someone if they'd seen his aunt, then decided to check the attic first. That way he wouldn't have to come back up if no one had seen her, and could simply leave a message with someone downstairs that he couldn't wait any longer.

As far as Peter was concerned, his aunt could have the entire contents of the attic, the house, the cellar, and whatever else she could haul out of here. Just get it out and be done with it and let him get on about his business of developing this site as should have been done years ago.

Peter found the small attic door, almost hidden in a shadowed hallway recess, groped around for the knob, and pulled it open. For a moment he stood, staring into the silence and quasi-darkness of the narrow wooden stairway.

A small dormer window at the top of the stairs bled droplets of afternoon light. He could no longer hear the muted sounds of preparation going on downstairs; there was a deadness to the silence around him, and a slightly sour mustiness that hung on the dust motes hovering about the attic air. No way was his Aunt Elizabeth up here; this place looked like it hadn't been disturbed for millennia.

Peter was about to close the door and go back downstairs when he heard the sound . . . a soft *swish-swish*, like old silk being brushed against the floor.

"Aunt Elizabeth?" He frowned. There was no response, but the sound repeated itself.

Peter scowled again, brushed aside a tendril of cobweb

that was hanging just inside the door, and started up the stairs. Despite their lack of carpeting, no creak accompanied his progress.

"Aunt Elizabeth?" Peter's rich, baritone voice sounded strangely deadened, as though resonance was being sucked from the tones.

"Are you up there, Aunt Elizabeth?" he demanded, feeling the breath quicken in his body—from the climb? from the oppressiveness of the air?

Again the swishing sound drew him, causing his steps to hasten, bringing a flash of ready anger. He'd had quite enough of her game.

"Ugh!"

A length of twisted cobwebs greeted him at the top of the staircase, brushing up against his face and clinging like some gummy old remains of a child's cotton candy. It slithered beneath his collar and began tangling around his chin and neck, not wanting to come off as he pulled and swiped at it angrily. Finally he rid himself of the stuff.

Moving on away from the staircase, Peter glanced around the dusky attic. Cobwebs were everywhere, draped from the rafters, filling the corners, matted across the boxes and trunks and odd pieces of furniture that covered almost the whole floor. There was no sign of his aunt.

The swishing came again. Jerking his head around, Peter moved toward the sound—and then saw what was making it: a length of cobwebs, a thick, heavy weave of them, brushing against a stack of old newspapers strewn in the far corner. Every so often a breath of air from some unknown draft would blow them back and forth over the paper, creating the rustle he had heard.

"Damn it all!"

Quite obviously, his Aunt Elizabeth was not up here. Peter turned to leave, disgusted with himself for wasting his time and prepared to vent that disgust on the first person who crossed his path.

A cobweb brushed his face . . . another . . .

Peter swatted at the straggling mass that suddenly seemed to be coiling about his neck and shoulders. Where he plucked at them, pieces of cobwebs were sticking to his hands, stringing out like thin white taffy.

"What the—"

From his left, a tangled mass of cobwebs drifted toward him, blowing leisurely around the arm he swung in an attempt to ward them off. Slowly they began twining around his upper torso and down around his hips and legs.

"Son of a bitch!"

Peter started to take a step forward. More cobwebs came spinning toward him, from all sides now—growing, multiplying at a fantastic rate.

Frantically, Peter spun his head this way and that, seeing stringy cobweb fingers reaching for him, encircling him, crawling across his skin and around his body. He began to curse—quick, volatile epithets spit into the silence and the shadows, little darts of fury and helplessness and disbelief. *What was happening? What the hell was going on?* He couldn't move—and now the horrible tendrils were creeping across his face, his eyes! *He couldn't see!*

Peter opened his mouth, and cobwebs flowed in, filling it, blotting his strangled cry like a thick wad of cotton. He coughed violently, trying to dislodge the sticky mass so he could roar for help, demand that someone come and get him loose from these things that were attacking him, wrapping his body up like—*like a cocoon, by God!* And now there were tendrils slithering into his ears and down inside his shirt, crawling into his nose! He began to choke, retching involuntarily. He couldn't breathe. *He couldn't breathe!*

Was this some obscene joke? Some game or setup for the Halloween House gone horribly awry? Would someone appear at the very last moment and set him free and they'd all have a good laugh?

And as the cobwebs enshrouded his body, filling his ears and mouth and nose and covering his head, gradually contracting, pulling him upward toward the rafters until he hung suspended two feet off the floor, Peter Beaufort's masterful control kept telling him that yes, this had to be a joke or game or setup, and yes, someone would come just in the nick of time, because things like this didn't happen . . .

And *never* in the daytime . . .

Dood Hopkins sat at a small table in the back of his shop watching smoke coil from his umpteenth cigarette of the day and shadows lengthen outside on Main Street. It was early yet, not quite five o'clock, but day was being bled dark by gathered storm clouds and encroaching night.

Dood toyed with the mug of coffee in front of him, now cold, took a final deep drag from his cigarette, and dropped the butt in the dregs.

The Closed sign hung in the glass-topped door; the room was quiet, the air was still; and thoughts like ragged scraps pulled from a random storage bin were laid out in Dood's mind for inspection.

Here, man, make something out of this.

Okay.

Piece: There was some *thing* at The Manse. Period. That was that. No doubt. He'd seen it.

Piece: For a while, this thing had been active. The two JDs. PoJo. Davy, even?

Piece: Pearl Rollins's visit to The Manse and what she'd told them.

All of it formed neatly into a pattern that spelled trouble, big time—trouble Dood had been expecting for months now. And yet:

Piece: Nothing had happened.

Since the night he had stood in the bitter cold with sleet beating down on him, and watched his version of reality get drawn and quartered by the boogeyman, nothing further had occurred. At least, he amended, nothing to his knowledge. For months now, the house had been quiet, quiescent, a veritable haven of innocence.

Dood had been sick to his stomach with dread as September eased into October and the Jaycee House of Horrors began. But all had gone smoothly; no tales from the dark side, no monsters from beyond, no episodes in the twilight zone. He'd kept close track, casually questioning people who came into his store. Just today he'd heard two more separate reports, carbon copies of each other, from Samantha and Tank.

Tonight was the final night of the Jaycee Haunted House. Tonight would ring down the curtain on The Manse. For good. The news was out that demolition would begin next month to make way for a modern condo unit being built by Mr. Peter Beaufort and partner. There had even been a picture in last week's paper, an architect's rendition of the new Beaufort House Condominiums, proposed completion date, this time next year.

Fine. Good. Tear the house down. If they could just get through this one last night without incident, the fear would stop, the thing would die, and the house and what was in it would be gone, taken apart, forevermore, amen. Just one more lousy night . . .

Why, then, couldn't he get rid of the feeling that something awful was about to happen? Something horrible; something that was waiting for—

"Jesus God!" Dood breathed the words, as suddenly the pieces all came together.

Just one more lousy night!

A shock wave of ice-cold fear washed down Dood's body, making him weak with the thought of what might happen tonight. Pearl Rollins had prophesied it a year ago—snatches of her words came rushing back: *elements being kindled, summoned up—a coming together—an egg nursing on fear, drinking in vitals—growing toward life!*

Dood hugged his arms across his chest, rocking his body slowly backward and forward. A soft moan came out of him with each shallow breath.

Was that why the thing had been so quiet? Was that why nothing had happened over the past few months, and everything was going smoothly at the 13th Annual House? Had it been biding its time, saving its energy, gorging itself on one last month of nightly horror feasts? And tonight—*tonight* on the big grand finale night, when the Jaycees reached for levels of terror they'd never plundered before—would the thing finally become strong enough to make its move, *to be born?*

A hysterical laugh bubbled out of Dood. *It's moving day, folks. Time to get going. It's been swell in this little hick town, but I gotta run now. Moving on up to bigger and better things.*

Am I crazy? Dood slung his head back and forth. *Please, God, let me be crazy!*

As quickly as the laughter spurted from him, it dissipated. Weakness flowed away. Dood felt resolve take hold, felt it look out of his eyes, steady his twitching hands, brace his spine.

If he wasn't crazy, then something had to be done to stop this thing or an unimaginable madness might be let loose on the world tonight. If he wasn't crazy, then someone had to act before this thing's strength equaled its need to live.

Incidents flashed to mind: increased feelings of discomfort in the house, abnormal episodes, stirrings of apprehension; faces flashed to mind: Davy Dawson, his brother Randy, PoJo. Had the thing been testing itself on them?

"It's getting stronger," Pearl had said. The thought was chilling.

Slowly Dood got up from the table. He knew what he had to do. This time there would be no turning back. If he wasn't crazy, then someone had to stop this—and there was no one else but him to try.

Chapter 18

Elizabeth Beaufort woke with a start. It was dark, so dark that for a moment she thought she'd gone blind. Elizabeth had heard of such things happening, something going wrong in your head and you wake up blind or deaf or paralyzed—she twitched her hands and feet—no, not paralyzed.

Slowly, Elizabeth sat up. Where was she? Not in her bed at *that* place. Her heart gave a slight flutter. She put a hand up to her chest and tried to still the breathing that had become too rapid.

Think, Elizabeth . . . Oh, yes, yes, of course—you're in Peter's room, you're waiting for Peter, waiting to kill him.

Confusion roamed among her thoughts. Had she done so? No. No, Elizabeth was certain she had not because— memory came seeping back—because Peter hadn't come.

Elizabeth remembered entering the house, slipping un-
detected through the dining room and large salon, up the
main staircase, down to Peter's room. She remembered
entering the room, remembered twilight lying thick atop
the dust and shadows. The room had been empty. She
remembered seating herself on the straight-backed desk
chair, sitting bolt upright and still for a long, long time,
until the waiting had become so heavy on her that she'd
had to rest. She'd pulled the dustcover back from Peter's
solid mahogany high-poster bed, taken off her fine velvet
cloak and smoothed it out to one side, then settled herself
across the bare mattress, closing her eyes only for a moment. She must have fallen asleep.

How long had it been? Elizabeth reached up and fingered the small timepiece pinned to the front of her bod-
ice. Although her eyes were becoming more adjusted to
the darkness now, there was no hope of seeing the watch
face. She needed light.

Sliding carefully to the edge of the high bed, Elizabeth
groped around and made contact with the night table beside
it. She fingered her way over to the base of the table lamp,
felt up the pedestal to the switch, and turned the lamp on.
Muted light spilled out around the lamp and brushed the
surrounding area. For a moment, Elizabeth's eyes squinted
against the sudden gleam, but it was not a glaring light
and after blinking a couple of times she could see clearly.

She glanced down at the small timepiece, lifting it for a
better view. So clever of her, she thought, to pin it upside
down so she could easily read it at a glance. Elizabeth
frowned. Ten thirty-five. The frown deepened, eyes narrowing, growing cold, as she realized her plan, so carefully plotted, had failed. Peter wasn't coming. Once again

he'd disobeyed her; just as he often had as a child, Peter had failed to do as he was told. Elizabeth's fury began to mount, small hands clenching into fists. Now more than ever, Peter deserved to die! Just like his—

"Elizabeth . . ."

Startled, Elizabeth swung toward the sound of her name being gently called, scanning the darkness beyond the lamp's soft glow. "Who is it? Who's there?" She could see no one in the shadows at the far side of the room.

"Elizabeth . . ."

This time the whispery voice seemed to be coming from beyond the door, out in the corridor.

"Peter?" Elizabeth's eyes sharpened. She glazed her tone with honey. "Peter, is that you, dear?"

Sliding quietly off the bed, she pulled her velvet cloak around her, quickly fastened it, and put the hood up over her head. She did not wish to be seen.

She moved around the bed, then slowly crossed the room. The hem of her cape brushed the floor, a dry whisper-sound of aged silk and old velvet. As she walked, Elizabeth removed from the cape's lining the long, slender hatpin she'd threaded there earlier. Its hand-carved ivory rose head always evoked memories of lovely large hats worn to gracious garden parties, and masses of coiled golden hair.

Clutching the tapered steel body firmly in her right fist, just beneath the rose—the way Cook used to hold the icepick when attacking a huge block of ice—Elizabeth moved to the door, stopped, listened, then opened it. No one stood there. The corridor stretched empty, dark, silent.

"Peter, dear?" Elizabeth moved out into the corridor, the hatpin held ready beneath her cloak. "Peter—"

A sudden burst of shrieks and screams poured from the

far end of the hall. Elizabeth's heart jumped in her chest and began beating crazily. *What was it? What was happening?* Thrusting her body against the wall, she inched away from the shallow light coming through Peter's open door as more sounds filtered toward her—moans, laughter, an undercurrent of jumbled noise and movement.

Elizabeth felt her heart pounding. She could even hear it beating, a steady throb like the beat of a drum, deep vibrations of sound coursing through her body. She placed a hand against her chest, feeling alarm. Was she having a heart attack?

"Elizabeth . . ."

The voice came from beyond her, weaving down the corridor like a wisp of smoke as the jumble of other sounds receded. Elizabeth's grip tightened on the hatpin, the carved ivory rose biting into the soft, pudgy flesh where it nestled against her curled thumb and forefinger.

"Peter?" Her voice sounded brittle.

Slowly she walked on, the soft swish of her cloak following along.

She reached the branch where the corridor met the upper hallway at the top of the long staircase to the main floor. She was hearing movement again—someone coming up the stairs—a bobbing, orange light.

Elizabeth flattened herself against the wall, backing into the corridor once more to wait. Her heart kept beating, beating, the sound of it drowning out the other sounds around her. She shook her head back and forth, trying to be rid of the sound, but it wouldn't go away. Any minute now it would betray her, burst out of her chest.

Screams! Cries of fright!

Eyes! There were eyes! Eyes all around her—eyes looking toward her, staring at her, seeing her in her hiding place!

Elizabeth's moans joined in with the rest, though she was barely aware of the other people in the corridor. All she could see were the gaping yellow eyes staring at her—

Like her brother Avery's eyes had stared at her as she'd stood over his bed, stared up at her—

The eyes disappeared.

Silence slowly settled back into the darkness. Laughter faded. Elizabeth felt herself go limp as the sound of movement receded.

"Elizabeth . . ."

The word scorched the silence, burning into it with a hiss of vitriol. The voice sounded like—

Elizabeth clutched her hatpin. "Avery? Avery, is that you?"

"Elizabeth . . . (Elizabeth . . .)" A second voice, quieter, joined the first.

"Avery! Susannah? Are you here too?" Elizabeth stumbled forward, feeling her way to the staircase, clutching at the banister. "Go away, both of you! You're dead! I know you're dead—as you deserved to be! As your son deserves now!" Elizabeth started down the stairs.

"I remember that afternoon, Avery. Papa's body was still laid out in the library, and I remember how you and Susannah quarreled about the money—you and your shrewish, greedy wife! You were going to sell this house, sell my heritage!"

Slowly, Elizabeth moved down the staircase, hearing again the raging argument that had taken Avery and Susannah from their bedroom to the top of these very stairs, she in the lead, he in pursuit . . .

"Neither of you saw me, did you, Avery? But I followed you, listening, hearing you plot to sell my home!"

Elizabeth moved down the stairs, remembering how Avery had overtaken Susannah that afternoon, grabbed her, shaken her roughly—angry enough to push her down the stairs.

Elizabeth had merely helped him do it, shoving him against his wife, sending them both plummeting to the hallway below. Susannah had broken her neck, Avery his back. He'd lingered for several days, completely paralyzed, unable to speak—but he'd known, Elizabeth had seen it in his eyes as she stood above his bed, seen the anger, the accusation, the fear. She only hoped he'd seen her satisfaction.

She'd reached the bottom of the staircase, leaving Avery and Susannah behind, dead and gone back where they belonged.

"Elizabeth . . ."

Elizabeth froze. The voice was a different one.

"Florence?" She stepped forward cautiously, looking toward the entry hall. "Florence, that can't be you. I left you back at that place. You can't be here . . . I made sure . . ."

Elizabeth flattened her hands against the side of the wall, moving down the long hallway toward the back of the house, away from the voice of her sister . . .

"You had to die, Florence. You know you did. If you'd just kept quiet. But you wouldn't have, would you? I knew you'd begun to suspect, after all these years. It was that girl and her questions, of course, dredging up matters better left alone. But why pick today of all days to accuse me, when I had Peter to take care of? You looked so peaceful lying there afterward. The pillow didn't hurt much, did it, dear? You only struggled a little. If you'd just kept *quiet.*"

Her heart was beginning to pound again, thudding in her chest, heavier, louder—Elizabeth thrust her hands up to her ears, careful of the hatpin still clutched in her palm. She tried to blot out the sound of her wildly beating heart, but it kept on and on, growing stronger.

"Stop it! *Stop it!*" she shrieked to the darkness.

And then other shrieks were joining in, people moving all around her, pushing her along. She was jostled against first one, then another, as a swarming tide of people flowed down the hallway toward the rear of the house. A horrible orange head floated by.

Somehow Elizabeth managed to get over to one side, out of the moving throng. She felt a door behind her, a doorknob, pulled it open. Light filtered out into the hall.

The basement. She could get out this way, go down the stairs, out through the cellar entrance.

"Elizabeth . . ."

Again a voice whispered her name, enticing, familiar—and once more it was different.

"Who? Who are you?"

"Elizabeth . . . Elizabeth . . ."

Elizabeth felt the breath catch in her throat. It couldn't be . . . No! Not— "Edward? Edward, is it you? Was it you all the time?"

Slowly she began to descend the cellar stairs, hatpin raised.

"I'm coming, Edward . . . I'm coming . . ."

Paul Oliver smiled as delighted squeals filled the room of mirrors. His own special pet scenario—for kids only—was proving a particular hit with the under-twelve set. Through eye slits in his concealing black cape, he watched

the small forms cavort from one mirror to another, performing all sorts of gyrations and contortions which the
mirrors gathered in, twisted into their own designs, then
spat back at the laughing children.

The popularity of the mirror maze would go a long way
toward backing up Paul's planned campaign to revamp next
year's House into a kid's carnival. They'd been losing
perspective with their Halloween show for the past few
years, performing increasingly gruesome, horrific scenarios,
going for shock value rather than titillation. Something had
to be done before this thing got completely out of hand.

Paul recalled the feedback he'd gotten following last
year's House. He still believed that a few of the more
gung-ho members of the club had irresponsibly embellished
the setups, though there'd been no hint of such free-
lancing this year. Apparently, Zack's token slap on the
wrist had been taken seriously, which rather surprised
Paul; he'd halfway believed Zack Dalton and his attack
pack responsible.

Paul listened to the happy sounds of children having
fun. He loved kids. That's why he'd become a teacher,
and a Little League coach, and a Scout leader. That's what
this was all about—what it was supposed to be about, and
he was going to spend the next two years trying to guaran-
tee it, before he aged out of the Jaycees and no longer had
the chance.

This would be the last House of Horrors at The Manse,
and before next Halloween, Paul resolved, there were
going to be some drastic policy changes.

Off in the distance, the slow heartbeat from the octagon
room began pumping vibrations throughout the house, sig-
naling that tour in progress. It did sound like a giant heart

beating, gave the feel of being inside something alive. Paul felt his spine contract as the dull thudding began to grow. He, for one, would be glad to move their program elsewhere. Something about this old house gave him the willies.

With an exaggerated moan, Paul entered the maze, adding his costumed reflection to the others being folded, spindled, and generally mutilated by the wavery mirrors. The tour guides were headless horsemen this year; standard-issue black capes fastened around a Styrofoam headpiece gave the open-neck look, evilly grinning jack-o'-lantern heads under one arm. They'd used real pumpkins, spending the day before opening night carving out the faces. Small flashlights tinted orange and mounted inside the fruits gave the luminous finishing touch. Paul had thought some of the heads too scary for younger children, an opinion voiced and, not surprisingly, joked aside. Perversely, he'd carved a smiley face for his.

Trying to ignore the rapidly swelling heartbeat, Paul swooped around a mirror, raising the tenor of his moan. The incessant beating made his skin crawl, an irritating sensation that provoked an urge to squirm out of it, slough it off like a dry, scaly husk. He shrugged his shoulders against the annoying feeling of fingernails scraping a blackboard and tried to concentrate on his role-playing. Only another hour or so and this would all be over.

Tension suddenly claimed him with a prick of alarm. Something was wrong. The thin film of perspiration oiling his body turned cold, became a layer of congealing wax. Had the laughter around him subtly altered? Did it sound slightly forced, unnaturally sharp?

A piercing scream erupted from the far side of the room. Paul's heart caught on a beat, hung suspended, then began to sprint out of control. That scream had been a child's—and it had been terrified!

Ripping the cape from his head and seizing his flashlight, Paul began plowing around the maze of mirrors toward where he'd placed the scream, hearing other frightened voices now, other cries, and panicky movement.

"Remain calm! Everyone remain calm!" Paul shouted over the wails and confusion, bumping into retreating bodies, having no effect whatsoever.

What was happening? What in the hell was happening? Had someone broken a mirror? Fallen through? Cut themselves? He hadn't heard a crash or shattering glass.

"My God . . ." The words were a whispered oath as Paul's body ceased forward motion of its own accord. Veins in his neck and temples began to pulse, swell, hammering against the contradiction of images that met him as he rounded a corner. A child was being pulled into a mirror—by her own reflection!

The pandemonium around him muted into a background drone as Paul's mind struggled to qualify what his eyes were recording.

Groping arms had emerged from the mirror, pushing the glass forward, stretching it like melted plastic. Misshapen child-hands were reaching, grasping, extruded fingers slithering about a little girl in a butterfly costume with silent, eerie grace. The child was struggling and crying—screaming!—as the grotesque pseudo-image claimed her, drawing her into the mirror.

As though suddenly released from paralysis, Paul found himself in motion, blindly stumbling toward the girl, shout-

ing over the frenzied sounds around him for the other
children to ''Run! Get out!''

Grinding his teeth against the delirium that threatened to
send him screaming from the scene with the hysterical
children, Paul grasped the little girl around her waist. There
was an immediate, gut-wrenching shock wave of resis-
tance. Paul's arms felt like they were being jerked from
their sockets as he tried desperately to hang on, pull
backward. He formed an armlock, closing his mind to
shrieking nerve endings as muscles were rended and convulsed. *And what would this be doing to the child?*

A sudden, vicious spasm of force sent him careening
backward, tearing his arms away from the girl's body with
a finality that wrung a cry of anguish from him. Blinding
light exploded in his mind as his head crashed against
another mirror.

Paul crumpled to the floor, fighting clouds of dizziness
and nausea and concussion; he lay there a moment, stunned,
trying to banish the sheets of blackness enveloping him. A
wave of unreality and disbelief crashed against the scene,
splitting apart and dribbling away like so many bubbles on
the wind.

Distorted arms and hands were continuing to slide around
the little girl, mingling into her body now, a liquid, obscene merging. Torsos met, melded together like thick
clotted cream; the skin began to buckle and heave.

Struggling to his feet, Paul staggered forward, moving
as though reeling through molasses, plodding, gasping.

In front of him, mirror-fingers lovingly fondled the
small body, folding it, embracing it, twisting it into impossible angles and curves; skin pulled taut over the writhing

form as the horror became a sickening collage of distended body parts. Paul couldn't seem to reach across the space between them, couldn't seem to get there.

A final scream was severed, lost in a spongy, sucking noise.

Paul's groping hands reached the mirror. Fingers clawed at the undulating smoothness, trying to get a grip on the cold, hard glass, but his hands kept sliding off, slipping away.

And then it began to contract—a hemorrhage of merging— back into the glass—a corruption of swollen, malformed limbs and—

Oh, God! the face—the head—it was reemerging from the mirror, eyes gaping, staring, trying to pull away, sever itself from the thing consuming it. Sluggishly, as if movement were a memory being slowly sucked down a tunnel, the mouth stretched open, lips crawling apart, jaw working in a silent, agonized scream, a scream held prisoner by the glass.

Paul fought to gain hold as gargoyle eyes locked onto him from inside the mirror, bulging fishbowl eyes, watching his futile efforts—and then one of the eyes ruptured with a gush of viscous, puslike fluid that splattered and ran down the inside of the glass.

Paul began to retch. His knees buckled; he fell to the floor. Around him, the frenzied screams, the tidal wave of panicked motion, began to fade away. An eerie silence shrouded the room, silence but for a thick, sucking noise and the heart beating in the distance.

Paul couldn't hear his own heart because the rhythm of

the house-heart had replaced it, impacting on the room like the tolling of a huge, muffled bell. *"Ask not for whom—"*

Slowly the paroxysm left him. He felt weak, wounded. He didn't want to look . . .

Forcing his eyes to obey the command dredged from some level of remaining sanity, Paul turned his broken, brutalized gaze on the room.

The bitter rush of bile resurged as his eyes took in the scene—a scene that could inspire a hundred Dantes, a thousand Poes. Around him, children caught before they could escape the room were being absorbed into the mirrors. Small, contorted bodies were merging with their mirror images, becoming monstrous, swollen child-things. Here and there a body part protruded, a reaching arm, a jerking foot, a silent, screaming head, wrapped in glass the way a spider wraps a fly, cloudy plastic bubbles of writhing bodies, innocent childfaces staring wild-eyed, features smeared, screams locked behind glass.

Paul's mind shut down. He became fascinated with the spectacle surrounding him. It was like watching a silent horror movie, one of the old, surrealistic ones, all blunted shapes and blending colors and merging scenes . . .

He didn't even flinch when something cold touched his back.

Seated on the ground outside The Manse, knees raised, shoulders and head resting against the rough bark of an old hickory nut tree, Dood heard the first faint change in the rhythm of the heartbeat. Not a difference exactly, more a subtle shift in timing, a heavier vibration. He kept his eyes

closed, listening, evaluating, and detected a deeper resonance, too, a half-step drop in tone.

Dood opened his eyes and slowly glanced around the
front yard. Clutches of people milled about, waiting for
midnight and the grand finale, but the line still to go
through the House was shorter. No one else seemed to
have noticed the slightly altered heartbeat, or at least they
were giving no indication of having done so. Perhaps
because he'd had his eyes closed and his mind open,
waiting for something like this to happen, he'd been more
attuned, more receptive.

Dood levered himself to his feet. In spite of being
folded against the tree for almost an hour, his body felt
poised and mobile. "Ready to leap tall buildings in a
single bound," Dood murmured, his tone devoid of amusement, laced with irony.

The heartbeat seemed louder now . . . not in volume,
precisely, but as though the sound had grown, spread out.
People were beginning to notice. Dood saw some look
around, pinpoint several outside speakers that the Jaycees
had set up to use for their big sound-and-light-and-monster
midnight rally finale. The few mildly curious appeared
satisfied with this explanation, although Dood knew otherwise. He was standing not five feet from one of the
speakers. It was silent. The sound was coming from the
house itself, as it had been off and on all night—but
different now.

Dood began walking toward The Manse. Every bone in
his body, every muscle, every nerve, cried out at him to
stay away. For hours he had heeded that internal cry; for
hours after arriving here just past dusk he had circulated

outside the house, slipping from this group of spectators to that, arguing with first one Jaycee then another, edging around the perimeter of the house in his efforts to seduce people away from the danger he feared lay waiting to erupt.

The spectators had thought he was part of the show— *Jolly good show, what?* The Jaycees he'd accosted had laughed, or jeered, or angrily brushed him off—*Igor the eyesore who's flipped his lid.* Finally, after someone reported what was going on, Zack Dalton, decked out in full Wolfman regalia, had come out and threatened to take him downtown and lock him up for the night if he didn't lay off. Since his efforts had been useless, and since from jail he'd be no help at all, Dood laid off. He'd taken up a wait-and-see position against the old hickory nut tree, where the ground was hard and the night lay still and his fear hung dry and thick as the eye of a storm.

And now the elements were coming together. He could feel it in the air, sluggish eddies starting to take shape, move into place—a maelstrom of elements being gathered and formed into . . .

Dood's mind balked at this final visualization. With his heart thudding an echo to the dull, steady sound now coming from the house, Dood climbed the front steps, walked across the porch and past the waiting line, and entered The Manse. He didn't want to. He had to. Had to try and do something, though in his wildest imaginings and despite the movies and books and TV shows, he had no conception of what one could do in such a situation— not when the situation was *real.* Somehow silver bullets and wooden crosses and plastic Jesuses seemed inane.

Darkness greeted him. He reached into his pocket and pulled out the small, high-beam flashlight that had been a constant part of his ensemble for the past several months. Flicking it on, he moved the beam around the entry hall, past the staircase, down the hallway. Maybe just being here, being prepared for something to happen, might make a difference.

A faint glow suddenly broke into the darkness from around the bend in the stairs, followed by a burst of screams. Dood flinched with the sound, but then came laughter, and he felt the quick tension that had claimed him relax its hold. Just an upstairs scenario in progress. Just a sudden glut of fright—fuel for the fire, food for the hungry.

Dood squeezed his eyes shut as a shudder wrenched his body, trying to close out the fear that was threatening to send him screaming from this place. He knew he had to control his fear—the damned thing *ate* fear, gobbled it, popped it in like salted beer nuts! But he couldn't stop shaking; he was trembling all over, to the point that his teeth had begun to chatter.

The heartbeat swelled slightly, as though responding to his fright. Dood felt his stomach churn and acid bite its way up toward his throat. He fought to control his fear and managed to back it down for the moment.

Inside the house, the heartbeat resounded with a hollow, dull thudding, less a sound than an invasion. It pulsed through Dood's body with an almost physical convulsion, a concussion of sound, like the shock waves from an explosion or the after-tremors of an earthquake.

Screams came again, a volley to his left, out on the sun porch . . . They sounded normal.

Off in the distance, other screams, mixing quickly with laughter, spattered the house—other groups, other scenarios taking place on cue.

For a moment, one group of screams seemed different—shriller, more frenzied. It sounded like a bunch of kids. Dood started toward the sound, but then it began to fade.

From down the hall in front of him another group came alive, more muffled this time, as though a silencer had been attached in an attempt to muzzle the sharp report of the screams. The sound buffeted dully about the hallway, impacting against the walls, seeming almost to pulse and surge with the rhythm of the swelling heartbeat.

Dood's eyes snapped open. Something was wrong. There was something wrong with the scenario—something *bad* wrong!

A sudden wail of terror wound into the air, curling around the screams and cries that were becoming frantic now, panicked. There was no letup of sound this time, no relaxation, no laughter. These cries bore no resemblance to the ones still filtering toward Dood from other parts of the house.

Forcing his feet into action, Dood moved toward the sound. Was it only a year ago he'd led groups down this hallway, thought nothing of bouncing rubber spiders off their heads and shoving plastic monster masks in their faces, playing the cool ghoul for all it was worth?

Veering to one side of the entry hall, he ran a hand up the wall several times until he found a light switch. As expected, no light came on in the hallway. Dood bit back an oath.

The sounds were stronger now: startled exclamations, too muffled to understand; curses; screamers becoming hoarse from repetition. They were coming from the octagon room—the small room in the middle of The Manse that was the Jaycees' "absolute highlight of this year's House"—its beating heart. Only now it was something more. Now something was happening inside that room that hadn't been written into the scenario.

A nameless dread sent Dood running down the hall to a door set beneath the staircase. There was no one outside the room. The Jaycee in charge would be inside with the tour group.

Dood flung himself at the door, flashing his light up and around the closed entryway. The door had been covered with thick white padding. Fumbling around where the doorknob should be, Dood found a slit in the padding, thrust his hand in, and grasped the knob. He tried the handle, turned it both ways, but the door wouldn't open. Throwing his shoulder against the heavy padding, he pushed and thrust at the door, still trying to force the knob. But the door was locked, stuck, jammed—*something* was holding it closed!

The sounds inside the room were wild now! Terrified, frenzied people—*children!*—trapped in a room where God only knew what was happening.

Dood caught words: "*Help us!*" "*Stop!*" "*Turn it off!*" He began to beat against the door with the base of his flashlight, shouting through the barrier for someone to pull while he pushed—help him from inside—*get the fucking door open!* But they didn't hear—or were past hearing.

Dood began yelling up and down the hallway, continuing to pound against the door, the walls.

Inside the room, the sounds began to change, become fainter, dying out.

Flashlight still clutched in one fist, Dood gave a final savage heave against the door, shoving his entire body into the attack, screaming, cursing the power that kept the door from opening, while his mind and stomach lurched with the horror of what he might see if it should. But the door wouldn't budge—it was as though a heavy pressure lay against it, like a million gallons of water crushing against a bulkhead.

Around him the thudding of the heart had swelled into a hammer beat that rammed his body again and again. Burning tears scalded his eyes and spilled down his face. His own cries were becoming weak and hoarse now, interspersed with great, hiccuping sobs of fright and fury.

Inside the room, the screams had stopped. The cries were stilled. A new sound had taken their place: a heavy sound, like water, lapping against the inside of the room . . . a thick, gelatinous slap crawling up the inside of the door.

Dood didn't want to think about this—his mind repelled it, refused to consider it. He held his breath as silence wrapped itself around him, tomblike except for the steady tolling of the heart and the *lap lap lap* against the inside of the door. The rhythm jarred his teeth together, flinched his body each time it came. He stood there in the throbbing silence.

Something moist touched his hand. Something warm
and sticky. Dood's subconscious mind knew what it was,
knew what he'd see if he peeled his hands away from the
thick white padding that covered the door . . . but his
consciousness said no. No, I don't want this knowledge.
No, I won't accept my fair share of the burden. No, I
don't want to know, don't want to see. No. No! *No!*

Dood slowly backed away from the door, not looking at
his hands and arms, until he was stopped by the wall
behind him. A gurgling sound oozed from his mouth. The
white padding was stained. Where he'd leaned against it, a
dark blotch formed a distorted outline of his body. Even as
he watched, the stain began to change, to grow, spread
out.

Almost without volition, Dood inched the beam of the
flashlight down from the ceiling, down to the white-padded
doorway that—"OhsweetGodmyJesus!"—had begun to
bleed!

The root cellar was cold, airless. What light managed to
find this far corner of the basement seemed to be instantly
gobbled up by the small pit that was the old storage room.

Poised on the descending steps, hatpin still grasped
firmly in her right hand, Elizabeth felt along the inside
walls for a light switch before remembering that they'd
never run electricity down here. The root cellar had become obsolete and much too inconvenient years ago, its
coolness unnecessary after the advent of the icebox, its
darkness of worth only if one wished to grow mushrooms—or
hide bodies.

"Edward? Are you here?"

No sound answered Elizabeth's question. No voice whispered her name. But Elizabeth knew where Edward was. He was right where she'd put him more than fifty years ago, right under this soft dirt floor, covering his body with garden lime like she'd seen the gardener do once with the body of Papa's old hunting dog. "Dissolves it quick, even the bones," the gardener had told the curious child. "Keeps it from smellin' too, and drawin' things." Elizabeth had asked what kind of "things," and received only a shrug in reply, but her active imagination had no trouble supplying a vision that crawled with adjectives like "slimy" and "squirming."

Sounds came from the basement behind her—muffled curses from the young man who had been totally involved with some sort of apparatus at the old furnace while she silently made her way across the back of the room. He hadn't even noticed the old woman in the black cape moving around the edge of the basement, so intent was he on his machine. She'd been sure he would at least hear the heavy thudding of her heart.

Elizabeth moved on down the steps, pushing the door closed behind her. The creak of long-disused hinges scraped across her nerve endings. She froze. Would they hear? Elizabeth stood immobile for a long, tense moment, feeling the darkness and the cold begin to seep their way past the fear that wrapped her body. No, she finally decided, they hadn't heard . . . and neither could she hear them, now— the beating of her heart seemed bent on drowning out all other sound.

The droning thud and the total darkness began to fray Elizabeth's composure. Her mind groped away from encroaching panic the way her fingers had fumbled to find a light switch. *Matches, candles!* Hadn't there been a supply of those kept always at hand? She inched sideways toward where the rows of shelving began, feeling cautiously around in the dust and rubble of years.

Ah, yes. There they were. Elizabeth laid the hatpin down beside the box her searching fingers had discovered, lifted its top, and drew out the stubby remnant of an old tallow candle. And here were matches too; still dry in their wrap of waxed paper and waiting to be used these many years.

With great deliberation, Elizabeth struck a match against the rough wood shelf, watched it flare to life, then touched it to the stubby candle. She held her breath when at first she thought it wasn't going to catch, but then the wick sputtered and lit. Blue-white flame flickered and swelled into the small chamber, throwing dancing shadows against the age-darkened plank walls in a crazy pattern of bobbing heads and craning necks. For a moment, Elizabeth felt as if she were in the midst of a circling mass of misshapen beings—dwarfs and elves and strange towering giants cavorting about. But then the flame began to settle into routine shedding of light and the figures disappeared.

Sudden heat drew her attention back to the match, which had almost burned down to her fingers. Quickly extinguishing it, Elizabeth dropped the remains to the ground and cupped her hand around the burning candle. She looked around the room, eyes traveling past dusty shelves with their dried remains of long ago dotted here and there, past trailing cobwebs that strung and overlaid forgotten jars and burlap potato sacks, seeking out a far corner beneath some

extra shelving no one had ever bothered to install, the
planks leaning against the back wall over a natural depres-
sion in the floor.

"Edward? Why don't you answer me? I know you're
here." Elizabeth took a step forward, eyes locked on the
far corner of the room. A smile rested serenely on her
face. "You've been here such a long time, Edward—and
you'll be here for a long time yet. You can't escape."

The coldness in the cellar seemed almost liquid. Beads
of it spread across her exposed skin, around her neck, over
the backs of her hands; small rivulets of liquid ice were
trickling down her back, her arms, her legs.

"It was warm that afternoon, Edward, warm in the
garden, with the birds and the flowers and the soft stirrings
of the wind. Such a beautiful day for you to spoil. I
wanted you, and I made you want me . . . until *she* came
between us. But I took care of all that, didn't I?

"You shouldn't have told me, you know. You should
have merely gone away. So convenient, your already telling everyone that you were going and would send for me.
I followed your suggestion to 'save me the embarrassment
of a broken engagement' and dutifully reported that you
had fallen ill while abroad, and then that you had died. So
fortunate that you had no close family to ask difficult
questions, and I satisfied the others quite nicely, never
letting on to Florence that I knew it was she who had taken
my place in your heart. Florence—my own dear sister!

"Were you going to send for her later, Edward? Would
you both have lived happily ever after somewhere far
away? But instead, here you are, and here you were all
those years ago when I watched dear, trusting Florence's

inner happiness slowly turn to anxiety, then despair, waiting for her lover to fulfill his promise—while all the time your bones lay rotting right under her foolish nose. She grieved and never married, Edward . . . but then, neither did I, though I did have the pleasure of talking about you from time to time. My 'dear young man who died' . . .''

Elizabeth took a step backward as suddenly the beating heart reclaimed her attention. It had crescendoed to a deafening boom, shaking the very walls around her, causing the ground beneath her feet to tremble, quiver. She glanced around the room, darting little looks this way and that. What was happening?

"Elizabeth . . ."

Elizabeth froze, staring at the far corner of the room. One of the leaning planks had started to shake—twitching, jerking, heaving outward as though some force was building up beneath it. One by one, the other boards joined the dance, knocking against each other, cracking, splitting down their lengths, across their widths. They began to splinter, blossoming outward in a sudden burst of escaping pressure, exploding into the room like jagged pieces of shrapnel.

Elizabeth tried to shield herself from the vicious assault that had come so unexpectedly. Pieces of wood showered around her like a rain of arrows, pelting her body, jolting a cry of alarm and pain and fright from her lips.

"Elizabeth . . ."

Elizabeth whirled around, hands still cradling the burning candle, eyes peering, squinting into the darkened corner . . .

The ground! The ground was trembling, forming little

fissures, sending small eruptions of loose dirt into the stale air. And now a larger crater sank inward, giving off a deep rumble that was sucked up by the wild beating of her heart, its vibrations joining the shudders racking her body. Fear gushed through Elizabeth, huge tidal waves of it, choking off the sob that almost closed her throat.

"Edward, no. No, Edward!" she cried hoarsely, backing away, eyes widening in disbelief at the sight of what was happening in front of her.

Slowly, from several places in the loosened earth, bones had begun to emerge . . . white, glowing bones, growing larger as they slid from the ground.

Elizabeth moaned, a small mewling noise that was lost in the cacophony filling every inch of space. The bones were rising from their grave, shaking off the dirt of years, reaching from the ground to point toward Elizabeth—coming for her! Lengths of them broke free, pieces horribly distorted, eaten away—a finger here, an arm there, part of one hip—disjointed, unattached bones, emerging singly from their tomb like pale, dead soldiers of the night.

Elizabeth continued to back away from the bones that were joining together now in a distorted shape—legs and ribs and shoulder bones, forming hands, giant, reaching hands made of bones, reaching out for her.

"No, no," Elizabeth moaned, shaking her head backward and forward, closing her eyes. "Go away! Please, please, go away!"

She stumbled against the bottom step. Keeping her balance, she began to back up the stairs, moaning softly, eyes squeezed shut.

"Elizabeth . . ."

Elizabeth stopped crooning, stopped her backward motion. Slowly she opened her eyes and turned her face toward the sound. Her frozen gaze slipped past the gleaming fragmented bones crawling on the air toward her, past the distorted, monstrous hands made from bits and pieces of Edward's skeletal remains, to—

"Oh, dear God, dear God, save me, save me . . ." Elizabeth felt the final terror rend through her. In the center of the reaching hands of bone, a gaping, smiling skull was floating—a living skull, *Edward's* skull, alive with all the crawling, slimy, putrid things that hadn't kept away . . . creeping toward her, growing, becoming larger, opening its swarming, festering mouth in a silent screaming laugh.

Elizabeth's hand flew to the door behind her. Fingers clawed, tore at the rough wood, grasped the handle. She gave a savage jerk, pulling the door open.

"Stay away! Stay away!" she screamed, thrusting one hand toward the skull—the hand that still gripped the lighted candle. Fingers spasmed open. The candle dropped, its flame momentarily disappearing in the folds of her cape, nestling against the rich velvet and spun silk of another time, another reality, the age-worn cloth that held all the brittle dryness of more than sixty years.

With the roar of a torch being ignited, the cape burst into flames.

================ Chapter 19 ===

The night came alive with squeals of fright, then laughter, as Tank Worley jumped from behind a tree brandishing his ax with all the enthusiasm of a cheerleader. Pealing forth a maniacal laugh, Tank charged the group just exiting The Manse via the sun porch, swinging his ax in a vicious semicircle of menace, backing them against the side of the house as blade slashed air.

He stopped about twenty-five feet from the cringing, giggling group and began to stalk them, giving his best to the performance, enjoying it thoroughly. This routine had proved his favorite yet, much better than the Frankenstein role he'd figured to get stuck with again. More comfortable too. Tank gave the air another chop, flexing his arms easily without the heavy clothing he usually wore. The plain white work shirt with its rolled-up sleeves emphasized his muscled physique and shone eerily in the muted outside lighting.

Loping toward the group, Tank again treated them to his sinister laugh, threatening them with detailed descriptions of what he intended to do with the ax, careful to shake the weapon at the proper angle for the spotlight to pick it up. Obligingly, the polished blade caught a beam and spit refracted light back at the crowd.

Right on cue, Micky Wainwright came running from around front, yelling, "This way! This way to safety! Everybody follow me!"

Tank roared with insane laughter once more, wiggling his toes inside his old size-fourteen Topsiders as the crowd surged toward Micky. Lovely.

Throwing a final exaggerated burst of ad-libbed threats at the retreating crowd, he returned to his tree cover, crouching down behind some bushes to wait for the next tour group. They should be winding down soon, beginning to congregate out in the front yard for the Midnight Surprise.

Sounds like a nightcap, Tank thought in amusement, or a David Letterman special.

He settled down to wait and immediately became aware of the heartbeat. It sounded wrong. For weeks he'd been hearing it, night after night, hour after hour; a background drone, relegated to a slot in his subconscious. It was no longer inserted there.

A frown creased Tank's brow; he stood up, knocking over his empty coffee thermos in the process. Tank let it lay, tuning all his senses to the sudden feeling of wrongness. He'd set up the sound equipment, given instructions to the two neophyte Jaycees assigned to monitoring duty, then dismissed the whole shebang from his mind to have fun with the mad-gardener skit. The rookies had handled it perfectly . . . until this moment.

Even as he listened, the beat grew louder, louder than anything they'd done before. And the rhythm was different, less syncopated, more . . . concise.

"Somebody's jumping the gun on the midnight show," Tank growled, starting for the house. "I knew I shouldn't have let those new guys—"

A tree branch flew in his way. Tank impatiently flung it aside and stumbled across a root. "What the hell?" He'd picked a fairly clear spot in the foliage for his hiding place, just beside a winding pathway to the yard, but he seemed to have veered off it somehow.

Bushes closed around him as he plowed his way through the trees. Low-hanging limbs reached out to snag at his clothes, his arms, almost like spindly hands grabbing, clutching.

"Shit!" One of the branches rebounded, lashing his bare arm. He rubbed at the welt and felt the warm ooze of blood.

A tangle of kudzu vines loomed toward him from the left, blown by a gust of wind that hadn't been evident before. They coiled around a branch, then came rippling forward, looking like giant black snakes twisting and turning. One of them whipped around Tank's neck, circling his throat as if it had purpose.

Exerting an almost superhuman effort, Tank grasped the tough vine and tugged it from him, throwing his body forward in a frenzied effort to escape the suddenly malevolent vegetation that seemed intent on impeding him, attacking him, holding him back . . .

Then he was through, bursting into the empty space at the edge of the back garden, falling to his knees in the damp grass and rising mist in an attempt to catch his breath and comprehend what the hell had just happened.

"What's going on!" Tank demanded of the night, trying to shake off the utter terror that had gripped him. "What the hell is going on?"

Mist rolled across the lawn, an ocean of sluggish white swells, a languid, eerie tide of soundless motion, dipping and spreading through the garden. Tank stared at the central fountain, which was bathed in a milky incandescence that made it look illuminated from within. Tongues of swirling mist were beginning to coil around the base and lick at the statue of the mermaid.

Tank pushed himself to his feet, feeling the dampness of the ground cling to him. The wind had grown, sending gusts dive-bombing through the yard and around the house in a moaning race with the swirling mist. A low rumble of thunder brought Tank's eyes heavenward; boiling clouds churned across the sky, blending gashes of deep purple and midnight blue with charcoal black.

Tank had the sudden, burning feeling of being trapped in a huge cauldron, of things rushing together in a scalding fury.

A jagged clash of lightning stung the sky, blinding him for a moment, causing him to throw an arm across his eyes. Thunder growled, vying with the heart that was beating insanely now, a great crash of sound that sent

shock waves through the ground and up the length of
Tank's body.

Then he saw the flickering light.

Fire!

Samantha gasped as the full impact of sound hit her.
Out in the kitchen annex the growing heartbeat had been
clearly audible, increasing as she threaded her way through
the back corridor to avoid areas in use—but here in the
front entry hall the sound was deafening.

She clamped her hands over her ears. What was going
on? Why were they starting the midnight show this early?
It was barely eleven-thirty. Didn't whoever was doing
basement duty know that the big sound-and-light finale
wasn't supposed to start until the stroke of twelve?

Samantha had been on break, and pleasantly involved in
a close encounter of the passionate kind with a certain
attorney who was unusually lighthearted tonight, despite
the macabre surroundings. The intrusion of the heartbeat
had finally been persistent enough, however, to send her
scowling from the kitchen to investigate.

"If they decided to up the schedule, the least they could
do is tell me," she muttered, starting down the hallway
toward a splash of light escaping from a fist-sized crack
where someone had stupidly left the basement door ajar.

Behind her, the front double doors swung open, then
banged shut.

"What the hell's going on in here?" Zack Dalton demanded angrily, flipping on a flashlight and sweeping its
beam down the hall toward Samantha.

The light pinpointed her, caught in the act of turning

around to see who'd come in. She flung up an arm draped
in gauzy white to shield her eyes from the sudden glare.

"Now I'm deaf *and* blind," she mumbled, then louder,
"Do you mind pointing that beacon in another direction,
Zack?"

Zack flipped the flashlight onto low beam and strode
toward her, eyes glittering through the slits of his werewolf headpiece. "What's going on? Where's Tank? Who
turned up the volume down there?" He stabbed the beam
from the flashlight toward the basement door.

"I was just on my way to find out," Samantha said as
he reached her; she found herself staring at his retreating
back—all business—as he strode past, heading for the
basement. She ran to catch up, sparing a cursory glance at
the door to the octagon room nestled beneath the staircase.
No one seemed to be about.

"Shit!" Samantha's feet had found a puddle of someone's spilled drink, or—worst thought of all—someone's
dinner that had gotten scared out of them. She lifted the
long, flowing skirts of her Lady Drac costume and tried to
see what she'd stepped in, but it was still too dark in the
hallway, even though Zack had thrown the basement door
wide open after stomping through.

"Ignorance is probably bliss," she muttered.

Holding her skirts up, she carefully extracted herself
from the puddle and hurried after him, wincing as the
horrible beating of the heart crashed around her again and
again.

As she reached the basement door, she had the vague
impression that someone called her name from the shadows behind her. She almost stopped and turned around,

then decided it must have been a trick of the hallway acoustics, an echo or distortion of the sounds coming from the basement. She stepped through the door and glanced down on the scene below.

"It's not *on*, I tell you!" a heated, slightly hysterical voice was shouting above the din. Matt James, the young Jaycee in charge of the audio equipment, was waving some wires back and forth wildly in front of the wolfman towering over him. "It's not even plugged in. Do you *hear* me, Dalton? It's not even fucking *plugged in*!"

Samantha felt a frown draw her eyebrows together as she moved down the basement steps, remembering to pull the door closed behind her so that none of the tour groups using the hallway would hear this commotion. What kind of uproar was Zack causing this time?

"What do you mean, it's not plugged in?" Zack was shouting. "I can hear it, asshole! You've got the amps on full—"

"I do not, you fucker!" Matt James screamed at Zack, cutting him off in midsentence.

Samantha came to a standstill at the bottom of the stairs, frozen in shocked disbelief as with a completely unexpected burst of savage violence Matt yanked the tape recorder out of the old furnace and smashed it to the cement floor. The heartbeat swelled around them.

"It's not on! It's not on!" Matt continued to scream, jerking out parts and pieces of their audio equipment and flinging them to the floor.

"Shit, man!" As though coming out of a daze, Zack stripped the hairy gloves from his hands, yanked the wolfman's head off and flung it toward a corner, then made a grab for Matt James, who was shouting and throwing things as if he'd gone instantly insane.

Sudden fear gripped Samantha—a bone-crushing, stomach-heaving paroxysm of fear—as every doubt, every dread, every insanity that had been carefully compartmentalized and stored away came exploding out. Around her the heartbeat crashed and split apart—a pile driver of sound hammering against the cement wall of logic she'd built up over the past months, sending huge chunks of it careening into oblivion. *There shouldn't be sound! The heart shouldn't be beating!* She'd seen the dangling wires Matt had torn from the equipment. She'd seen the recorder dashed to the concrete floor, pieces of it erupting in all directions. *There shouldn't be this pounding, relentless sound!*

What in God's name was alive in this hell house? What was alive in here?

Movement caught her—a flash of motion from the steps above. She glanced up, and immediately recoiled. There at the head of the stairs, poised like a study in scarlet and incomprehension, stood Dood.

As Samantha stared up at him, he began to descend the stairs, slowly, hands extended in front of him. He was looking at his hands, studying them as though he'd never really seen them before.

His hands were red. The front of his shirt was red. The undersides of his sleeves were red. His jeans. Deep, cloying red. Thick red. Dripping red. *Blood* red. He was turning his hands and arms this way and that, looking at first one, then the other, then back again, as if he'd sought out this light to study himself.

All at once he glanced up, focused on Samantha's stare.

Samantha shrank back from the look in his eyes—a look of
profound, oblique knowledge. Nothing in her life had ever
terrified her as that look now did.

"The room is full of blood," Dood remarked matter-of-
factly. The words cut through the crashing heartbeat like a
laser's pulse. "They drowned, of course. All drowned in
the blood." He spread his hands apart. "I couldn't get the
door open." He took a step downward. "I couldn't get the
door open." Another step. "I couldn't get—"

"*Zack!*" Samantha screamed, pushing her body against
the basement wall behind her, flattening her hands against
it on either side as if to push through the wall, away from
what was happening here. "Zack! Zack! Zack!" She
squeezed her eyes shut against the insanity closing in
around her, screaming his name again and again.

"Sam, what's—*Christ Almighty!*"

Samantha's eyes flew open at the explosive change in
the timbre of Zack's last two words. He had started to
move toward her, but something had caught his attention,
something on the far side of the basement. Even as Samantha
turned to see what it was, Zack uttered an oath and started
running across the room toward the fireball that had erupted
from some nether region at the back end of the cellar. A
flickering, ominous light was already crawling along the
far wall.

Flames leaped from the blazing pillar, and screams,
inhuman, nightmarish screams! Smoking fragments of fire,
detached from the moving sheet of flame, were being
flung to the sides and behind a writhing, lunging, *shrieking*
figure. A human figure, grotesquely distorted in the midst
of the fireball—black against orange, scarecrow arms flail-

ing wildly as it ran a zigzag pattern toward the stairs
leading up into the house.

Samantha found herself moving sideways, away from
the stairs, toward the furnace where Matt James lay sprawled
in oblivion. Zack must have punched him, Samantha
thought, as she knelt beside the younger Jaycee. Wide-
eyed and helpless, she watched Zack rush toward the
burning body, which, *unbelievably,* tried to evade him, to
elude his help!

And then from Samantha's left, another form burst onto
the scene, trying to head off the fireball. It was L.J., jolted
from whatever edge of insanity he'd been teetering on,
back into the reality that was filled with the kind of
madness you couldn't escape.

Samantha realized she'd started to shake Matt, pull at
his prone body. Fire stung her vision from a dozen points.
Beyond the figures madly chasing each other about, fire
blazed and danced.

"Matt!" She shook him roughly, screaming, "Matt,
we've got to get out of here!" But he wouldn't come to.

She glanced around wildly. Would she be able to move
his unconscious body?

In the far corner of the basement, flames had begun
consuming the walls, moving inward. The wooden windowsill and the door to the outside staircase had already
caught fire. There'd be no escape there. Pieces of burning
cloth and flesh continued to rain through the air as the
blazing form threw itself toward the inside staircase . . .
and the stench, oh, God, the stench . . .

Zack and Dood had managed, finally, to intercept the
human torch, Zack kicking the blackened legs from be-

neath the fiery torso and throwing his body down on top of the burning pyre in an attempt to smother the flames.

"Zack! No!" Dood yelled, trying to pull the huge man in the hairy costume away from the flaming body. "Your suit! You'll catch fire too!" Dood yanked at the wolfman's suit, at the same time trying to beat out the flames with the jacket he'd torn from his own back.

"Zack!" Samantha jumped to her feet as she saw flames take hold of the costume, joining her scream to Dood's. "Zack, get off!" Without thought, she took several steps forward.

Around them sound was a thing alive. Inhuman shrieks from the mass of flames, her own screams, cries and curses from both Dood and Zack, who, mercifully, had finally understood his own imminent danger and rolled off the burning form, then brutally stripped away the now flaming wolfman suit. Relentless sound pounded the room, blending, merging, running together . . .

. . . and overlaying all, the frenzied, maniacal beating of the heart.

Tank began running toward the breezeway entrance, plodding through the swirling sea of mist that was up to his calves now. Each step felt heavy, thick; his leg muscles strained with the effort of lifting and stretching, as if the ground were covered in a gummy residue that stuck to the bottom of his shoes. Mist stroked and curled around his legs like soft, cool fur, the way a cat will arch and rub its body against a standing object. It felt like fingers, caressing, alive.

Desperately he scanned the yard for other Jaycees, seeing

no one. He was trying to decide if he should yell "Fire!" Moments might make the difference in escaping the house, despite the fire drills' emphasis on calmness, control—but it might also start a disastrous stampede. Praying they knew what they were talking about, he opted to follow the fire code, clamping his teeth on the shout that threatened to erupt.

He dashed around the corner of the house, glancing behind him one last time for possible reinforcements, and almost missed a step at what he thought he saw. *No. Not possible.* He kept on running, to the breezeway door now, blocking off the vision of a swelling contortion of mist and bulbous, gleaming eyes—teeming eyes—*just a costume—kids—a group of kids.*

Up the steps. In the door, banging it behind, still seeing no one. Tendrils of mist entered with him, curling through the air like ropy coils of smoke. Abstractedly he brushed one aside, then recoiled when he seemed to feel it slither against his skin as though it had substance.

For a moment he thought the inside door was fastened; he couldn't get it to budge. Then he wrenched it open and was through, sprinting down the corridor that ran straight to the main hallway despite the fact that they were supposed to avoid the tour areas. He vaguely registered that he was still gripping the ax.

The air was pungent here, overlaid with a sour, rotten smell. His ability to move seemed compromised, slowed. He had the sensation of running in half time, moving to a slow-motion cadence in rhythm with the pounding heartbeat.

This wasn't real . . . he'd fallen asleep outside in the woods and this was a dream . . .

Tank glanced to his left as he passed an open door—
Paul Oliver's mirror maze—and saw the shifting, distorted
reflections of a dozen or more children in the eerily silent
room . . . but where were *they*?

On his right a grinning monster mask glowed wickedly
in the darkness, installed over a wall sconce to light the
way while keeping in line with the decor. It suddenly
looked like a disembodied ghoul's head with slitted green
eyes that gazed directly at him, moving to follow his
progress. As he passed by, it began to laugh. *No, no, that*
can't be. We didn't set up anything like that unless Zack
or J.T.—of course, they did it, they did it without me
knowing . . .

Peals of diabolical laughter followed him down the corridor, and now a second mask-head turned to watch him,
its burning red coal eyes shifting his way, thick blackened
lips twisting into a smile.

Don't look don't hear don't think just run—run!

Thoughts became as plodding as steps; sounds began to
merge, becoming one long sequence of throbbing heart-
beats as Tank groped toward the front hall, seeing the
ominous flickering light, hearing snatches of terrified screaming, smelling the first acrid stench of smoke.

Something touched Samantha's leg . . . something cold.
She looked down. An electrical cord lay curved across the
cement floor, stretching from the furnace to her left foot,
disappearing beneath the hem of her long skirts. As she
watched—dumbfounded, held immobile by some sort of
grotesque fascination—she realized it was moving, slowly
inching, slithering serpentlike over the floor.

Samantha couldn't move—couldn't scream—couldn't seem to breathe. She was mesmerized by the snaking cord, by the feel of it slipping over her foot, around her ankle— cold wire in a plastic casing, pulsing with the rhythm of the heartbeat, breathing against her skin, *coiling up her leg!*

"Zack." Had she shouted his name? Murmured it? Thought it?

But he was turning toward her, his expression hardening as it caught hers, eyes narrowing as though stung by her gaze, locking onto her horror-stricken gaze and holding it for what seemed an eternity until she realized he was closing the distance between them, coming to take her away from the madness that was cascading in from above and below and all around . . . and then he was here, grabbing on to her, holding on to her like he'd never been away, gathering her against his chest, and how could she have ever thought he'd try to hurt her . . .

A sudden, gentle tug on her leg ripped through Samantha. The thing was around her knee!

"Zack, it's on me! Get it off! Get it off!"

Gripping Zack's body with a strength born of madness, Samantha tried to jerk away from the coiling wire.

Zack was fighting her. "Sam, let go! Dammit, I can't—"

Zack tore away from her. The break was a rupture of physical agony, a severance from the lifeline she'd embraced physically and mentally.

Grabbing at him wildly, she tried to pull him back, her fractured mind caught on a jagged thought that he might be leaving her, abandoning her to the nightmare that could send an electric cord coiling up her leg.

But he was bending down, thrusting aside the long skirts
with a curse, grappling with the cord that had firmly
twined its way around two thirds of her left leg.

"What *is* this?" he yelled. "What's happening here?
What the hell's going on?" And then, "My God . . ."

He was looking past her. She followed the look; the
breath in her lungs froze. Matt James was a mass of
writhing, coiling, twisting wires. Black electrical cords
were wrapping themselves around his twitching body, pulling it toward the old furnace. Matt was awake now, awake
and aware of what was happening to him. It was, God,
like an octopus with its long black tentacles coiling and
waving and—

Samantha stopped looking at Matt. She didn't want to
look at Matt. She could hear him screaming, or was it her
own screams rending the air? Zack was working furiously
now to free her leg, casting glances toward Matt between
bouts of cursing and confusion. "Dood!" he yelled over
his shoulder. "Help me!"

Samantha twisted to see Dood still frantically beating
the spreading flames. He'd abandoned the blackened crea-
ture beneath the stairs—Samantha averted her gaze from
the charred form, the thing that *had to be* dead—and was
desperately attempting to turn the fire back from the staircase, their only remaining means of escape.

Smoke billowed to the top of the room like heavy black
storm clouds strung over their heads. Heat and fumes stung
her eyes. She squeezed them shut, feeling tears swim
across the gritty insides. A red haze began to form in front
of her jammed-down lids. Sound became pain; thoughts
became visions. She could see the scene around her im-

printed on the inside of her eyelids like a tabloid nailed to
a board . . . becoming nebulous now, misty . . . fizzing
like the bubbles on a soda . . . wisping away like cigarette
smoke through an open window . . .

If she opened her eyes now, would she see a blank
screen? Couldn't this, please, God, be a dream and let's
all wake up now and go home.

Something changed. She could feel the sudden shift in
the air—a pressure building—a subtle movement of air
currents around her, sucking inward, brushing her face.
Sound, too, was being altered, becoming muddied, muffled, deadening into one central drone, becoming one with
the air and the night.

Someone grabbed her arms. She screamed.

"Samantha!" Dood's voice. "Samantha, help us get
you loose."

Only then did she realize that a battle was going on
around her, a struggle for her body against an enemy that
was steadily gaining in strength, pulling her toward it,
reeling her in like Matt. *Like Matt!*

She started to fight then, joining in the battle with every
ounce of stamina she had left, kicking and tugging and
straining against the force that would take her—

"Jesus—Matt!"

Samantha pried her eyes open at the tone of Zack's
words, then wished she hadn't. Matt James's body had
been pulled into some sort of *vortex* where the furnace had
been. No, the furnace was still there, she could see its
distorted outline through the swirling, sluggish whirlpool
that seemed to be forming in front of it, or around it, or—

"God, no," she whispered as Matt's body began to

swell, the cords twined about it snapping off to snake upward through the whirlpool like hissing, spiraling serpents on a Medusa's head. The body grew, expanded, cracking and splitting open, organs spilling into the churning whirlpool of air and sound and mist, blending into the swirling vortex.

Fire lapped at the edges of the expanding pool, tongues of flames licking at the vortex, being fanned by the rushing air. Fingers of fire were spreading all around them, reaching out to stroke, caress.

Samantha felt herself shoved *violently*. Something gave way. She stumbled forward into Dood's arms, free.

"Get her out of here, Dood," Zack was yelling. "Get her out!"

She looked back at him in confusion—why wasn't he coming?

"Zack! No!" She swung at Dood. "We can't leave him! Dammit! Dood—" She began to fight, kicking, scratching, screaming at Dood, who was managing to hold on to her, pulling her away from Zack—Zack, who had saved her life, but at what cost?

"Samantha, we can't help him, it's too late!" Dood shouted.

She twisted back around toward Zack. He was struggling furiously with the cords that encircled his body. The one that had held Samantha was coiled about his arm now and moving up toward his shoulder. Other cords—hundreds of them, it seemed—were slithering across the air or were already crawling about his body, wrapping him up as they had Matt James, pulling him into the cyclone of sound and corruption that had opened behind him.

"Dood, let me go. Damn you, let me go!"

Relentlessly, Dood forced her away from the scene. Her
gaze remained locked on the struggle; she watched Zack
being sucked into this swirling, boiling abomination coming alive in the basement. His face was contorted with the
effort of the fight he was waging—the face she'd held
between her hands and kissed. His body strained against
the tightening cords—the body that had lain with her,
touched her, loved her. The sky-blue eyes swept back and
forth, the gaze searching, seeking, trying to understand; in
it swam fury and incomprehension and pain, but not
defeat—it would *never* occur to Zack that he might lose.

"Please, God," Samantha whispered, *"please . . ."*

Zack swam before her eyes—not the writhing, expanding body being dragged into the maw, but another Zack: a
sleeping Zack, snoring so loudly one night that she couldn't
sleep and after what seemed like hours finally hit him with
a pillow, which had awakened him, which turned into a
pillow fight, which turned into a wrestling match, which
turned into . . .

A laughing Zack: handing her a bouquet of dandelions
on her birthday, rubbing them on her nose, then pulling a
single long-stemmed red rosebud from behind his back,
that horrible cap cocked sideways on his mop of blond
hair . . .

A playful Zack: clad in the old green gym shorts she'd
always hated, and the crazy T-shirt he was wearing now,
one of a pair he'd bought as a joke, his with a finger
pointing sideways saying "I'm with Stupid," hers saying
"I'm Stupid." They'd always mock-fought over who had
to wear the "I'm Stupid" one, with her always losing.

Zack: focusing for one horrid instant on her, seeing her grappling with Dood, Zack shouting, "Get out, for God's sake, Samantha!"

"No, Zack, please," she whimpered as with a final wrench, Dood thrust her toward the blazing staircase.

An abstract portion of Samantha's mind debated the question of how much horror a human brain could absorb before curdling into permanent mush. Had it already happened? Was this horrible vision only a dream conjured up by her insanity? Please, God, let it be a dream . . .

The wooden staircase was fast becoming an inferno, the railing a latticework of leaping flames and burning support posts. A stream of liquid fire ran down the banister and swirled in little eddies around the newel-posts. The lower steps were alight in places, but about midway up the fire had taken full control. A sheet of solid flames stretched across the stairs, spreading as Samantha watched, cutting them off from the door to the hallway.

"We can't get through!" she screamed, balking at the insistent hand still shoved into the middle of her back. "Dood, the stairs are already crumbling."

"We've got to," Dood yelled back. "There's no other way. Keep to the left."

Samantha pulled her gaze left and saw a narrow strip of steps against the wall that might still be solid enough to hold their weight.

"Here! Throw this over your face and head."

A T-shirt was flung across her shoulder.

Samantha started to glance back. "But you—"

"Do it!"

She took the shirt and wrapped it around and over her

head, holding the loose end across her face. It was getting harder and harder to breathe. Her lungs and throat felt as if the fire were being dragged inside her.

Together, they moved as close to the wall as possible, taking one stair at a time, going up as quickly as they dared, while around them the flames were fingers reaching for them, giant hands trying to close around them, trap them within a burning embrace.

Sudden, blinding pain surged up Samantha's left leg. At the same moment she looked down, she heard Dood exclaim, "Jesus!"

She was on fire! Flames bounded up the long white skirts of her costume.

Without a thought other than to rid herself of the fire and pain, Samantha started ripping away the cloth, feeling Dood tear at the material from behind.

"Keep going," he hollered at her, shoving her forward once more—and then a stair gave way, and Samantha felt herself falling, tried to put out a hand to brace against the wall. For a suspended moment she dangled in space, neither up nor down, but simply hung there, waiting to fall. Around her the flames howled and thundered like surf against a cliff; below her the screaming roar of that *thing* was growing, expanding, seeking to overtake its two escaping victims.

Dood grabbed her, holding her above the chasm that yawned beneath them. Flames licked at her legs, her arms, her body; fire danced in glittering waves before her eyes. She felt consciousness sliding away down a tunnel of raging heat and sound.

"Samantha! Reach for it! Reach across the gap! Look up—*dammit, Samantha!*"

Something automatic in her responded. Her head jerked back, eyes spanning the distance, hands trying to follow that visual link.

Above her—in the doorway—

"Nathan!" Dood's voice sounded harsh, dry-rotted, cracked from the burning fumes that were pouring down their throats with each ragged breath.

"Nathan, goddammit, man! Grab her! Pull us up!"

Why was he just standing there? Samantha wondered. She posed this question to a mind gone slack, even as her body strained to reach toward Ted and safety. Her eyes found his, locked on; his look was glazed, uncomprehending. He wasn't looking at her, she saw, or at Dood—but at the *thing* below them. It was as if reality had burned away.

With the blood congealing in her veins, Samantha saw him take a staggering step backward.

"*Ted!*" The cry tore from her, exploding out of her with the ferocity of desperation and torment and despair. Was he going to leave them here to die? She clasped Dood's arm in an agonized grip.

Ted's hands suddenly found her, fastened on roughly, jerking her up through the flames and past the chasm to the top of the stairs. Somehow she managed to hang on to Dood, pulling him with her as she went, feeling like the middle link in a chain between opposing forces.

A tremendous, roaring crash opened up behind her.

Samantha felt Dood's grip on her arm begin to slide . . . slipping away in a dragging, vacuous dissociation as though it were happening to someone else, somewhen else.

She turned her head toward the basement, saw the dark hand slide to her wrist, her hand.

"L.J. Noooo!" Her cry was lifted, carried away on a monstrous blast of wind that imploded toward the basement, sucking everything inward, almost tearing her from Ted's grasp—a whirlwind of sound and heat and motion that wrested Dood from her, claiming him, spinning him into the vortex as she watched, helpless to stop what was happening. She saw Dood's body torn away, ripped apart by the swirling forces consuming it, a voiceless scream frozen on his face.

And then hands were drawing her forward, beating at her clothing, tearing away the remaining strips of burning cloth, pulling the T-shirt from her head and neck.

"My God, my God," Ted was intoning in a litany of disbelief and horror.

When he tried to pull her away down the hall, she twisted out of his grip, screaming "L.J." as she turned back toward the stairs, her mind rejecting the vision searing it.

But there were no stairs now—there was no basement. Beyond the door there was only a raging, swirling, roaring furnace of hunger and madness and fury.

Beyond the door was Hell.

Dazed, Samantha stood there gazing into the inferno while around her the house began to come apart. Blazing timbers separated from flaming walls, crashed across the hallway; burning chunks of wood and debris fell like incendiary bombs.

Ted held her tightly, struggling to fight his way forward and at the same time anticipate which way the dripping fire would land. Pieces of burning plaster rained down on them, singeing arms and hair. Pain became a constant, a blurred sensation of heat and agony and fear.

Ted stumbled, pulling her down with him as a huge beam crashed across their path scattering burning debris everywhere. "Samantha, get up!" he demanded, trying to jerk them upright and beat out the flames in front of them, get them an escape path.

But they weren't going to make it. They were going to die here just like Matt and L.J. and Zack.

From out of nowhere a huge body loomed over them, ludicrously wielding an ax, kicking burning wood aside, tossing the ignited pyre left and right as he swept a pathway through the midst of the flames toward them.

"Tank!" Had she said it? Had Ted?

Tank was grabbing for them, manhandling them forward, forcing their stumbling bodies down the disintegrating hall . . .

Perhaps she fainted then. Perhaps her mind shut down, turned off, fled. Everything stopped—her thoughts, her physical sensations, her emotions. Nothing existed in the shell that was Samantha Evers. Nothing lived there anymore. Nobody home . . .

The shell that was Samantha let herself be rushed outside. The shell that was Samantha allowed her body to be wrapped in someone's coat. The shell that was Samantha made no objection to being placed upon the front lawn. It watched The Manse ignite and perish like a stack of dry kindling before the wail of fire trucks even sang in the distance. It listened to the screams and cries of the survivors, saw them strewn in bundles across the yard. It even failed to shudder when the thin, inhuman cry began above the still-beating heart.

Only when the heartbeat began to flutter, to fall off its rhythm, only when the piercing cry swelled in mindless rage—like a knife stabbing at the night—did a semblance of life return to Samantha Evers. It was the *thing*! She knew! The *thing* screaming. Dying!

A smile curled her mouth as she watched the house decay in flames. *Burn, baby, burn! Burn the pestilence away. Burn the horror and the fear and the rotten, cankered thing forming from it. Burn the rafters and the walls and the very foundation from the ground. Burn, burn, burn!*

As she listened, the cry became a reedy shriek of sound, a banshee's wail . . . The heart grew slow . . . slower . . . It threaded away into the night.

She saw Tank wander across the yard, glancing around him quietly as though looking for something else to do, someone else to save. He seemed diminished somehow, his unnatural silence melting layers from his huge body and leaving only a wasted core.

There was J.T. Hunsinger, huddled by the ticket booth, rocking back and forth and hugging his knees. Janet Weims cried silently beside him.

Where was Micky? she wondered, mildly interested.

Phil Handy dashed from group to group, checking, giving orders, being resourceful. Other Jaycees did the same . . . Martha was comforting a child—where was Teresa?

Samantha's glance roamed on, moving away from the house, stopping momentarily on a dark figure standing beside the old hickory nut tree. It looked like an old woman, an old black woman. Firelight shimmered on

ebony skin, flickered in glittering, tear-stained eyes.
Samantha thought the woman looked familiar, but she just
couldn't seem to remember . . . The old black woman was
slowly shaking her head.

"Samantha?" She flinched as someone touched her.
Ted. He drew back his hand from her shoulder. Agony and
confusion lacerated his voice, chafing the blessed silence.
"Samantha . . . what . . . ?"

Slowly she turned her head and met his shocked and
searching eyes. She spoke as if to a child. "It's all right,
Ted. It'll be all right now. Fire cleanses, you know. Fire
cleanses."

She turned away from him and looked again at the
house that had nurtured and bred something that had tried
to come into this world and failed. In abstract interest,
Samantha watched the blazing structure begin to collapse
. . . and with a violent crash that spiraled fire and belching smoke into the air, The Manse folded in on itself.

Only then did she begin to cry.

Notice in *The Merrillville Weekly*,
November 4, 1987:

Samantha Evers, five-year veteran feature writer, will
be taking an extended leave of absence from the
paper. During this time, we welcome Scott Gladden to
our staff on an interim basis.

Excerpt from *The Merrillville Weekly*,
November 11, 1987, Scott Gladden, Staff Reporter:

. . . and the small town of Merrillville is still reeling
from the tragic events that occurred October 31.

State Bureau of Investigation agents on the scene
now conclude that Elizabeth Beaufort was solely responsible for the fire that destroyed her former resi-
dence and killed thirty-seven people. It has been
determined that the eighty-two-year-old Miss Beaufort, apparently having become seriously deranged
after the year-long legal battle that saw her declared
mentally incompetent, murdered her twin sister, stole
a vehicle from the nursing home where they both
resided, and drove to their former home, where she
had arranged to meet her nephew, Peter Beaufort.
She then set the fire which killed him and thirty-six
others, including herself.

Although the investigation has not been officially
terminated, no new evidence is expected.

Excerpt from *The Merrillville Weekly,*
September 14, 1988, Scott Gladden, Staff Reporter:

. . . and due to right-of-survivorship clauses held by
Peter Beaufort's former partners, the development company of John H. Brinker & Associates has announced
its intention to proceed with construction of the Beaufort House Condominiums on the site of the old estate
house struck by tragedy almost a year ago. Work on
the project is slated to begin October 1.

EPILOGUE

The Manse: October 31, 1988,
Halloween Night, 8:42 P.M.

"I wish they still had the House of Horrors here." Bobby Case kicked at the loose gravel that marked the entrance to what used to be the driveway leading up to the old Beaufort estate house.

"Yeah," Tom Gilliam agreed. "That school shit was really nowhere. Peeled grape eyeballs and cold spaghetti guts—gimme a break."

"I'm glad we left." Bobby glanced up the hill toward where The Manse once stood. "Were you here last year?"

"Naw. We were out of town . . . You?"

"Yeah, but we went early and my folks wouldn't let me stay for the midnight show. Good thing, I guess . . . Hey, you hear something?"

"Where?"

"Up there, in the yard."

Tom peered into the darkness that was broken in places by slivers of ghostly moonlight. "Didn't hear anything, but I thought I saw something move—look, just past that bulldozer. Does that look like somebody's head?"

Bobby began to make a soft moaning sound. "*I am the spirit of those who died . . . Come to me . . . Commmme to meeee . . .*"

"Knock it off, asshole. You're about as scary as the school carnival."

"Hey!" Bobby lowered his voice. "I'll bet it's Andy and Vant up there hiding in the construction equipment. Come on, let's sneak around behind and give them a little something to remember Halloween by."

"I'm with you. Let's go!"

Excerpt from *The Merrillville Weekly*,
November 2, 1988, Scott Gladden, Staff Reporter:

The search continues for two Merrillville youths last
seen in the vicinity of the Beaufort House Condomin-
ium project Halloween night.